I0670898

SOULTIME

a novel

Michael R. Patton

Peace Mill Publishing
Myth^Steps Productions

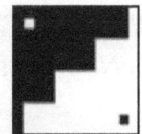

about the author:

Michael R. Patton, in his own words, "likes to make stuff". This stuff includes novels, new fables and myths, poetry, cartoons, essays, and videos. The ideas that run through that work can be found in the titles of his books. For example: "Searching for My Best Beliefs". Basically self-taught, he describes his slow, tedious journey of discovery as "crawling blindfolded through the labyrinth". He has lived and worked all over the United States.

POETRY COLLECTIONS
My War for Peace
Searching for My Best Beliefs
Common Courage: poems of our story
Butterfly Soul: poems of death & grief & joy
Glorious Tedious Transformation: poems of change
Myth Steps: searching for the new mythology
Listening to Silence: poems of meditation
Survival: documenting the fight
What I Learned While Alone
The Truth of the Dream
Poet, Heal Thyself
finding Beauty

NOVELS
The Raven's Way
Soultime

NONFICTION
I'm Responsible

STORY COLLECTIONS
40 New Fables

note to reader:
Two spaces are used between the period at the end of a sentence and the beginning of the next sentence for ease of reading.

acknowledgment:
Writing a novel, with the aim of creating a work of literature, is a challenging and sometimes humiliating task.   What I hoped might raise me high has, instead, humbled me.

Nonetheless, I still take pride in the goal of my quest: I wanted to add to our culture.

SOULTIME

ISBN 978-1-953996-09-1

© copyright 2020, Michael R. Patton

Hound dog howlin'
Bullfrog croakin'
Everything is broken.
          -- Bob Dylan

Chapter 1 : In The Beginning

In the beginning there was an argument. That's why things are such a mess. This argument involved the earth and the sky, except that in the beginning the two were one: a massive swirling mix of white sparkling light and dense black dust.

But in time, the earth became aware of its own nature and wished to separate to express that nature. So it heaved a great sigh, then pulled itself away and down from the sky, to settle into solid ground.

This made the sky angry; the sky did not wish to be separate. But the earth had its own desires and the earth refused to reconcile.

So...the sky folded inward until it'd melded into a single spike of pure white fire. Then it plunged down into the earth, to spear the earth and try to become whole once more. A rough and shoddy business, yes, but that's how the world began.

Time and time again, the sky speared the earth, hoping to regain the whole. But finally—finally—the sky gave up and billowed back out to become the same blue dome that covers us even today.

But the earth did not recover so quickly. It reeled and spiraled in dizziness; it wheezed and hacked and spat out its sickness, the sickness the sky had given it. This sickness came out as its many children: the ragged mountains, the sagacious lakes, the somnolent grazing plains, the mad roisterous oceans. And still the earth regurgitated: producing rocks that contained the mother's fiery core, and ice so blue it could turn your dreams inside out. And still the earth regurgitated: goats and sheep issued from the maw of mountains; the waves crashed together, creating flashes of fish; the prairies groaned forth antelope and bison.

Life poured from the earth like blood. And when all was finally said and done, a lively peace pervaded the place.

Then, amidst all this wonder, man and woman appeared: they fell from the first tree, the tree at the center of the world. For awhile, they just sat there, looking stupidly at one another, and at their hands, front and back, and at the clumsy feet attached to their knobby legs. They did not seem completely of this earth; alone among the animals they had the awareness of something beyond themselves, though at the time, this awareness was but a dim buzz in the far black space of midnight.

Chapter 2 : The Good Life

Before my tribespeople knew who they were—before they became Matarians—their chief salvation and only tool was the flint rock. They spent much of the day just sitting around, chipping away with dull stupefaction and delight.

It was a good life.

It was a good life...until I came along, that is. Yes, I give myself much credit. You see, I'm the one that had the dream, the dream that changed our way of living, our way of being.

In those days, we resided in the yellow grass savannas. Our clan consisted of thirty or so adults and twenty-five or more children. (These adults were by name: Aar, Ack, Ap, Aruk, Boq, Bruk, Dat, Dith, Ert, Kar, Kol, Kur, Lar, Lia, Lur, Lut, Mok, Nea, Naw, Ool, Oroo, Parn, Pren, Purl, Ter, Tor, Tur, Ur, Yar, Yer, Yor, and myself, Amar. I'm not even going to bother naming the children. Half of them didn't make it anyway.) Though our elders told of times when provisions had run short and small groups had broken away from the tribe, we knew of no other bands besides our own.

Yes, it was a good life. We lived free and naked beneath the sky's blue dome. Our tough hide and thick splintery hair helped ward off briars and mosquitoes.

At night, we all slept together in a loose conglomeration like a pride of lions.

Though the rain gave our bare bodies a salamander's chill, afterwards we'd luxuriate in the sun's crystal warmth. We accepted the rain, we accepted the sun, and never asked too many questions. All we knew was that the world had begun with an argument; that was enough for us.

Like I said, we had a good life...until I had the dream, that is.

Chapter 3 : The Dream

I run through the tall grass in pursuit—the antelope zigging and zagging ahead of me. Deep night, but I can see those white flanks bobbing up and down, up and down. When I try to move faster, it moves faster. But if I slow down, it slows down.

And so, in this way, the animal stays just out of spear range.

The cool wet air harshes in my lungs. The earth seems to grab at my feet. My leg muscles are all knotted up. But I push myself, push myself on.

Then without warning, the antelope plants its hooves in the earth. The long body sways forward, then rocks back, fighting its own momentum. Startled by this sudden stop, I stumble and hit the ground hard on my stomach. It feels like someone just punched me in the gut.

As I regain my breath, I see the antelope stands at the edge of a precipice. Moonlit fog pours over the lip of this cliff. The creature dips its head in the cloud and gazes down into the chasm.

I began to slide forward on my belly. I can feel the fog condensing on my face. For some strange reason, my prey now seems oblivious to me. Soon I'm but a few steps away from this elegant wild thing.

Ever so slowly, I rise to my feet. I cock my arm back, testing the balance of the spear. I plan to jab my weapon between the third and fourth ribs, then dig my heels in, lest the beast drag me over the ledge. I steady myself; I take a deep breath.

But before I can plunge my spear, the creature turns its long neck and looks back at me.

This is no ordinary antelope: in place of the elongated snout and jaw, I find the face of my favorite partner, recently deceased—Ellar!: coarse black hair hanging down the jut of her forehead; the loose lower lip exposing a hazard of brown teeth; the deeply-socketed eyes exuding both warm mystery and mock innocence. She was my lover, truly my lover.

I drop my spear. I open my arms to her. But in that moment, she turns and leaps from the cliff. I throw myself forward, but my arms only flail at the air and again I smack the ground.

Sucking for my wind, I crawl to the edge and look down into the depths of that blue canyon, into the swirls and eddies of fog below. I wait and wait, but hear nothing. Finally, I toss a rock out into the chasm. The stone diminishes to a mere speck, then is swallowed by cloud. Except for my own stupid breathing, the silence is complete.

At that point, I woke up feeling absolutely miserable. I had lost Ellar at the time of the last new moon when a red spider bit her on the heel. For three days and nights, she had writhed and moaned and cursed until, finally, she let go and gave herself to death. Now, with this dream, I had lost her once again. I felt so helpless. If only I could reenter the dream. This time, I'd grab her in my arms before she could jump; then I would love her as I'd loved her before—antelope or not.

Of course, everyone in the tribe, at some time or another, had come upon a dearly departed one while dreaming. From these visitations, we had deduced that a part of ourselves entered a new world after death. The Otherworld, we called it. But besides its name, we knew little about the place.

Like the rest of my tribes-kin, I usually shared my dreams freely. But that morning, as I sat in a circle with six other men, sharpening spear tips, I could not bring myself to speak. The strong feelings of the dream constricted my throat; the shock of it still had me dazed. Why had Ellar come to me? What was she trying to do?—torture me?

Abruptly, blood gushed from my thumb. Then the pain began: hot little jabs. My chipping stone had slipped. I plucked some weeds and wrapped their leaves around my thumb, then gave a nod to my brothers to show that I was okay. But as I continued flaking the flint, I could feel Mok watching me; I could feel his tiny eyes boring into me. Deep-set under the shelf of his brow, those eyes glittered like silver minnows seen through dark water. Mok was our best hunter, the tallest among us, the strongest of limb, the least stoop-shouldered. Based on these virtues, he qualified as our leader. Though I did hunt, I was the weakest of our seven. To Mok, I was an irritating fly. And he loved to take his swats.

Soon, the others picked up Mok's cue and turned their eyes to me. These men were Boq, Dith, Dat, Lut, and Aruk: short, quick names because our palates had not yet developed; our mouths could not mold sophisticated words. For that matter, at the time, we had but a handful of words with which to express ourselves. But though we were young, that didn't stop us from being complex. So, for the sake of clarity, I'm giving my people language which approximates their thoughts and feelings. Otherwise, you would not recognize them as your kinsfolk.

Finally, I lifted my eyes from my work and met their gaze.

"Don't worry about the thumb," I told them. "It's no deep cut. I'm okay. Just a little slip of the rock, that's all."

"Just a slip, Amar? I think not," said Mok. "I sense something from you. What words lie behind your silence?"

"Yes, Amar, what lies behind your silence?" echoed Aruk and Lut.

I had nothing against Aruk—except that he was Mok's good buddy. They complemented each other: whereas Aruk was dull and honorable, Mok was ostentatious and under-handed. As for Lut—well, I guess the name says it all: Lut. He was neither the best of us nor the worst of us. In that way, he typified my tribes-kin.

Ordinarily, I could have slid away from such a confrontation. But the dream still churned within me; confusion choked off clear thought. Before discretion could intervene, I found myself telling the dream.

"Yes, there she was," I said, repeating the sad conclusion of my tale. "Those dark eyes staring back at me one last time. Then she was gone."

I looked to my comrades, hoping for a glimmer of sympathy. But they just studied the ground, examined their chipping tools, and dug their heels into the dust.

Then Mok stood up. He scratched his crotch. He rolled a pebble with his big toe. "I know what your dream means," he said.

"Yeah?"

"Ellar is in the Otherworld, right?"

"Yeah, so?"

"So the antelope must be in the Otherworld as well. That's where they go when they're not here, when we can't find them. That's the message of your dream."

"I'm not too sure about your interpretation," I said. "It doesn't quite resonate."

"You must find Ellar again," Mok continued. "Go to her in your dreams tonight. Have her to talk to the antelope. She must convince them to return to us."

For one full cycle of the moon, we had suffered in the hunt. The antelope had deserted the plains. Though our women could gather enough fruits and nuts and dig enough roots and grubs to sustain us, without the antelope meat, we somehow seemed less than ourselves.

"I might not be able to find her."

"Well, you're going to keep trying 'til you do."

"I don't know," Boq interjected. "Ellar hasn't been dead that long. The antelope might not know her that well. Yes. They might not listen to her."

Boq made up the rules of life as he went along. But his logic was innocent.

"That woman had honey in her voice," Mok said. "Tell her to sing to the beasts. Tell her to do whatever she has to do. We've got to get the antelope back."

"Yes, we've got to get the antelope back," echoed Aruk and Lut.

I opened my mouth, but couldn't think to speak.

Mok then hefted his balls with both hands and spat from the corner of his mouth—his way of signaling an end to all further discussion.

That evening—after another unsuccessful hunt—Mok informed the others of my special mission. No one had ever attempted such a dream communication before. For the moment, I was something of a hero.

But heroism has its price.

As the last campfire sparks drifted upward to the stars, my tribespeople gathered together for their nightly repose. Elbows, knees, feet, and buttocks protruded from the loose conglomeration of our sleeping pile. As usual, I snuggled in amongst my tribes-kin. However, each and every one of them now shouldered me away. The old woman Ool dug her thumbnail into my sternum just to make sure I got the point.

Finally, I gave up and wandered over to the tall grass.

"The tribe respects my mission," I told myself. "They realize that I need solitude to perform the task at hand."

But I knew the truth: they now saw me as different. I was venturing into unknown territory; that made them apprehensive. So, for this night at least, they would keep me at a distance.

I had another good reason for not wanting this job. If the antelope didn't return soon—and I had no cause to believe that they would—I'd get the blame. That's probably why Mok had foisted the job on me in the first place. This way, he didn't have to take responsibility for our failure in the hunt.

As I bedded down in the tall grass, I considered how best to handle this precarious situation. If I was good at anything, it was wheedling out of trouble.

In a flash, the answer came to me: tomorrow morning I'd tell the tribe that I had indeed found Ellar in my dreams. I'd tell them that she knew of our plight and had spoken to the antelope already. But the antelope had told her, in no uncertain terms, that they would return only when good and ready. And not until.

With this plan in mind, I began to relax. I lulled into sleep with an almost peaceful feeling.

Then something nudged my shoulder—something soft and wet. In my drowsed state, I tried to ignore this irritation. But then it breathed warm air all over my neck. I jerked up and started slapping the air like a man plagued with gnats. But my hidden foe was out of striking range. So I cooled myself down and peered into the darkness.

Clouds slid away from the moon. The field came alive with a pale white glow. A passing breeze sighed through the grass. Then all was quiet.

Perhaps I could return to the tribe now. Surely, they'd all be asleep. I could shift in amongst them undetected; I could rest in peace.

I crept through the hushing grass, looking for the pile of bodies. I knew that my people slept only a stone's throw away, yet I couldn't locate them in any direction. Finally, I held myself still and strained to hear the harmony of their mixed breathing. But this moment of repose brought a new awareness to me. I now felt a slight tremor running through the earth beneath my feet.

Just to be on the safe side, I moved a little to the left. However, the ground here shuddered with greater force. The vibrations hummed all the way up my frame. So I slid over some more.

But now the quaking grew so strong that it rattled my teeth.

"Maybe I'd better stay put," I told myself. "Give the earth a chance to calm itself."

But the earth would not quiet down. The ground shook so hard that the stars jiggled. The moon smeared its white shadow over the night. I began to fear that a torrent of fire and rock would burst from the earth's bowels at any moment.

So I made like the wind; no, I'm not ashamed to say that I ran, yes, I ran, and as I ran, something strange began to happen to me—a new power began to course through my body. I was no longer a clodding thud. No, I now bounded through the air with speed, strength, and grace. As soon as my feet touched the ground, they sprang right back up again. It seemed as though my legs had multiplied by two. And my lungs could drink twice the normal dose of air. I soared above the earth. Such an exhilarating sense of freedom! What had happened to me? I knew that fear could quicken my heels; I'd run scared before. But never before had I felt such elegance and stamina in my body.

The ground thundered beneath me.

Then abruptly, everything jumped to halt. Some inner force held me frozen. Wind rushed over my face from below. I found myself at the edge of a precipice. Beyond the ledge, blue fog swirled and eddied in a bottomless chasm.

Four dainty black hooves stood on the slab of rock beneath me. I gave my body the once-over. Yes, you guessed it—I now "wore" the sleek design and sturdy build of an antelope. But I would not fret. "You are dreaming," I told myself. "So enjoy your time as an antelope. In the morning, you'll be human once more." Again, I gazed into the luminous blue fog below. "Ellar is down there somewhere," I thought. "I sure have missed the girl. Yeah, I've been with nearly every woman of the tribe and they are all fit and fine. But there was something different about Ellar...some unnameable something; with her I felt a special charge, an elation of spirit, an elevation within. I would truly love to meet her in this dream. Our powerful antelope bodies would collide in a seizure of passion."

Desire welled up inside me. I could be with Ellar again if I would only jump. Yet I hesitated. Though I knew that I dreamt, a chasm is still a chasm.

But then I pictured those dark eyes of hers, so full of warmth and mystery. Maybe now I could pierce through to their secret.

And so, I closed my eyes and took a deep breath; I gave up all care; I leapt from the cliff.

Abruptly, the bubble of my dream world broke. Damp grass brushed against my cheek. A red sun bled over the horizon.

I shook the dream webs from my head, squeezed a sorrowful sigh from my chest, then pulled my all-too-human body into a sitting position. Steam rose over the morning savanna.

I stumbled to the campfire, scratching myself and yawning, ready to suck down a few dried grubs and get on with the day. But as I stepped into the tribal circle, the people looked to me in expectation. I suddenly recalled my mission. How could I appease my tribes-kin? I started to tell them that the antelope would return when good and ready, but then something prompted me to share my dream, to speak its song, to describe the power that had pulsed through my body. I told of how I'd given chase to the night and of the great courage, born of desire, that had propelled me down into the blue mists in search of my beloved.

When I had finished this strange tale, I turned my gaze outward again and studied my congregation. In their glazed eyes I could see my story reverberating. The young ones had even stopped throwing dirt clods to listen. It gave me pleasure, knowing that I'd held them under my spell, if only for a short time. A self-satisfied smile kept trying to curl my lips.

But then Boq stepped in.

He broke from his ruminations and sprang forward onto his hands and knees and cried, "Oh my brother, what a wonderful thing you have done!"

"Really, you flatter me." I giggled and bowed my head.

"You became aware in your dream," he continued. "You conquered your fear. Yes. You conquered your fear the way the antelope must conquer their fear when they lay down their lives for us. Yes, there's a message here— I can see it clearly. Yes. We can get the antelope to come back if we honor their sacrifice. Yes—we'll get them back by doing what you did in your dream."

"Huh?"

"Tonight, under the full moon's light, we'll run through the tall grass the way the antelope run. Yes. And we'll put little sticks on our heads to imitate antelope horns. Yes. And when our feet strike the ground, we'll knock rocks together to mimic the pounding of hooves. Yes. For this one night, we'll become antelope—just like you did in your dream."

"You don't plan to jump off a cliff too, do you?"

"No, but we can go to the bluff by the river and throw a carved antelope figure down into the water. Yes, yes. By performing this reenactment, we will honor the way the antelope sacrifice themselves for us."

"And that's supposed to bring them back?" grunted Mok.

"Sure," Boq said. "And Amar will lead us."

Everyone looked to me and then to Mok.

Mok held up his palms and shrugged. "Okay," he said, "why not? I mean, I don't quite get the connection, but hey, if it brings the antelope back, I'm all for it." Then his dark, silvery eyes focused on me. "And it'd better bring them back."

My stomach twitched.

Yes, I'd gotten myself into something of a fix.

Chapter 4 : The Ancestors

If this little ritual—the Stick-Horn Dance—hadn't worked, I might be telling a different story today. But it did work. Or rather, the dance happen to coincide with the antelope's return. The day after our first performance, a full herd moseyed right up to the thicket where we hunters crouched. It was almost too easy. For the first time in a long time, the tribe feasted on antelope meat and had the pleasure of a bloated stomach. The women presented me with the choicest cut.

In a clan with no official rank, I had suddenly become an honored person. And that made me nervous. The tribe now wanted me to lead them through the dance every full moon. But what would happen when—as was inevitable—the antelope stopped showing up again? Well, for the present, I decided not to worry. I would enjoy my moment in the sun.

From that time on, the tribe made me sleep away from the pile every night. However, most evenings, one of the women would visit me in the tall grass before bedtime. They now believed that I held special powers. As such, they wished to partake of my magic.

In addition, the hunters no longer let me go out with them. They told me to save my juice for the antelope dance. I did not even have to chip spear tips anymore.

The easy life, right? Wrong. For some strange reason, about this time, my dreams became a swirling flood. Amid this nightly chaos, I began to fear for my feeble mind.

These nightmares all had the same scenario: I would find myself standing in an empty black space, unable to see the ground beneath my feet, unable to locate even a single star above me. Though I strained my ears, I could hear nothing—not one creeping thing. I dared not step backwards nor forwards for fear that I'd drop into some unknown abyss.

Then the faces would come at me—masks as pale as death—floating in and out of the darkness, scowling and howling and snarling their teeth. Among these twisted spirits I saw many who I'd known before their demise. But that didn't make them any less scary—on the contrary that made them seem all the more real.

And so, I'd soon decide to risk that abyss and take off in blind run. But no matter how hard I ran, I couldn't escape the faces; they clung to me; they roiled about me like leaves caught in a wind funnel. Their shrieks and moans burrowed down into my brain, down into those places where fear lives unimpeded.

Though I knew that I was dreaming, I couldn't break out of the dream and I couldn't make those faces stop screaming; I couldn't stop my fear. I couldn't see where was I going. Each step felt like stepping off a cliff.

Then somewhere along the line, I'd stub my toe and plunge forward headfirst. But no, I wouldn't hit the ground, I'd just keep falling, all the while anticipating the moment I'd strike bottom; all the while feeling the cold wind blowing through my weak woozy stomach.

But I'd always wake in the tall grass before I struck down.

After one of these dreams, my arms and legs would ache as though beaten with a stick. I'd try to rub the burn from my eyes, try to spit the dead-fish taste from my mouth, but to little effect. The heavy nausea that pervaded my body would weigh on me the rest of the day.

Yeah, those dreams had me in a bad way. But what could I do? I would've given up all my new privileges just for some peaceful sleep.

"If only I could rest amongst my tribes-kin again," I thought, "then I could escape this horrid dream life."

But I knew that was out of the question. Somehow, someway, I had to strike a truce with the dark world of my dreams.

So finally one night, before bedding down, I knelt in the tall grass and begged mercy from my tormentors, from those who now lived in the Otherworld of dreams. "Why do you haunt me, dear ancestors?" I cried. "Why do you tear at my heart? Please don't plague me so. Please, let me rest. I need my strength. The people depend on me now."

This pleading soon exhausted me. I collapsed on the ground and wept like a young bird weeping for its mother.

Finally, I gave up all care and wandered into sleep.

Strangely enough, the next morning, I awoke dreamless and refreshed.

Thereafter, I begged for mercy each night and each night I slept contentedly. This happy state continued for seven days running. I began to believe that I was free.

Then one evening as I sat at the campfire circle, preparing to thank our antelope brethren for feeding us, Mok came up and stood directly behind me. I could feel the heat from his groin on the back of my neck.

"Oh Amar, how we praise you," he said to all in the circle. "How we value your gift. But Amar, dear Amar, I think you've hidden something from us."

My stomach twitched. "What can you possibly mean?" I asked. "What I have, I have given. Actually, it's not that much and I can hardly take credit."

"Sweet words, Amar, sweet words," Mok said. "But last night, while I was relieving myself in the bushes, my ears picked up the faint sound of your voice. Drawing closer, I found you in the moonlight on bended knee, speaking aloud to the ancestors."

His body heat had disrupted my thinking. "So? Everyone here has lifted a voice to the ancestors at one time or another."

"But you thanked them for answering your request —something about letting you sleep at night. Again and again, you thanked them."

I could hear my tribespeople draw in their breaths.
"So?"

"So the ancestors never answered anyone of us. They must actually listen to you. Why you didn't tell us about this little deal of yours?"

"They told me not to tell."

"Oh, so you can hear them as well. You converse back and forth."

"Why would they tell you not to tell?" Boq broke in. "That doesn't make sense."

"They said their world wasn't your concern," I said. "They said that you needed to concentrate on life in this world."

"That is true, Amar. That is true." This pronouncement came from an old woman of forty named Ur. She had a wide bottom that spread across the ground like a puddle when she sat down. Mok might've been the muscle of our tribe, but Ur served as its wisdom. "Yes," she continued, "we should pay attention to business in this world. That is why the ancestors keep their distance—they don't want to distract us from our daily tasks. But if we were to communicate with the ancestors through you, Amar, that wouldn't really be a distraction, now would it? I mean, you have nothing better to do. Yes, that's it— that's why they've come to you. They want to get through to us through you. Amar, you must help them communicate with us; you must help us communicate with them. Don't you want to help them, Amar? Don't you want to help us? Is there something you're afraid of?"

"Nothing," I lied.

"Well, okay then. I'm sure everyone here has something they'd like to say to someone in the Otherworld."

"Okay, I'll talk to them tonight. But if they catch you spying on me—" I turned my head to look at Mok but only caught an eyeful of his crotch—"they won't say a thing."

"Very well," Ur said. "Now who wants in on the action?"

A flock hands shot up.

Again, my stomach twitched.

That night, after checking to make sure that no one lurked about, I again begged the ancestors for mercy. But I did not bother them with any messages or questions or requests from my tribes-kin—I didn't want to pester the spirits too much. For that matter, I was half-afraid that they might actually answer me.

That night, my ancestors again respected my pleas and let me sleep.

The next morning, as I approached the campfire, the faces of my tribes-kin all turned to me in expectation. However, I ignored them with an air of nonchalance and settled down at my usual place in the tribal circle.

I picked out a slab of meat and gnawed off a hunk.

"Well come on!" Ur finally said. "Don't be sly, Amar. Did you talk with them?"

"Yes, I did. Don't worry, I relayed all your messages."

"But what did they say in return?" Ur scratched the puddle of her buttock.

"They wished you all good health and good hunting. They will help with requests whenever possible. But just remember—it's not always possible. They said that they can see you from their world; they watch over you and your children every day and every night."

"All the ancestors said the same thing?" Boq asked. "That doesn't make sense."

"They spoke the message to me in unison, a chorus of voices in the night." The tribespeople stared at me blandly. I realized they weren't about to let me off the hook that easily, so I added, "And yet I recognized many of the voices: Lar...Poz...Mulk...Muz...Clrrr..."

"Url?" asked Ur.

"Yes, that man you once favored so sweetly sends you a special greeting."

"What about Murk?" asked an old man with glaring ribs named Purl.

"Oh yeah—Murk said to tell you hello. She still remembers your honeyed times together under the baobab tree."

The questions began to fly at me. I answered them with cunning. The ancestors who I had not known personally, I knew from stories, so I could guess what they might say. But one thing was certain: all the dead folk had gushed fond remembrances of loved ones left behind. The tribespeople ate it up. By the end, when I was all talked out, I felt I'd done a good thing; through my subterfuge, the people had touched warm memories.

This trickery helped to lift my status yet another notch. I had become someone special in the eyes of my people.

I had never been special before. My feet could never find the rhythm of the dance; I had the grace of a bird wounded in the wing. I couldn't sing—I couldn't stay in key. I frequently disfigured the flint pieces that I chipped. My spear missed the mark more often than not. In view of such mediocrity, perhaps you can forgive me this breach of faith.

For three mornings in a row, I came to the tribal circle bearing sweet greetings from the ancestors. And I guess I was getting a bit too puffed up. Maybe the ancestors were tired of my lying ways. Anyway, for whatever reason, my dreamworld erupted once again.

Once again, I found myself stranded on a shrouded plain. Once again, twisted faces rushed at me from the darkness. And, once again, I became a scaredy cat, except that this time, before I could run, some unseen force took hold of me and threw me into a black spin; I twirled about, quickly picking up speed, and all those shrieking faces swirled with me. I was a sneeze in a windstorm. My arms and legs flapped about like palm fronds. A weak pink feeling bled through my stomach and drained away all my will. I just wanted to give myself up; I just wanted it to end.

The faces mocked me with wind-torn laughter.

Then abruptly I got my wish—everything slammed to a halt. I'd hit something hard, flat, and definite. The faces all broke into fine chips and flew away. I seemed to be resting on a slab of rock. I seemed to be horizontal—at least, I seemed to be; somehow I'd landed horizontally. I didn't feel too bad, but I didn't feel like moving either, so I just lay there on my back in the dark, hoping that I'd soon wake up.

Then I began to get the oddest sensation: an irritated tingling filled my frame. My body now fluoresced a blue-white glow. It seemed to be made of powder. Was I just dust?

I thought I should do something, so I tried lifting my left arm. But at that moment, a breeze raked over me and blew all my hand granules away. I felt sad about the hand—life would lose some of its texture.

"Oh well," I sighed. "Oh well—I guess I'd better stay put, lest I tempt the wind again."

However, the zephyrs now began dragging across my body. I could feel my sand drifting off. I begged the air to let me be. But little gusts continued to sweep and spiral over me, sending my particles spinning into a thousand different directions. Soon I lacked even the will to think and had no center of being, nor enough spark of life to care.

That's when I finally awoke.

I was glad to be back in the tall grass, back in my normal body. Only my body didn't feel so normal at first. My limbs and trunk quivered and hummed as though still partially diffused. I felt like one good puff could blow me away and I did not want to live life as a loose, lost dust mote. Nor did I wish to continue living a lie. I wanted to rejoin my tribes-kin, to sleep amongst them again and receive no special privileges. Yes, I would tell them the truth; I would confess my deception. Sure, at first they'd be mad at me. But then, when they saw that I was just an ordinary fool, with no particular magic, they'd relax and let me back into the fold.

That morning, as I approached the campfire, I avoided the hopeful eyes of my tribes-kin. I sat down before them, put my hands on my knees, and bowed my head. I wanted to create a solemn atmosphere and, at the same time, hide the shame in my eyes.

I had rehearsed my confession to the last phrase. But before I could begin, Boq hit me with his logic again. He scratched his neck, cocked his head, squinted up one eye, and said, "Amar, if you can call the antelope back with a ritual, shouldn't you be able to call the ancestors back as well?"

My stomach twitched. In an instant, I forgot all about my little speech. (Maybe I wanted to forget.)

"Call them?" I said. "But I call to them every night."

"No, I mean, return them to us. By doing a ritual. Yes. That makes sense to me."

My mind ran in circles, searching for an answer. "But, ah, you see, ah, the ancestors prefer the

Otherworld. They have good hunting there; food is plentiful. And they don't have to worry with ticks and lice. Why should they want to return to this life?"

"Ah, come on, they wouldn't have to hang around that long," said Dith.

"Yeah," said Dat.

Dith and Dat–don't even ask me about those two; don't even ask.

"If you can bring them back, Amar, you must," Ur said. "If I could just hear one more syrupy murmur from Url! Can't you at least try for us?"

"Why yes," Mok said, ever so sweetly. "Come on, Amar, try for us." The silvery light danced in his eyes. He spat into the fire.

The entire tribe now chorused the same desire. Finally, I agreed to give it a go. I would perform an ancestor-calling ritual that night at the campfire.

"I'll confess my lies later," I told myself. "What difference will a day or two make? In the meantime, maybe my dreams will calm down again."

That evening, I waited until all the tribes-kin had gathered at the campfire before I made my entrance. As I strode into the circle, everyone grew quiet. I did not say a word, but seated myself near the flames, closed my eyes, elevated my chin, then crossed my arms across my chest.

However, I soon discovered that I had sat too close to the fire. My face felt scorched. I feared that my hair might combust from the heat. Yet I remained motionless, knowing that I needed to maintain a dignified bearing.

During the afternoon I'd hit upon a plan, a plan that would allow me to save face and, at the same time, satisfy the tribe's demands.

I could feel the suspense building as my audience watched and waited. Finally the time seemed ripe, so I went into my choreography: I held my arms straight out to the side, raised my face to the moon, and paused for a beat.

Then with a great shout, I brought my arms down and leapt to my feet.

But my legs had cramped; I stumbled. A pebble rolled under my heel. I slipped backward and had to twirl my arms to regain balance. Then as I bowled forward, I accidentally stepped into the fire. Though I hopped right back out, my feet throbbed from the burning.

After I'd managed to compose myself, I gave a look of great gravity to the faces around the circle. Then I reached into a gopher-hide pouch strapped to my waist band and extracted a thin strip of meat.

"Our ancestors are hungry," I said. "So they shall eat." I extended my arm over the fire, holding the meat strip between forefinger and thumb. "Ancestors, this is for you." I dropped the offering into the blaze. The meat quickly shriveled into a blue ball. A fine stream of smoke shot up from the flames.

I waited a moment, then cupped a hand to my ear. "What's that?" I asked. "What's that I hear? Oh, that's nice—the ancestors say they enjoyed the taste of that smoke. This offering will bring them closer to us. I will feed them some more."

With great formality, I dropped another strip into the fire, then another strip, then another. But though I kept my chin perched in the air and my eyelids low, this haughty expression belied the fact that I felt like a complete fool.

I emptied the pouch, then backed away from the campfire until I'd reached the periphery of its light. Then I spread my arms out again and threw my head way back. I held myself in this ridiculous position for several ceremonious moments before I spoke.

"I can feel them, I can feel the ancestors—they are near us. Can't you feel them, my brothers and sisters, can't you feel them near us?"

I dropped my arms again and spun on my heel, then jumped into the tall grass and went into a crouch. Oh how my keen eyes did peer into the darkness! I jerked my head about like a nervous rabbit, ever watchful. My audience studied me with some concern for my sanity.

"They are here," I said. "Our beloved ancestors have arrived. Look at them. Their dreamlike forms emerge from the night. Join with us, dear ancestors, join with us again. No, they say they must keep their distance. They can not fully enter our world. They belong to the world of dream. Too bad for us. Too bad for them. But hey, look—over there—" I pointed to the right— "it's Url. See him grinning like a happy monkey? What's that, Url? What's that you say? He says Ur's luscious buttocks always make his stick bob and bounce. Nice sentiments, Url. And look who else's here—" I pointed left— "it's Muz. See how he still hooks his finger on his lower lip? What's that, Muz? You say you've missed the beauty and dignity of our circle? What a lovely thought. And oh, who's that over there? That you, Murl? Well yes, it most certainly is. Look, they keep emerging from the darkness—I see Bzzz and Plzz and Frah. Greetings, dear ancestors—welcome back."

31

I kept this patter going on for some time. Though my audience strained to see what I saw and hear what I heard, their imaginations could not create what wasn't there. They remained silent.

Finally, exhausted by my efforts, I cried out, "Wait, wait, what's this? The ancestors—their images grow faint. They're fading away. Wait, ancestors, wait! No, they say they must go. They wave a fond farewell to us. Now the darkness swallows them once more. Goodbye, dear friends, so long. Thank you for blessing us with your presence. Thank you."

Let it be known that at that moment, I hated myself. I felt weak within. But how could I drop the ruse now?

I turned back to my tribes-kin and looked at them with wide, excited eyes.

"Wasn't that wonderful?" I asked everyone.

The tribespeople all searched the ground for some suitable answer. Finally, Ur cleared her throat and gazed at me with sad gray eyes. "Amar, I didn't see nor hear a thing. And I don't think anyone else did either."

The others grunted in agreement.

"But their forms were right there," I said. "How could you miss them?"

"I really tried to see them, I really did," Ert whined. "I stretched my eyelids apart and stared until my eyes burned. But no luck."

The others grunted in agreement.

"Strange, strange indeed," I said, tapping my chin. "You couldn't see nor hear them, yet I could. What's going on here?"

"It's simple," Ur said. "The ancestors have dream bodies. Because you have merged your dream world with your waking world, you can see them while we can not. I keep telling you, Amar: you have a special gift. I'm so proud of you."

This explanation seemed to satisfy everyone. My plan had worked. I had escaped unscathed.

But my relief was short-lived. I now found that I'd only added to my burden. Though they couldn't see nor hear their ancestors, the tribe liked the idea of having the dearly departed around our campfire. So they made me conjure up those ghosts every night.

The performances drained me. People started asking the ancestors questions. I had to think on my feet. But through some skillful dissembling, I was able to provide my tribes-kin with answers they could accept. In a pinch, I'd tell them that the ancestor's reply was but faint.

Yes, I had found my calling: I was a liar without equal.

I tried to believe that I was helping my tribe-family. I told myself that these fake communiqués gave them solace, returning to them for a few brief moments that which they had lost. And so, I lied to myself just as I lied to my people.

Though my status rose yet another notch, the gain wasn't worth the pressure of performing. But the tribes-kin were hooked. The charade would have to continue. However, to my relief, the whirlwind dream had not returned. I could sleep in peace.

Then one night, the ancestors played a trick on me.

That evening, as usual, I went through the meat-strip ritual. But when I peered into the darkness, damn!—I actually did see a luminous shape amid the trees. It hung there like a glowing white shadow. At first, the apparition was only vaguely human. But then, slowly, a shrunken, bony body took form, softly florescent as though an inner light shone through translucent skin.

As the mask of the face grew more distinct, I recognized the flat, flaring nose and rock-hard chin of our ancestor Url. His sharp eyes stared a hole right through my head.

I looked over my shoulder at my tribes-kin. But they gazed at me, not at Url. They didn't seem to see him.

I was staggered. This ghostly vision had knocked me off-balance.

"Url?" I whispered. "Is that you?"

"Of course, it's me," he snapped. "What the blazes do you want with us?"

Again, I checked the tribe. They looked at each other and shrugged. No one had heard Url.

"What do I want? Ah, well, nothing much, old man. Just saying hello."

"Well, if that's all you want, why do you keep bugging us?" Url dug a finger into his ear.

"I didn't mean to bother you...but the tribe misses you guys."

"Can you see Url yet?" Ur asked.

"Ah, yeah," I said. "He's here."

"Well what's he saying?"

"That he longs for you and all that other stuff."

I didn't mean to be abrupt, but I was a little distracted. Ancestor forms kept emerging from the darkness. Ten of them had drifted out from the trees. They dangled in the air just a few steps from me, their toes barely brushing the ground. Among them was

Lub, Grob, Ptah, Plzz, and Bzzz. But no, to my disappointment, I did not see Ellar.

The spirits glared annoyance and boredom at me.

"What's wrong?" I asked them. "Aren't you glad to be back with your tribes-kin?"

The ancestor Mul floated towards me. His lower lip still extended from his gum like a like a leaf from a stem. "This world is okay," he said, "but we've all seen better since we left. I mean, life here had its benefits, but really, we were just getting by."

"You make it sound so paltry."

"You're telling me that you're happy, Amar?"

"Yes," I lied.

"Then why do you play these silly games?"

I now recalled Mul's blunt-headed belligerence, how he enjoyed ruffling your feathers. "I'm not playing games," I told him. "I'm trying to help my people."

"How? By lying to them? Why don't you try a little honesty for a change? Let them know how your dreams torment you. They might actually understand."

"Amar, what're they saying!" Ool shouted.

"Hold on, old women," I yelled over my shoulder, then turning back to the ancestors, I told them, "If you guys hadn't tortured my sleep, I wouldn't be performing these tricks."

"We never touched your sleep," Url said.

"You can't fool me," I said. "I recognized your faces."

"That wasn't us."

"But I saw you...I saw your faces...I mean, I did see faces...I thought it was you...I mean...you sure that wasn't you guys?"

"You're just chasing yourself, you fool," Mul said.

"Amar, why're you whispering?" Ur hollered. "What Url's saying? Does he still miss his honey blossom?"

"That woman was insatiable!" Url sighed.

"Look, Amar, if you keep bugging us, you'll be sorry." This warning came from that old spider, Muz.

"We mean business," added Lub.

"So what do I do? I won't bother you anymore, but tell me, how can I make my tribespeople happy? They've become so demanding."

A little boy with a crooked spine wafted towards me. I recognized this lad as Emo. I'd always had a great empathy for this ill-fated child. Perhaps his outward deformity mirrored a deformity I felt within.

"Amar," he said in a small, thin voice, "let your people do the work. If they wish to talk with us, they can summon us in their dreams."

"No, I know what they'll say—they'll say they don't know how, they'll tell me they just can't do it."

"But they can and you must convince them."

"How?"

"Do a group ritual."

"Okay then, what do I put in this ritual?"

"Just make something up. That's what you've done before, right?"

"It doesn't matter what I say?"

But the boy had already turned his back to me. He dissolved into the darkness.

The ancestor forms now began to grow dim. I watched the night consume them one by one until only their silhouettes remained. For a brief interval, these silhouettes were a deeper darkness amid the shadows, then even these last traces faded, leaving behind an onerous void.

"Dammit Amar, what's going on!"

Purl's impatient bark broke my stupor.

"They're gone," I said.

I turned to face my audience. The way they glowered at me could've stopped hyenas from mating.

So I put on a false face and pumped myself back up. "Great news, my brothers, my sisters!" I beamed. "The ancestors say they wish to speak with each of you. Individually. You know—one-on-one."

"Amar, stop your fooling," Ert whined.

"Now wait, now listen...tomorrow night, we'll perform a special ritual, a ritual given to me by the ancestors themselves. This ritual will allow all of you to contact your dearly departed. You'll be able to call them forth in your dreams. Then you'll be able to talk to them and remember everything. It'll be just like they're right there, which of course, they will be."

The whole tribe groaned in unison.

"Oh, come on, you can do it. You'll see. Anyway, the ancestors demand it."

Still, the tribes-kin grumbled. What a bunch of lazy butts!

"But we don't have your gift," they kept complaining.

"Don't worry, after tomorrow, you will."

But I neither convinced them, nor myself. However, for the time being, I saw no other way out. Besides honesty, of course. But I wasn't quite ready for that.

Despite all the upheaval, I slept well that evening. The next day, I kept myself hidden away, hoping to add a touch of mystery to that night's proceedings.

Then at twilight, I approached the tribal circle.

My carriage conveyed a certain grandeur and pomposity. Such high-handed behavior just seems to be a part of ritual.

I sat down at my usual place and surveyed the circle.

But though I regarded my tribes-kin with lofty reserve, I could not ignore the love I felt for these people. Before all this rigmarole about dreams and ancestors began, I'd breathed as they breathed, thought as they thought, and felt as they felt. Now all that had changed. I had become special, different, separate. Now I had to shroud my thoughts, hide my feelings, and cover my moves. When you throw a spear, if you err a little at the beginning, you're way wide at the end. My lies were pushing me farther and farther away from my people.

"I must confess to them right now," I told myself.

But then a small conniving voice within me said, "No, wait; this ritual might fix everything. If you can get the people to believe that they share your abilities, they won't think of you as special anymore. Then you can return to the sleeping pile."

"Let us all join hands," I said softly.

I took Ur's hand in my own. The feel of her dry, bristly skin reassured me. That gentle hand had guided my youth.

"By joining hands, we become what we are: we are one, with one mind and one heart," I told the circle. "So close your eyes now and feel the oneness within yourself."

I let the moment dangle. The campfire seemed to crackle with new life. My ears picked up a finely-pitched hum.

A peculiar energy now began to pulse through my hands. It pulsed through my arms; it pulsed through my whole body. Where was its source? Did it come from me? No—after focusing for a few moments, I realized that the current merely used me as a conduit; it hopped from Ur to me, then to Kol, then continued on around the circle—a lively wave with wild crests and troughs, a wave with no beginning nor end. It came from no one; it came from us all. My body stiffened against its surges.

I swallowed hard, then choked out the words I'd rehearsed that day: "Now everyone take a deep breath. Breathe deeply. Breathe the night. When we sleep at night, we breathe the night. So breathe the night now and go to that place within yourself where dreams are kept. Go to that place that connects you with the Otherworld, go that place and stay there—don't move."

The current really sang through me now. The wave bounced up and down like a crazed antelope. I fought against its centrifugal force. Its high-pitched whine razored my ears. I felt ready to burst.

But I managed to hang on long enough to pass through that agony; I hung on until the current quieted down; I'd arrived at a finer state of being. As I grew still inside, I found myself sitting in the center of a cyclone funnel, the proverbial eye of the storm.

Faces floated within the white whirlwind. I scrutinized them sharply. But no, this time they really were my ancestors: Url, Mul, Muz—the same batch as last night. Except that now they exuded a roisterous good cheer: Url gave me a gap-tooth grin and Mul laughed so hard I could see his uvula.

Then Ellar's lustrous face appeared. The hair drifted about her head as though resting on water. I gazed into her dark, knowing eyes and found there something soft and loving. I could see that she felt hurt and frustrated by the distance between us. "Why did you leap from the cliff?" I asked her. "Why did you leave me?" But my words did not make sounds.

Then suddenly, a white explosion cleared the scene and I was lost for an indefinite moment. When my mind and vision returned, I found myself cradled within a translucent blue-white cocoon. I was a helpless babe; I had no weight. My arms and legs danced softly in the air, floating. I felt pleased and ignorant; I felt dumb as a stunned calf. I looked at my hands and feet as if seeing them for the first time.

But this womb was too pure to last. At the end of a deep extended sigh, I was blasted once again—a jagged white flash shattered the cocoon, splintered that shell. The force of this blow propelled me up into the night sky, toward the thick morass of stars. My stomach was a weak, empty sack that dropped beneath my feet, then kept on falling.

"I am ready to die," I said to the stars, I said to the sky. "I gladly give up. Take me, please—take me back. The ancestors are right: this human life is not a fit place to live. Each sucking breath sears my lungs. With every step I take, the earth harshes against my feet. The least puff of wind grates my skin. I don't belong here; we don't belong here. Take us now and be done with it!"

I opened my arms to the stars. But those distant crystal eyes just regarded me with boredom. And that's when I realized: it didn't make any difference. Whatever new world I might find after my death would still be a part of life. Life was life; I probably wouldn't feel any better anyplace else. I–me—Amar—that was the determining factor.

Round about this time, the bottom fell out of the whole experience. The energy that had carried me upward—so powerful just a moment ago—now fizzled, sputtered and spat. I became a limp, wet thing spiraling wildly downward. But, strangely enough, though my body felt puny and uncertain, my mental state was as calm as a root.

"Oh well—so I guess this is some kind of ending," I thought to myself. "Such a fall could destroy me completely. Beyond all life. I might never return to consciousness. Is that possible? Ah well. Whatever will happen will happen."

But then, after a long whistling sigh, I struck down with a gentle, insignificant...splat.

When I came to myself, I was sitting at the campfire again. My legs felt tingly and cramped. I had to swallow hard to keep my supper from spewing. Around the circle, my tribes-kin rocked on their haunches and blinked their eyes. We all seemed to have crashed at about the same time.

For awhile, we just sat there silently, our eyes echoing this one question: "What...what was that?"

I looked to the children of our tribe: their heads wobbled on their necks as they struggled to regain equilibrium. Why had I allowed them into the circle? I knew why—until now, I didn't believe that a ritual could have such power.

Despite the ragged state of my body and mind, I managed to force out these words: "And so tonight, my good family, before you go to sleep, ask your ancestors to visit you in your dreams. The ancestors—we have drawn closer to them. Can you feel them? I'm sure you can. Tonight as we sat in this circle, we breathed the night, and as we breathed the night, we joined with the night, and as we joined with the night, we joined with the world of our dreams—and with the world of our ancestors. They can hear you now. Call to them."

At this point, I did not wait around for any questions or comments, but blurred the air with a hasty retreat.

That was the last time we ever joined hands during a group ritual. And that was the last time we ever experienced that magnificent power.

Despite the commotion of that evening, I slept contentedly.

However, the next morning, when I came to the campfire circle, I found my brothers and sisters all hollow-eyed and empty-headed. Their jaws hung slack. Their feet dragged the ground as they walked. They stared at me like I was a curse and a pox.

Feigning cheerfulness, I sat down by the fire and slapped my knees. "Everyone hale and hearty this morning?" I chirped.

Ur scratched her flabby buttock and said, "Amar, you did a bad ritual last night."

"Bad? Did you say 'bad'? I didn't mean for it to be bad."

"Well, the experience during the ritual itself wasn't all that rough. Sure, that white cyclone made me a little dizzy, but nothing I couldn't handle. I managed to keep myself together. Until I went to sleep, that is. That's when it hit me. Oh boy, how it hit me!"

"What a ferocious dream!" Boq slapped his forehead. "I don't know where the rest of you went, but

I found myself in a dark place with a bunch of ugly faces chasing me. Yes. I couldn't get away from them—they infested my ears and crawled down deep inside my brain. It was monstrous."

"The same damn thing happened to me!" said Dith.

"Yeah, me too!" said Dat.

One after the other, the tribespeople echoed Boq's nightmare.

"Well anyway, you all look okay now," I lied. "It's always a little bumpy the first time. Tonight it'll be much gentler. Those faces you saw were actually the ancestors. You shouldn't have run away from them. That's what caused the problem—you ran away. But what the heck, everyone got through it, right? It'll go a lot easier tonight, I promise." I tried to smile, but my mouth felt weak.

The tribes-kin stared at me with narrowed eyes. I felt myself shrinking.

"What about you, Mok? You weren't afraid, were you?"

I regretted that question as soon as I'd asked it. Mok glared at me with that silver fire in his eyes. He hated to admit fear.

"That ritual's no damn good," he grunted. "Look, Amar, here's how it is: each one of us has a job to do. I'm the leader of the hunt. That's my great talent. But you, Amar, what can you do? You're pathetic in the hunt. You bust your thumb chipping flint. And any women here can dig twice the number of grubs in half the time. This business of talking to the ancestors, it's not a necessity. But still the people enjoy it. The antelope dance, in that we will assist you. But calling the ancestors, that's your job. And you're not putting it off on us."

To punctuate his point, Mok jabbed the campfire with a stick. Sparks spun into the sky.

Still I pressed on. "Just thought you guys'd like to talk to the ancestors yourselves, that's all. Really, it's not that hard once you get the hang of it. Trust me. Why don't you give it another—"

"Enough, Amar!" Ur shouted. "Mok speaks the truth. You have your job. So do it. I'm trying to feel proud of you."

A weak feeling floated down through my stomach —the sigh of a leaf falling from a tree.

"Well okay," I said, "but I can't call the ancestors every night. They don't always have the time, you know."

"That doesn't make sense," Boq said. "Yes, I mean, being that they're dead, what else have they to do?"

"They do the same things we do except in a different place."

"Well then, if we have time enough to call them, they should have time enough to visit us. Yes."

Though Boq didn't contain a drop of malice, his logic could be deadly.

"You aren't trying to get out of it, are you, Amar?" Mok sneered.

"No, but I'm warning you—if we keep bugging them, they may stop coming."

"Well they'd better show up," Mok said. "Or else." And with that, he got to his feet, hefted his balls with both hands, and then spat—signaling an end to all further discussion.

Chapter 5 : Matar

Through the heat of that day, I wandered the grasslands, wondering how could I escape the trap I'd set for myself. It was too late to reveal my lies. If the people found out now, they'd never let me live it down. Mok would see to that.

On the other hand, I didn't dare risk raising the wrath of the ancestors. I knew they meant business.

I was ashamed of my lying ways. The guilt weighed on my shoulders until my legs nearly buckled. I felt small enough to crawl into an ant hole.

I couldn't go on living this life. I couldn't stay here. As I now saw it, I had no other choice but to turn away from the only world I'd ever known. I would the reject the company of my tribal family and set out across the savanna alone. Perhaps, in time, I would return. Perhaps when I did, my tribes-kin would rejoice at my homecoming. Perhaps they would then see fit to forgive my transgressions.

It was an action hitherto unthinkable; an idea that chilled me to the core. However, the thought of remaining here frightened me even more.

Nonetheless, I could not leave without a last farewell to my people.

So I kept myself hidden away until the tribe had turned in for the evening. Then I tiptoed over to the sleeping pile. Bathed by the sighing moonlight, this conglomeration of heads, arms, backs, breasts, buttocks, legs and hair breathed as one, with tender crests and troughs.

"Goodbye," I whispered. "So long. You're better off without me."

And so I began my journey across the savanna. With no other point to guide me, I aimed myself toward a star near the horizon. Feeling my shame, the moon veiled itself behind a cloud, leaving me in total darkness. Twice I stubbed my toe on a rock. The spikes of pain only served to reinforce my loneliness. I cried for all that I'd endured these last few days. I cried for all my foolish behavior. I had broken the chain. My lies had broken the chain. How could I ever go back again?

Morning found me leaning against a dead tree on an empty, scorched plain—I had walked all night long.

The horizon wavered in the heat. I knew it would be my death to continue on across this wasteland. Nevertheless, my feet kept leading me toward the far horizon.

The sun began its lonely arc across the sky. Soon, sweat started to sting my eyes. Wind gusts whipped up sand. The sand burnt my face, slipped between my teeth, and etched its way down my throat. A fiery coal smoldered in my scalp.

Such harsh treatment helped me to regain a sprinkling of sanity.

"If you turned around now," I told myself, "tomorrow morning, you'd be back in the grasslands, under the cool trees by the plentiful river. Why punish yourself? What'd you do that was so wrong, anyway? You gave your tribes-kin what they asked for, that's all. They wanted something in their lives besides hunting, gathering, eating, sleeping, and fornicating, and you gave it to them. What's so horrible about that?"

But my feet were immune to such weak-willed logic. My feet kept on dragging me across the desert.

The sun at its zenith pounded my head. My mind spiraled outward and upward. I was losing myself. I moved merely by rote now with no real feeling in my body. I didn't know in which direction I traveled. But I'd ceased to care. I didn't care about anything anymore —including my life, including my death.

My brain rattled around in my skull like a dried nut.

"I can no longer be as one with them," I repeated in my delirium. "No one but me to be with me. I was once one with them and they with me—we were we—but the world started with an argument, so now I dry in the desert. Why am I to blame, am I?—the damage was done before my birth—it was the argument, the argume

Sometime in the afternoon, I completely wilted. My legs melted under me. Mother earth pulled to her bosom and my cheek slapped the ground.

An arid wind raked my skin.

I slipped into oblivion.

When I first awoke, I thought that I lay in the tall grass, just a stone's throw away from my people. But then I smelt the sand beneath my cheek and remembered: I had done the unthinkable, I had left my tribes-kin. What had possessed me?

"You lost your wits, that's all," I told myself. "You'd better stop this feeling guilty and get on back to your people."

I pushed myself up, knocked the dust from my swollen lips, then looked about, trying to gain my bearings. I found that I now inhabited a twilight desert, a dead gray landscape shrouded in fog. To my right lay a ragged boulder. On my left, a scrawny tree clawed the earth. A hare skittered past me, flicking sand back with its hind feet.

I walked on, expecting either night or dawn to arrive soon. But the sun did not rise nor did the moon. The twilight remained twilight.

"I don't know which way to go," I said to myself. "I'll just have to trust my feet to guide me."

But then I stubbed my toe—the same toe—again. Small strokes of lightening fired across my brain. I hopped about, holding my foot, though that only seemed to increase the pain. Then I landed wrong on the other foot, lost my balance and fell to the ground. My humility was all worn out. In fact, I was ready to let loose with a long stream of expletives when I looked up to find a most splendid sight: an antelope stood just ten paces from me—calm and attentive, as typifies their kind.

"Hello my friend," I said to the antelope. "Perhaps you can help me. I am lost here and need to get back to my people. You must know them—your breed has nourished us through many a season. I thank you for all that you've done for us, I bless you, and I hope that, through the goodness of your being, you will assist me."

The antelope blinked its dark round eyes. Those eyes lured me with a magic beyond description. Within their orbs, I found both a sparkling night sky and a womb of deepest earth; I beheld the mysterious essence of the Universe. I wanted to dive in, immerse myself, lose myself forever in the pool of that night womb.

"This just might be a good time to die," I thought to myself. "At least as good as any."

But then the antelope began to talk, moving its lower jaw loosely as though chewing cud. "Wake up, Amar, wake up," it said. "Can't you see me?"

Did my ears fail me or was that the cool, spritely voice of Ellar?

"Ellar? Can that be you? It can't be you," I said. "Where's your face? I see nothing but antelope snout."

"Take another look, Amar. I became an antelope after my human death."

I examined the creature more closely. Yes, I had to admit, those long, gentle cheekbones did suggest something of Ellar. And the smile that played about the black, furry lips teased me in a manner familiar and warm.

"Forgive me, dear Ellar. How could I have been so obtuse? Yes, now I can clearly see you through the antelope. Especially in the eyes, the eyes especially. You must've grown up quickly. I mean, you haven't been dead all that long."

"You're in the Otherworld now, Amar. Time works differently here."

"Wherever I am, I'm just glad that we're together again. I only wish...I only wish that you weren't so antelope, or that I wasn't so human. Then we could renew the pleasure of our coupling."

"Ooooo, but why can't we?" cooed Ellar. "True, we are different, but why let such differences curse our love?" She then rotated on her forefeet, swinging her white hindquarters into view. The pointed tail twitched, both bewitching and beseeching me. I could never say 'no' to Ellar. Her spirit was equal parts wind and fire.

So I took the big leap.

As Ellar's soft cocoon stretched around my stick, my entire being was held entranced. My arms and legs spread out wide in a paroxysm of skyward ecstasy. For a moment there, I could see infinity.

But then Ellar began to move. And I don't mean the lapping, coasting movements of sex; no, I mean she fastened onto my stick with a tight grip, and then bolted. I don't know why she did what she did, but this was typical Ellar: spontaneous and inexplicable. I had no choice but to run with her.

Since I couldn't match her swift gait, my feet skipped over the ground. The toe stubbed before was now stubbed many times more.

"Whoa, Ellar, whoa! Please my darling, whoa! I say stop, please stop!"

She glanced back at me. The corner of her long mouth curled into a smile. "Something wrong, my love?" she called, all sweet and innocent.

"I can't keep up. I can't continue. Please my dearest, let me rest."

But she merely shook her head and kept on running. A low laugh echoed within her elongated neck. Finally, I gave up and wrapped my arms around her underbelly, then I lifted my feet off the ground and held on for dear life.

Why didn't I just pull out? you ask. Was her inner organ all that muscular? you wonder. Well, no and yes. What I mean to say is: something even stronger held me, some deep force within me. I had lost her once—twice actually—and in the process, had lost part of myself. My desire to regain the whole—that was the power that held me.

How long we ran in this manner I can't even guess. As I managed to adapt and grew more comfortable, I burrowed my face into her warm fur and tried to enjoy myself as much as humanly possible.

In fact, I'd just gotten cozy when we slammed to a halt. My forward momentum shoved me deeper into her for an all-too-brief moment. But then, on the rebound, my stick spat back out and I landed on my haunches in the dirt. Though bruised, I felt beatified by the afterglow of love.

Then as I stumbled to my feet, I felt a wave of animal heat swarm against my face. Several sets of glossy black eyes now gawked at me. A cluster of antelope stood just a few paces away. Ellar shuffled in amongst them. When I caught her eye, she dipped her head as though demure.

The graying elder of the group walked up to me. He stuck his snout in my face and sniffed. Then he stepped to the left, then he stepped to the right. "Well well well...what do we have here?" he drawled.

"My name is Amar."

"So what'd you come here for?"

"I came here for Ellar, to claim her and take her back to her people."

"Is that so? Well, not only do I happen to be head of this herd, I also happen to be Ellar's father."

"What do you mean by that? What's a 'father'? I'm unacquainted with the term."

"She's my daughter, knucklehead."

"But you are not a female. You can not give birth."

"From my seed she was born, you idiot."

"Your seed? What seed? You're not a plant."

The elder glanced over to Ellar. "Is this boy as dumb as he pretends to be?" Then he turned back to me. "Yes, from my seed. The seed of my loins."

"Sure, whatever you say, old timer."

"So what were you doing with Ellar just now?"

The antelope whispered among themselves. Though sexual acts in my tribe often drew an audience, I couldn't help but feel embarrassed. "Ellar and I were running together, that's all. Just running, running like the wind."

"You had your stick in her, didn't you boy?"

"Okay, it happened. So what's wrong with that?"

"You mated with an antelope, you fool!" The elder's wet, black nostrils flexed and steamed. "That's wrong, boy, that's just wrong. Don't you know that? Antelope must mate with antelope and men must mate with women. Your filthy human stick has defiled her innocent womb. No telling what abomination might be born from your hookup."

In that splendid moment, the mystery of procreation suddenly revealed its secret to me. Now I understood what the word 'father' meant. My mind reeled. I rocked on my heels. "So that's how it's done!" I yelled. "Glory be!"

The women of my tribe used numerous techniques to induce pregnancy. Sometimes, the hopeful one would hop backwards around a huckleberry bush, or dunk her head underwater three times at dawn, or eat puff balls and mushrooms while sitting in a eucalyptus tree.

But now I knew the truth. How had we missed such an obvious connection? Within my two soft shells, precious seed resided, waiting to be stirred from slumber by woman's warm enticement, waiting to jump forth into her dark pool—to dive to the depths of her being—where it would then produce a child. I was a creator. From the flooding of my river the generations would sprout forth. Now I wanted Ellar more than ever.

"Most gracious old one," I said, "don't call our conjunction an abomination until you see the results. The offspring of our union will have both the best of man and the best of antelope. Two fine creatures in one fine body. Just so our children don't try to hunt themselves—ha ha."

The elder snorted at my rude joke. "Leave the sight of my eyes," he said.

"I will, but only if Ellar comes with me. To be mine and mine alone. We'll bring forth a new race. Human-antelope. Antelope-humans. Or some such thing."

"No!" The father stomped the ground. "Antelope are antelope and humans are human. It'll never work."

"But Ellar used to be human, and as I look among you now, I see many that I once knew as human. I don't know how I recognize you, but I recognize you. I guess it's the eyes. Yes, it's eyes. You there—the one with the drippy nostrils—you remind me of Thog. What a man you were! Some say you once put out a brush fire by peeing on the flames. And over there—the one who keeps twitching her ears—I don't know your name, but you used to tickle my toes when I was just a babe."

The old father raked the ground with his hoof. "Don't you understand anything, son? When your human life is done, you return to life as an antelope."

"But the ancestors I saw the other night had human forms."

"They just took those shapes so you'd accept them as your own."

"Well, I don't see any of them among you now."

"Trust me, they're around here somewhere."

"So then what happens after you die as an antelope?"

"You come back as a human again."

"I rejoin my tribe?"

"The possibilities are greater than that, short eyes."

"Okay, okay, stop...let me think...I want to return Ellar to her tribe and, well, I can't really bring her back as an antelope. Is there some way to make her into a human again without her having to die?"

"Well yes, there is. I actually do possess the power to change her into a human," the old one said. "But unfortunately, I just can't let her go right now. I need her with me; I need her help. I'm not quite myself these days...ever since..." —he sniffled— "ever since I lost my golden horn. Yes, I still have two regular horns, and they do their job just fine. But I used to have a third horn, a golden horn, that sat upon the crown of my head. Though I'm still quite astute, my wisdom just doesn't shine as bright since I lost my golden horn. It's not only important to me, it's important to the whole herd. Without the horn to guide us, we might not find the hunting grounds again. And then where would your tribe be?"

"And then where would I be?" I thought to myself. "They'd blame me."

"Okay, I think I get your drift," I told the father. "If I find this gold horn for you, Ellar can run off with me."

"You're so perceptive."

"So where is it?"

"A beast known as Matar stole the golden horn from me. Despite my personal greatness, that is one beast I can't defeat."

"So what makes this one so tough?"

"It's big, it's strong, it's a malevolent bastard."

"Oh, okay."

"But more importantly: Matar's the one who created us all, who created everything on this earth. For that reason, no one can defeat Matar."

"I thought everything came into being when the sky had its way with the earth."

"Well yeah. But who do you think created the earth and the sky? Matar, that's who."

The task before me was a black thundercloud ribbed with lightening. But I refused to show fear. "So where do I find this Matar beast?"

"You don't find Matar," the father said sweetly, "Matar finds you."

"I don't have to go anywhere?"

"You just have to go."

I figured the old coot only wanted to get rid of me. But it was too late to back out now. So I puffed up my chest and I said, "Then for Ellar I will find Matar."

I glanced at my beloved. She stretched her neck and lifted her chin, urging me onward. Her white hindquarters still glistened as though wet with dew.

And so I bid farewell to the antelope family and began my search for the one known as Matar. I realized that Matar might not even exist. I could wander this twilight world forever, hunting for a nonexistent creator.

"Well, at least my life will have a higher purpose," I told myself. "I can live with honor for a change."

And so I walked. I walked without direction. I walked without rest. I walked like the blind man that I was.

The earth sighed beneath my feet. Gray haze hovered like half-remembered dreams over a weary landscape. The monotony was relentless.

For awhile, the memory of Ellar's deep antelope eyes helped to motivate my legs. Then I considered her finer human features—the soft roll of flab that hung from her belly, the downy hair on the inside of her thigh. The way she would dip her head and give me that coy look, a prism hanging from each eyelash.

But then ever so slowly the rhythm of my soles slapping the hard, dry earth worked to erode my mind. In time, expectation died, as well as desire. I became free of all care. I could walk forever.

But of course, nothing ever remains the same. Eventually, a change in the air awoke my benumbed senses. My nose detected the scent of moisture. A fresh breeze stirred my blood.

As new vigor crept into my limbs, I picked up the pace, happy to feel alive again.

However, that breeze soon grew into a stiff wind that made me squint. Wet, putrid air filled my nostrils. But I was not to be deterred—I leaned into the blast and pressed ahead.

"If this path offers hardship, I must be headed in the right direction," I told myself.

Wild gusts tore at the spare sprigs of grass. Strands of fog raced past me as if fleeing destiny. My heart pounded with glad welcoming. I felt certain that I would soon meet my deliverance—though it might also mean my doom. But whatever it was, it'd be a real event.

Thunder rumbled within the earth; the ground shuddered. Tension gripped my body. I stubbed my toe; I stumbled; I slammed to the ground.

The blazing wind now became so fierce that I couldn't regain my feet; I had to crawl on all fours like a beast. The gale pulled my cheeks into pockets and drew my hair out straight. Bits of grit collected in my teeth. Through the streaks of my tears, all I could see was darkest night.

"Yes, this is definitely the right path," I told myself.

Finally, the strength of the squall forced me to press my chest against the ground and wiggle along like a lizard.

"No, you won't get me," I cried to the shrieking wind. "You can rip the flesh from my bones, but you still won't get me!"

As if to mock those words, the wind then grabbed me by the arms and legs and with one mighty heave, tossed my body to the sky. I shot straight up into the ecstatic black storm. A weak feeling bled through me all the way to my toes. I could feel my guts spiraling out, leaving not a whisper of bravado. My significance became the difference between a pebble and a speck.

As I entered the clouds, the hot mist swarmed against my face. Dark fog whipped up all around me. Veins of blue lightening sizzled through the billows. I could feel energy building.

Then suddenly the air shook with the sound of a rolling belch. A giant egg cracked and the white explosion knocked me spinning.

And that's when my lights blew out.

The next thing I remember is slapping down flat on a sandy beach. By some strange magic, I had survived the fall intact—at least, in the physical sense.

I waited until my head and body had ceased their internal swirl, then sat up and took stock of my surroundings. A few paces from me, the surf slid up the sand, then sighed back down. A blue body of water stretched all the way to the horizon. Waves heaved and hoed with a dull, powerful somnolence. The scent of brine bit my nose.

"This must be the ocean," I told myself.

I'd heard of the ocean from campfire tales.

It sure did look luxurious. I had a hankering to dip my poor feet into that luscious water.

But before I could take one step, a long shadow fell across my path. With utmost trepidation, I peeked over my left shoulder.

On the crest of a sand dune just twenty paces away stood the most hideous thing that I'd ever seen.

I mean, it was ugly.

From top to bottom, this eyesore was nine times my own height. It looked like a gigantic stump. The trunk was all sticky, glistening gray and speckled with big black pores. Ever so often, one of those orifices would open and out would plop a fat wad of yellow pus. These excretions dripped down the slimy trunk like a herd of slow-moving snakes.

Feelers that resembled long, fleshy flower petals curled outward from the top of the stump. These languid tongues lapped at the air.

Feelers also protruded from the base of the stump. Sliding like drollops of syrup, they eased over the sand toward me.

I believed the thing to be more plant than animal. So I figured I'd be safe as long as I stayed outside its field of reference. Towards that end, I took one delicate step backward.

But at that exact moment, a large eyelid popped open near the top of the trunk, revealing. an eye that looked just like a big fish eye—an eye with a dilated, round black pupil surrounded by a thin penumbra of white.

This eye didn't seem to focus on me or on anything else, so I took another delicate step backward. But as soon as I set my foot down, the dark orb began to swim back and forth in its socket. Finally, it honed in on me.

"Run, Amar, run!" I shouted in my head. "Move your feet or this slimy beast will slurp you up with its syrupy feelers."

But I could not stir a single toe. Had fear paralyzed me? Or did this monster possess some special magic?

A whistling bolt of white steam shot up from the top of the trunk. Hot mist stung my skin. The smell of burnt hair filled my nose.

A deep rumbling shook the stump, then all the orifices opened at once and a voice came forth—or rather, many voices speaking as one, and not in the thundering tones you'd expect from such a colossus, but in a piercing high-pitched squeal neither distinctly male nor female.

"You there—yes, you—why have you come to the Land of Matar?" the voices shrilled. "From far away I saw you. Despite the great wind of my flatulence, you pushed ahead like a fool. Why did you defy me? Why did you defy the all-powerful Matar?"

Fear and nausea weakened my frame. I fought to regain my composure—though this creature might be the Creator, I couldn't let myself be bullied.

Nonetheless, my voice fluttered like a butterfly as I spoke. "Gee, I'm sorry. I didn't know I was defying you."

"You're here looking for something, aren't you?"

"Not really."

"Yes you are. What is it? Speak up!"

"Okay, okay—I'm looking for a horn, a golden horn. But no, wait, now that I think about it, I don't need that silly old horn after all. Sorry to bother you. I should be going."

I kept trying to pry my feet loose but to no avail.

"Well, you just can't come in here, invade my domain, then run off without anything happening." The voices now rose to an even higher octave. "That's just not the way it works!"

My ears were ringing.

"Again, I apologize," I said. "I made a mistake, an innocent mistake."

"So why don't you want the gold horn anymore? What made you change your mind?"

I moved my lips, but could not speak.

"I'll tell you why—you're afraid, that's why; scared stiff. The magnificence of my presence frightens the pee out of you. Am I right or am I right?"

"Well after all, you did create the world, didn't you? Both the earth and the sky?"

"That's true, that's true. But you'd think that a being as powerful as myself would inspire courage, not fear."

"Yes, you would think so, wouldn't you?" I squeaked.

"In fact, you ought to be downright delighted to see me," the voices sang. "Because any being as potent as myself—not that there is one, but if there was—should be able to produce a golden horn upon a whim."

"Well, okay then. Can you do that for me? Can I get the golden horn from you?"

"Sure you can. But which golden horn do you want?"

"The one that once belonged to the old antelope."

"That sorry coot? What'd you want his damn horn for?"

Seeing that Ellar's father was not in good favor, I answered, "To trick him."

"Well, in that case, it's all yours."

"Thank you."

"Now lie down flat on the ground, face up."

"Huh?"

"You heard me. Lie down and close your eyes. Do it, if you want the golden horn."

Of course by this time, I no longer cared a whit about the horn. I just wanted out of here. But my choices did seem limited. Matar had me. What could I do except lie down?

But though I appeared to close my eyes, I kept them open just a sliver.

"Oh no," Matar's many voices chimed. "You must close your eyes all the way."

"So what's the plan here, if you don't mind my asking?"

"Like I said, I'm going to give you the golden horn—smack dab in the middle of your chest!"

I sat bolt upright. "You're going to stab me?"

"Yeah."

"But that'll kill me!"

"Well, it's the only way you'll ever get the horn. Now lie back down."

"And if I don't?"

"But you will."

I knew I was doomed. I couldn't go anywhere—I couldn't move. But after all I'd been through of late, I was only half-afraid of death. And so, with a weak sigh, I collapsed on the ground and closed my eyes.

"Okay now, relax," Matar said, "and spread your arms and legs out wide."

With a great force of will, I managed to open up my arms and legs the weest bit. My body shook until I could hear the bones rattle.

Thunder pounded within the stump. The orifices gurgled and hissed.

I kept reminding myself that I would soon join with Ellar in my new antelope life. But under the circumstances, that thought was of little comfort.

A cool shadow washed over me. Despite my best effort, one eye sprung open. I could now see the gleaming tip of the golden horn high above me. Hands that resembled black claws held the horn—the trunk had sprouted two long, spidery arms.

Matar's big fish eye glowed with gleeful malice.

"Move, damn it! Jump!" I yelled to myself. "Or you're a dead man!"

But some strange power held me fast.

A golden flash split the air. My chest erupted in a volcanic roar.

For an infinitely-intense moment, searing heat pierced the tatters of my flesh. I traveled to the farthest reaches of white-hot pain in a single breath. Then nothing. Stillness. The absence of pain. I floated on a bed of air in limitless black space.

I started to move, then stopped myself. I would wait; I would luxuriate in this cool peace and just see what came.

"For once, you're at rest," I told myself. "So why trouble the situation?"

But then a vague uneasiness crept over me. I realized that I couldn't feel my feet, nor my hands, nor my arms, nor my legs, nor my chest. Once again, I experienced myself as a loose mass of dust motes. And though I tried to draw myself back together, the tiny particles of me just drifted farther and farther apart. I could feel my mind dissipating.

"So this is death," I thought. Then I could think no more; I was too far gone.

I don't know how long I stayed gone, but I guess it doesn't matter. When I came to myself, my body was intact and had no tattered flesh.

However, I no longer lay on a beach by the sea, but on dry, cracked earth. A wet circle on the ground showed where I'd peed in my sleep. Powdery dust covered my skin—it looked like I wore soft brown moth hair.

When I stood up, my legs wobbled and my body listed from side to side. My head felt as light as a dandelion ball.

I thought of Matar, the malicious creator. I thought of antelope Ellar. And the old coot, her alleged father.

"You must've passed out and dreamt the whole thing," I told myself. "You'd better stop this woeful silliness and get on back to your people. Being untethered is unhealthy. A human mind needs to root among the common things of life. This desert is empty, so your imagination tries to fill the space."

But then I looked down to find a golden horn resting on my palm. The gold was not shiny, but frosted and deeply luminous. Though it barely measured the length of my hand, the horn had a solid weight to it, a serious density.

The gray haze of this twilight land had brightened to a white glow. With only my feet to guide me, I began to walk. I would trust my feet; my feet would lead me back to Ellar.

By fortune's chance, fate waited just beyond the next hill. There, at a quiet oasis, the antelope family grazed. As I topped the dune, I held the horn aloft to display my victory. But those of the herd merely lifted their heads, gave me a look, then went back to their business. Except for Ellar. She bounced on her front hooves, then turned and wiggled her white tail at me. I felt both pleased and embarrassed.

The old father was honing his horns against a palm tree as I approached him.

"Oh Honorable Father," I said sweetly, "I have something for you. Something I'm sure you'll enjoy."

He narrowed his eyes at me. "So you got my horn, huh?"

I extended my palm. "If this be it."

"Took you long enough. Now set it on my head."

"What? Where? Won't it fall off?"

"No, dummy, it's magical."

I set the base of the horn on the crown of his head between his other two antlers. To my surprise, the golden horn adhered instantly.

"Now if you don't mind, I'd like to get on back to my tribe," I said. "We had an agreement, remember?"

"Of course, I remember. You think I'm feeble? Ellar, come here."

But she already stood right beside him. Her pointed tail twitched with excitement.

"So you can make Ellar human again, right? Otherwise, I don't know how my tribes-kin might react."

"Just turn around," the father told me.

"What?"

"Do as I say. Close your eyes and turn around slowly. Take it slow, slow—don't rush."

Though I didn't trust the old geezer, I knew that I had no other choice but to obey him. I rotated cautiously on my heel, expecting the worst.

But to my delight, when I'd completed the circle, I found Ellar standing before me in fine human form. Her belly roll was a pillow for my weary soul. I looked for the old father, to thank him, but he and his antelope family had disappeared, along with the oasis.

"Amar, I'm back," Ellar whispered.

The light downy hair on the inside of her thigh awakened many warm memories.

But my joy was short-lived. All the hubbub must have pushed my puny mind past its limits. Whatever the case, I suddenly went into a swoon.

Responding to my weak, slumping form, Ellar extended her arms to catch me. But I had too much weight for her. She shuffled backward, trying to hang onto me. My spine slid against her pendulous breasts and into the soft pool of her abdomen. The heat of this friction helped to rouse me. I braced my legs and tried to stand. But something now tugged the flesh of my back.

Ellar gave a sharp shriek.

"Hey, what's with you!" I snapped. "You screamed right in my ear." But then I added gently, "Though indeed, it was the most mellifluous scream, full of perfection and truth,"—for I did not want to ruin our precious reunion.

"Oh Amar! We share the same skin," Ellar groaned.

"That's true, we are close."

"I don't mean that. Here, look."

I turned to face Ellar, but to my surprise, this movement threw us both off balance; we fell sideways together. My elbow hit deep into her biceps as we landed. She yelped again and let loose with a torrent of expletives.

"Ellar, what's going on! Why didn't you let go of me?"

"I can't, Amar. Don't you see? Father tricked us. Yes, he granted your wish, but in his own spiteful way. You asked that we be joined together, so that's what he did—he joined us."

By craning my neck and looking from the corner of my eye, I ascertained the problem. The flesh of my back, from shoulder to hip, had somehow bonded with the skin of Ellar's front. Though we twisted and pulled, we could not break the connection.

"It's no use," Ellar cried.

"We've got to find your father."

"No, I know him. He'd separate us only if we agreed to abandon each other. I'm not ready to go back."

"Well then, we must walk."

"I think that'd be a little difficult right now."

"But how else can we find our destiny?"

"Well, okay then. Let's walk."

"At least we're together, dear Ellar."

"Yeah," she sighed. Then she gave my cheek a wet kiss and raked her nose along the nape of my neck—this latter gesture being a vestige of her antelope life.

It took some huffing, heaving, and cursing, but we finally managed to climb back onto our feet. And so our search began.

Though we tried to coordinate our movements, we walked through the dunes with a hobbled, erratic gait. And as we walked, Ellar's furry bush kept brushing the bottom of my buttocks in a manner that could not help but entice. Yet I knew that my stick, having attained a heightened state of awareness, could not possibly reach her luscious interior. I thought about asking for her hand, but at the moment, the situation between us was just too testy.

Despite our love, Ellar and I had often rubbed each other the wrong way. The abrasion was part of our chemistry, I guess. Ellar was ember and spark to me; she was candidly sly and soulfully mysterious. Yeah, she was a little shadowy, but that was okay—pure light never attracted me; I always liked a whiff of smoke in the blaze.

Of course, such a woman can be daunting even under the best of circumstances. Under the worst, she is a storm.

Though I tried to be careful as we ambled along, I couldn't help but step on her toes. And too often—much too often—her toenails raked my heels. Her warm breath, so pleasurable in the past when it'd curled into my ear, now raised hackles on the back of my neck. Too often—much too often—our legs got tangled and we tipped, tottered, and crashed to the ground. The sharp sunlight razoring down only added to our misery.

But through it all, I gritted my teeth and held my tongue.

Ellar, however, showed less restraint. First, she whined, then she raged.

"Your hair keeps getting in my mouth," she barked, time and time again.

Finally, ever so sweetly, I said, "Then why don't you shut your mouth, my darling?"

Frayed as she was, Ellar's reaction was cruel impulse: her knee shot up between my legs.

In an instant, a fiery spear went all the way up from the base of my spine to the center of my brain and I did a little jump that took us both off our feet. We landed in a pile of arms and legs. I fought to keep from spewing. A hot coal throbbed in my groin.

"What're you trying to do to me!" I squeaked.

"I can't take this anymore!"

"Oh yeah? Well, I'm the one that just got punched in the bird's nest. What's gotten into you, anyway? You've changed. Where is that strong, sprightly woman who used to run through the fields with me? The one who used to pour flower petals over my head and stroke my belly with her long nails until I leapt upon her in the grass? Through you I once knew the best of myself. But now...but now..."

"Give it a rest," she said. "I've had it. I mean, what's the use? I'm done with walking. I'm just going to lie here until I perish in the desert. In the meantime, let's try to get along. You made a mistake. I accept that."

"Your father tricked me."

"You should've known better than to trust him."

"I wanted you."

"You wanted me to save you from your sadness and self-loathing."

"I sacrificed myself for you. You know that? Matar took that golden horn and burst my heart asunder. And the whole time I didn't even blink an eye. Now you say I made a mistake. But if you'll recall, it was you who came to me. You dragged me to your antelope family."

"No, Father found us. You can't hide from him."

"I never had that sadness until you left."

"Sadness can improve you. Eventually."

"So you think I need improving?"

"I know all about what happened between you and the tribe," Ellar said. "I know how you lied to the people. I can see it all from over here."

"They wanted my lies, so I gave them what they wanted. What I wanted was to tell them the truth— really, I did—but things kept getting in the way. I didn't hurt my tribes-kin—I hurt myself. This job they foisted on me is just too big a burden. I'm just too ordinary."

"You wanted everyone to think you were special. That's what got you into this mess. If you didn't feel so guilty, I couldn't accept you."

"Well, whatever the case, it looks like we're stuck with each other."

"That's supposed to be funny?"

"No," I said. "It's not."

But we were just too frustrated—we had to laugh. Through our anger and our tears, through our sobs and our moans, we laughed and we laughed.

I could feel Ellar's ribcage vibrating against my back.

When we finally calmed down, the peace between us was like the afterglow of love. Ellar kissed my shoulder and raked her nose along the nape of my neck.

"You're right," I said. "Why should we drag ourselves to the four corners? I just want to lie here with you. Let the shifting sands bury our bones. The heart of the desert will be our grave."

"Despite everything, I'm glad I'm here," she whispered.

So we just lay there, caught in the web of fate. What was there to worry about anyway? When we died, we'd both return as antelope, right? And then, when we'd finished our antelope lives, we'd be human again. I had to admit, the system had a comforting monotony.

Ellar and I had dissolved into quietude; in body and spirit, we were at rest.

So, of course, there came a change in the wind. A cool breeze prickled our skin. At first, we felt refreshed. But this soft zephyr soon grew into a rude gust. Sand stung my face and burrowed between my lips.

"And we'd just gotten comfortable," I said to Ellar.

The sky was now an imperious black. Dark clouds swirled and tore against one another.

The gale roared in our ears. We hunkered inward and held tightly to our love. Far in the distance, a cyclone funnel churned across the desert. It bounced here and there over the dunes, yowling like a wounded hyena. We both knew the cyclone would find us soon.

"Think we should try to make a run for it?" Ellar asked.

"You know that won't do any good. You can't flee from destiny. Besides, in our present condition, we're too slow."

Sand swirled about our heads. We covered our eyes and hoped for the best. Way down deep in my bowels, the little man howled loud and long.

Then abruptly, all grew still.

Ellar and I struggled to our feet and blinked the sand from our eyes. The cyclone had vanished. The clouds above had calmed. The world was as quiet as death. Yet we couldn't help but feel a difference. Our ears then detected a sluggish slurping sound. Wet, putrid air pushed into my nostrils.

"Amar, turn around," Ellar whispered.

"I really don't want to."

"But you know you have to."

"I know, I know."

We shuffled our feet until we both faced Matar the stump. That big fish eye glared down upon us with palpable disgust. The orifices hissed and spewed pus.

I could feel the gooseflesh rise on Ellar's skin.

"What is that?" she asked.

"That is Matar," I said. "Just relax and let me do the talking. Okay?"

"Oh, you again," the many voices sang in high-pitched harmony. "Who's that with you?"

"A friend," I said.

"Well the two of you look awfully cozy. But enough small talk. I want my gold horn back."

"I don't understand," I said. "I thought you gave it to me for keeps."

"Oh no. No, I just wanted to annihilate you with it. You weren't supposed to live. You weren't supposed to take my golden horn. Give it back to me and you can go free."

At that moment, I spied the wellspring of opportunity. I realized that Matar had the power to separate Ellar and me. True, the consequences could be dire. But I saw it as our only hope.

"About the gold horn," I said, "there's a little problem."

"Yes, go on," the voices shrilled.

Was this creator dumb or what? Why couldn't Matar—the all-powerful, the omniscient— see my devious plan?

"It's like this: I can't exactly get at the horn right now."

"No problem. Just tell me where it is."

"Well, if you'll look closely, you'll notice that this woman and I are stuck together—my back to her front. The old antelope did this to us, that conniving coot. But before he did it, he placed the golden horn between us. For safe keeping, I guess. So anyway, the horn now lies buried betwixt our two skins. I can feel it rubbing against my spine even as I speak."

"Oh, I am so sorry for you," the voices chimed. "I really am. That old goat's a real bastard—yes, he is. He needs a good talking-to, that's what he needs." As Matar spoke these words, five long, spidery limbs sprouted out from the trunk's gray flesh.. They dangled down, bent at the elbow, a jagged claw at the end of each.

"What's it going to do to us?" Ellar whispered.

"Uh," I said, "uh." I tried to swallow, but couldn't clear the lump from my throat.

In the next instant, the trunk buckled, creasing its midsection and bending nearly in half. The top feelers descended toward us. We couldn't even think to move. When the feelers touched ground, they created a shadowy cage around us. The stench took my breath away.

"I'm not so sure about this idea of yours," Ellar said.

The claw arms then snaked through the interstices of this cage, moving as if guided by scent.

"Uh," I said. "Uh."

The pinchers hovered in the air for a long frozen moment. Then...they jumped us—they bit into that tender zone where her front met my back and commenced chomping.

Let it be known that fear does not reduce pain. Quite the opposite. The first bite of the first claw sent a lightening shock all the way to my core. As the nippers sawed and hacked through our joint flesh, Ellar and I rocked with convulsive spasms. We danced like fishes kicked from the water. Our bodies sang with electricity. In a few brief moments, I traveled through countless eternities.

Then, when I'd finally ceased to feel or care, the claws drew away. Their jagged edges drooled wet pieces of flesh.

The cage now lifted from us as the trunk righted itself. Ellar dropped to one side; I dropped to the other. Oddly enough, not a drop of blood had been lost.

Yes, Ellar and I were free from each other; however, we were not yet free from Matar.

The beast gave its top feelers a little shake to work out the tangles. Then once again, that big black fish eye focused down upon us.

There was a fuzzy numbness all across my back. Just below the surface of that numbness, the pain was buzzing, waiting for a chance to break through. A dozen dizzy birds circled my head.

"So what happened to the damn horn?" Matar screeched. "It wasn't there."

"What? That's odd," I said. "I bet the old hoof-hopper took out it when we weren't looking."

"No, you tricked me, you little toad. How dare you mess with your Creator!"

73

"I have a question," Ellar broke in. "Father told us that you created both the earth and the sky."

"Yeah, that's right."

"But then where'd you come from?'

"From nowhere. I came from nowhere. And from everywhere at once."

"What kind of answer is that?" Ellar often lacked discretion, even in the most precarious situations.

"All you need to know is this: before me there was nothing. Then I came into being and then everything else came from me. And I mean everything."

"But the earth and sky are bigger than you are. How could they've possibly come from you?"

"A child can grow larger than its mother and father, right? Besides, this is only one of my many forms. You can't even begin to imagine how big I am."

"Well if you're the Creator, why don't you just make yourself another damn horn!"

"Ellar, please," I whispered.

"You obviously don't understand how I work," the voices shrilled.

"Oh yeah? Well, I think you're making it all up. I don't think you ever created anything in your whole life."

"Listen to you! Such impudence! Oh, I'm going to get you; I'm going to get you good."

I thought Matar would strike us dead right then and there. But no, in the next moment, the monster folded in its spidery arms, then wrapped its top feelers together and clapped its big eye shut.

Again, the wind began to blow. Sand swirled up around Matar's trunk. Ellar and I had to shield our eyes and take a step back.

A funnel of whirling sand now enveloped the entire stump. The cyclone funnel began to hop over the dunes, moving away from us. It soon disappeared against the distant horizon.

"Well, Ellar," I said over my shoulder, "I hope we've seen the last of Matar for awhile. Anyway, we're free now."

No reply. I coughed the sand from my throat.

"Ellar, did you hear me?"

I turned all the way around. Ellar now stood before me in her antelope form. She blinked her eyes. A long tear streaked her furred cheek.

"Matar got me," she said. "Yes, Matar got me good."

"Look, it's okay. We'll work it out. Here—come here." I reached for her, but she shuffled away.

"No. I'm sorry, Amar. I must leave you. That's just how it is and how it must be."

"But Ellar, we can still be as one."

"No, you have to go on. I see that now. It was my mistake. Sorry, but I can't bear to stay any longer. Goodbye, sweet Amar."

"Ellar, wait!"

But she had already turned from me. Sand flicked from her heels as she skipped across the dunes. Soon she had vanished amid the heat waves.

I sank to the ground. The breath choked in my throat. Again, I had lost Ellar. With her beside me, I could tolerate anything—even senselessness. Loving her was enough for me. Even her storm clouds had beauty.

I curled into myself and wept.

When I'd finally settled down some, I began exploring the skin of my back. To my surprise, it seemed to have healed and was not overly sensitive to touch. A narrow strip of scar tissue ran just beneath my shoulders, down the sides of my back, and then across the top of my buttocks. The skin of this strip had a puffiness to it. But that was all the damage done.

"Hard to believe that such a vengeful creature could be our Creator," I said to myself. "But then again, maybe not so hard to believe. Because when I look around me, it's not such a friendly world I see."

There was nothing left to do then except pick myself up, knock the sand off, and start walking again. I tried feeling mad at Matar—particularly for what he/she/it had done to Ellar—but my anger soon fizzled out. Somehow, I knew that Ellar was right—we no longer belonged together.

At this point, I wasn't concerned about returning home. If my feet took me back to the tribe, then fine. But I refused to worry.

I knew that, one way or the other, I'd find something for myself, sooner or later.

As twilight shifted to night, I bedded down on the bare ground. I just wanted to sleep off the day and forget.

At dawn, I brushed the dreams from my mind and continued on my journey.

And perhaps due to my relaxed attitude, I soon came to that stretch of dozing savanna where the tribe made its life. I found my people crouched around the mid-day campfire, gnawing bits of gristle.

I felt such joy that I could not contain myself. I strode right out of the tall grass and spread my arms to them.

"My brothers, my sisters!" I cried. "I have come back to you."

But they just stared at me with dull expressions. Mok flipped a bird bone into the fire and spat. "Where've you been?" he demanded.

"Oh my friends, I have wandered far from here. In fact, I believe I entered the Otherworld. It is a strange world, the Otherworld, yet a world made more real by its very strangeness."

To my surprise, they told me I'd been gone for two complete cycles of the moon. Time certainly did work differently in Otherworld.

"And while you were out fooling around, Ur took sick," Ool said. "She writhes and moans in a state of half-sleep. She has called for you many times, though no one can understand why."

So I went to the place among the trees where Ur lay dying. Soft fronds covered her body. I knelt down beside her.

"Ur, it's me—Amar," I whispered. "Are you still with us?"

Her eyelids twittered. "One foot here, one foot dangling," she hoarsed. "Where have you been, dear Amar?"

"I got lost and wandered into the Otherworld. While there, I met a being named Matar. Matar claims to have created everything, including the earth and the sky."

"I don't know about this Matar of yours. Sounds like a bit of braggart."

Ur suddenly went into a raw fit of coughing. I caressed her hard, dry hand. Though she'd been tough on me of late, I knew that I was still her favorite. Her loving gaze had been the rainbow of my youth. She would never let anyone else pick my lice.

At this point, I should explain something about how we raised our children. Each newborn belonged, not to its mother, but to the entire tribe. It was considered bad etiquette for a mother to recognize a child as her own.

Nevertheless, I had to ask the question. "Ur, tell me, am I your son?"

"Of course you are."

"I thought so."

"And Mok as well."

I felt something inside me collapse.

"Yes," she said, "you two are twins."

The word 'Noooooooooo!', amplified, rang through the caverns of my mind. How could I have shared the womb with that blunt-headed bully!

"Oh, is that so?" I said, as calmly as possible.

"I just thought you should know," she said. "So what else did you find in the Otherworld?"

The tribes-kin were all crouched behind me; hanging on to our every word.

"Well, I discovered that children come from men as well as from women. We are the seed, you are the soil."

"Yes, I know," she wheezed. "All the elder women know."

"You knew?"

"How could it be any other way?"

"But why...I mean, if you knew...I mean, how...I mean, why...I mean...I don't know what I mean."

Our matriarch went into another paroxysm of coughing. "We didn't want you men getting too big for yourselves," she managed to choke out.

"And why would we do that?"

78

"Well, you see, it's like this: before you guys go out to hunt, you've really got to pump yourselves up. How else could you rise above your fear? Trouble is, when you return from the hunt, you're still in that heightened state. Yep, you boys sure do strut. It gets tiresome, at times; it sure does. So I guess that's why we never told you—you think enough of yourselves already. But now...now, I feel maybe it's good you know."

"Why's that?"

"I suppose it has to do with this creator you mentioned—Madar, or whatever its name is. It just sounds like trouble to me. From here on out, you boys may need all the pumped-up courage you can get."

With that, the poor woman again began to sputter and hack. I wanted to tell Ur how much her tender caring had meant to me, but fumbled for the words. Then, just a few moments later, this ancient of forty summers, my dear mother, heaved a great sigh, then gently collapsed into herself as the breath of life emptied from her body.

The death weighed heavy on my tribes-kin as they went about their tasks the remainder of that day. Ur's life had been our life. Somehow I understood that we would never be the same.

At twilight, we buried Ur beneath the first tree—or one just like it. I said a few inadequate words in her memory, then scattered new leaves over Ur's grave.

No one spoke of conjuring up ancestors that evening.

After dinner, I crept off to the tall grass to sleep alone. The moon was nearly full. Tomorrow I would have to lead my people through another antelope dance. Our horned friends had disappeared during my absence. Naturally, I received full blame.

I seemed to have only dozed for a moment when I woke to find a tree before me where no tree had been before. Its branches and leaves formed a perfect green sphere. Such full and succulent foliage! A profound intelligence emanated from the tree, a deep and silent knowing.

I rose to my feet, drawn to the gentle goodness of this tree. I wanted to feel the security of its strong limbs and listen to the hum of its falling mist.

It was then that I noticed the apples. They hung heavy and voluptuous among the thick leaves. Such audacity in those apples! They dangled down before me, inviting sweet mischief. Their golden hues melded with the richly layered shadows of night—a seductive mix of darkness and light. Mesmerized and salivating, I reached for an apple.

"Ah ah ah!" the tree warned in a playful voice, a voice which somehow managed to combine the deep tones of the male with the high notes common to the female—a magical voice.

"Excuse me?" I said.

"Look, yes, but touch, no." The alternating notes danced around me.

"But I'm dazzled; I'm warmed."

"I came here to talk with you and nothing more. Rest easy and hear my words, dear one. My name is Matar."

"Matar!" I yelped. "I met a Matar in the desert, but that Matar was nothing like you. Fasten another name to yourself. I don't want to think of that pustulous stump when I gaze upon your elegance."

"But I am that same Matar."

"But you can't be that same Matar."

"But I am." The golden apples rang with laughter. Mirth shook the leaves. "You see, I have many forms; there are many versions of me. I need those forms because if you saw me as I really am, the spectacle would explode you. I am the Creator. So I can assume any shape I wish. This time, I used one of my milder forms so as to cool your fear and gain your trust. You see, we have much work to do, you and I. You must lead your people and show them my designs."

I felt hurt; I felt deceived. I did not want the lovely tree to be Matar.

"I couldn't lead those people if I tried," I whined.

"But you can. And you will. Yes, you will. Your people must change their ways. We must have rules. From now on, only one woman for each man. And only one man for each woman. What I mean to say is: women and men must now join together as couples. No more casual commingling as in the past."

"They won't like that one bit."

"But how else can a father know his son? Or his daughter, for that matter? From now on, fathers and mothers must recognize their sons and daughters. And sons and daughters must recognize their mothers and fathers."

"Couldn't you tell the tribe this yourself?"

"You are my messenger."

"Well, alright." I could hardly think to speak. Though I'd tried to fight the feeling, that shadowy gold had intoxicated me. I couldn't summon enough energy to disagree.

"And another thing: your people have to stop running around naked. From now on, you must drape yourselves with animal hides. And in so doing, be sure to cover your precious parts."

"That sounds kind of uncomfortable."

"But it's the right and proper thing to do."

"Well, it's not going to go over."

"Just tell them that it pleases me."

Matar's dark, warm, musical tones pooled in my ears. I gave up my feeble argument.

"Well," I sighed, "if it pleases you it pleases me."

"Remember, Amar, I am the Creator. My laws are the laws of the Universe. And you can't say 'no' to the Universe. My laws must be obeyed."

"Whatever you say." I could feel a silly, sloppy grin spreading across my face.

"Your people have lived in ignorance for too long."

"Ignorance? I don't understand. What is ignorance?"

"That means you just don't know any better."

"Well, perhaps it's better not to know any better."

"But without knowledge you can not suffer."

"But I don't want to suffer." I felt a tiny pain in my chest.

"Sorry, but you must suffer. For without suffering, you can not learn, and unless you learn, you can not know."

"But the more I know, the more I'll suffer."

"You see the beauty of the plan? How it feeds upon itself?"

"No, I don't see the beauty of the plan." Despite its loveliness, I was beginning to dislike the tree. "What's the value of all that?"

"It pleases me."

"To see us suffer?"

"To see you learn."

"I still don't get it."

"That's because it's beyond your understanding. Don't ever try to understand your Creator, Amar. I'm too much for you to understand. If you tried to fit all that I am into your little mind, it would surely flip your lid."

What could I say? I was caught in the net of too many words. I felt exhausted. "Well okay, Matar. Sure, Matar. Whatever you say, Matar."

"And another thing: stop wasting your time conjuring up ancestors. Each night at the campfire circle, dedicate a ritual to Matar instead. You and your people must now turn your attention to me. You must give thanks to your Creator."

"What exactly should I say during this ritual?"

"Oh, anything will do. You're good at making stuff up. But enough for now. I must be going."

"Wait. One last question—if you have so many forms, why'd you choose something so hideous the first time?"

"Who said it was hideous?"

"Ah, nobody."

All of a sudden, the tree pulled away from me. It receded into the night shadows, then, in a flash of gold, it vanished. The darkness was now complete. I could feel myself falling, falling backward, but for the moment, I had given up all care.

I jolted awake.

I looked all about me, but could not find the lovely Matar tree. It was already morning. The sun burnt the edge of the earth. My eyelids scratched my eyes as I blinked.

83

I began to recall the rules Matar had given me. Upon consideration, they seemed to lack practicality.

But I knew that any breach of those laws would cause problems. Matar didn't like having his/her/its authority tested. For me, the first Matar—Matar the stump—would always be the real Matar. I regarded the wonderful tree as a merely a ruse.

Whatever the case, it was all too much for my puny mind. I was reeling.

Nevertheless, as I approached the campfire circle that morning, I fixed a cheerful mien to my face.

The tribespeople regarded me with narrowed eyes. They had not yet accepted me back into the fold.

To try to regain their favor, I told them all about my Otherworld journey, though I didn't mention meeting Ellar, nor the antelope family, nor of my search for the golden horn. For one thing, the pain of these memories was still too fresh. I was in no mood to hear Mok's rude comments.

And of course, I wasn't about to tell my tribes-kin that they hunted their own ancestors.

However, I did say that while taking a stroll one afternoon, I'd gotten lost and woke to find myself in a land of shadow and fog, and that while in that land, a windstorm had tossed me high into the sky, but that somehow I'd landed safely on an ocean shore, where I'd met the one known as Matar.

"And Matar made it clear to me that we must stop pestering our ancestors," I told the circle

"Why's that?" Boq scratched his chin.

"Because Matar requires our full attention. We must worship Matar now and devote all our rituals to him/her/it and give thanks to him/her/it for his/her/its blessing."

"Why's that?" Boq scratched his chin.

"Because Matar is the Creator. From Matar came the sky and the earth and every single thing on this earth."

"I thought everything came into being when the earth and the sky had an argument," Mok said. "That's what the elders always told us."

"But who you do think created the earth and the sky and made them to argue? Matar, that's who! Matar's done an awful lot for us. So I think the least we can do is honor Matar's wishes."

"Just so he doesn't ask for too much," old man Purl said.

"Only a few things that're for our own good."

"Such as?" Ool cracked her knuckles.

"First of all, from now on, only one woman for each man. And only one man for each woman. We all have to pair off. Like on a permanent basis. And the couples must keep to themselves in regards to the sexual pleasure. We can't share as we've shared in the past."

Oh, the cacophony of cursing and lamentation that greeted this news! The people wrinkled their noses, stuck out their tongues, and pouted their bottom lips.

"What's Matar's reason for that?" Ert whined.

"Well, as we all now know, when a man plants his seed into a woman, he creates a child. Just as we must honor Matar as the giver of life, each child must now honor the parents who gave it life. And to do so, that child must know who its parents are, right? That child must know its father, as well as its mother. Therefore, only one woman for each man and only one man for each woman."

To my surprise, after a few thoughtful moments, all the tribes-kin nodded their heads and grunted their assent. Even Mok seemed satisfied with my explanation.

But I had one more idea I had to sell. And I knew it was a doozy. "Oh, and another thing before I forget...Matar also said that we must cover our bodies with animal hides."

Oh, what a chorus of groaning and moaning welcomed this announcement!

"Wait, now think about it," I cut in. "Since we are limiting ourselves to one partner, I don't think we should be going around presenting our precious parts for easy access. Now should we? No. Nor should we display our physiques in a manner known to be attractive."

After a moment of reflection, my tribes-kin again nodded their heads and grunted their assent.

However, as usual, Mok could not leave things well enough alone. "All that is fine and dandy," he said. "But Amar, the antelope have deserted us since you left. We tried performing the Stick-Horn dance on our own, but they won't listen to us. You want us to wear hides? Okay, we'll give it a try. But you have to bring the antelope back. We're holding you responsible for that."

"Whoa now." I held up my hands. "It's not me who wants you to wear the hides. It's Matar."

"Whatever. Just get the antelope back."

"I'll try my best." My stomach twitched.

"You get them back here—or else."

I thought of the antelope family, of the ancestral echoes within their dark eyes. When we ate the antelope, we ate ourselves. Actually, the idea had a nice symmetry. Still, I hated to think that when I chowed down, I might be taking a big bite of Ur or Ellar.

"So how do we decide who couples with whom?" Boq asked.

"Well, if there's someone you like special, that'd be a good place to start. Let your heart guide you. Approach the person, talk it over, work something out, make an agreement. Just let the others know who you've chosen. Otherwise, somebody might, ah... invade, if you know what I mean."

On that note, I begged leave of them, using the excuse that I needed silence and solitude before the antelope dance that evening. In truth, all this reasoning and justification had exhausted me.

That night, I tied sticks to my head and led the tribe through the dance once again. Tender moonbeams strobed our backs as we leapt through the tall grass.

But the next day, the hunters again returned empty-handed.

"You must give our antelope friends time to respond," I said. "Trust them."

Fortunately, the people still had plenty of roots and grubs with which to stuff their stomachs. Plus, the business of coupling helped to distract them.

Though I had expected a little difficulty during this transition phase, other than some name-calling and the occasional black eye, things went rather smoothly.

However, my own efforts to find a mate fell short. Having assumed a leadership role, I now felt responsible for the well-being of each and every tribe member. As such, I thought it best not to disrupt any potential unions. Yes, I realize that this approach goes against the usual standard for leaders—those in charge generally take what they want when they want it. Perhaps that is why, ultimately, I failed as a leader.

I was kind of sweet on a pretty young thing known as Aar. She had big feet with splayed toes, red bulbous knees, and dark eyes that you could fall down into forever. I knew that she could never compare with Ellar; even so, I felt a little hurt when Mok picked Aar for his own.

I thought Mok might start treating me a little bit better, now that he knew we were twins. But alas, things did not play out that way. In fact, he might've even treated me worse.

Within three days, the coupling had been completed. On the evening of the last day, having failed to make a match, I slunk off to the tall grass alone. I just lay there, staring into the nakedness of space, weighed down by the longing in my soul.

Suddenly, my ears picked up the sound of approaching footsteps. One foot dragged the ground as though the leg had fallen asleep. I knew that lame gait well. Bruk had come to me before, though I usually tried to avoid her. True, she was a generous woman. But she was also old and stale and excessively hairy. Her breath hinted of rotted fish. However, for the time being, I would accept my lot. I was that desperate.

Nevertheless, I would not go easy.

I pretended to sleep.

Bruk snuggled down beside me and dug her hair-spiked chin into my shoulder. She then began muttering a warm stream of enticements into my ear. Despite my best efforts to resist, this salacious nonsense prickled my skin and stirred my tired blood.

Nonetheless, I managed to remain inert. But then her gnarled hand delved down until it found my personal slug. Age might have knotted those hands, but age had given them experience as well. Bruk's hand soon transformed my clammy thing into a happy stick, then her hand kept on whittling that stick. In a few short moments, I forgot my pride and just about everything else about myself: my head rolled back; my tongue flopped out; my eyes spun in their sockets. I was about ready to bust when she yanked off the stiff animal hide that grated my skin, then leapt upon me like a cat pouncing on its prey. Her inner self seized my outer self with a coil of sharp intelligence. That coil played fiercely with me, yanking me this way and that. My arms and legs jerked about in paroxysms of pleasure. I reached for her swinging, pleated breasts, not as an act of passion, but in the frail hope of regaining some stability.

Then something hit me down deep and kept on hammering its way up until it came to my stick. With one last fatal gasp, I let go and burst into a shower of stars.

When I opened my eyes again, I found Bruk smiling down upon me with a gaped-tooth grin. I tried to smile back, but my mouth hurt.

"Bruk," I said, "we must tell no one of our union."

"And why's that?" she rasped.

"You see, I have certain responsibilities...which preclude marriage."

"You're a crazy boy. But I like you. Don't worry, I won't embarrass you. I won't say a word. Not one chirp."

She stroked my cheek with her claw-like fingers.

I felt ashamed and had to turn my eyes away.

From that night on, Bruk crept to my spot in the tall grass whenever she felt that I needed comforting. Though her desiccated body emanated only trickle of warmth, I welcomed her with open arms.

The coupling brought with it many changes. For one thing, the tribe no longer slumbered together in one heaving pile. Each loving pair now built their own private hut. These dwellings were made from animal hides tied to a framework of limbs and twigs. An ingenious design, but not without its flaws. On a scorching summer's day, it was like being inside a red-hot coal. And when it rained, the roofs leaked and the dirt floors became compacted mud. Nevertheless, having slept in the open with little or no protection, my tribes-kin believed these shelters to be the finest luxury.

As for myself, I rejected hut life and continued to sleep beneath the naked sky. I preferred to bathe my face in starlight and watch the moon swim through the silhouettes of leaves.

Four days passed without any sign of the antelope. All through dinner on that last night, Mok drilled me with his dark silvery eyes. The tribe felt the tension and grew quiet.

"Mmmm, these tubers sure are tasty," I said to everyone. "Where did you dig them, my sisters?"

Mok spat a mouthful of fiber into the fire and stood up. "My people want antelope steak," he snarled at me.

'My people'—that's what he'd called them. I was starting to feel like nothing more than a hired hand.

"The antelope fills us with its power," Mok continued. "If we only eat tubers and grubs, we'll become nothing more than roots and bugs. Our feet need the springing step of the antelope; our eyes, its keen vision; our ears, its sensitive hearing. Why are you keeping them from us, Amar?"

"The antelope will return to us in proper time," I said, as calmly as possible. "Matar guides such things. And I assure you, Matar knows just what he/she/it is doing, though at times it may appear otherwise."

Mok put his hands on his hips. "Name one good reason for Matar to keep the antelope away."

"Well, you see, it's a test."

"What'd you mean by that?"

"Is not the hunt a test of courage?"

"Yeah, but—"

"Well, we as a tribe are tested just as the hunter is tested. Matar gives us many tests. Matar tests us all the time."

"So why does he do that?" Mok demanded.

"Yeah, why?" Ert whined.

"Well...Matar tests us because—...because..."

"Yeah, go on." Mok spat into the fire.

"Okay, it's like this: we are each of us a grass plant, lifting our leaves to the sun, spreading our roots down into the earth. When winter comes, we shrivel and die. But when the spring rains fall from the sky, we sprout forth once more. And so, in this manner, we are born anew, returning to this world—or one like it—season after season, with each new life bringing further growth. And when our stalk grows tall enough and our roots go deep enough, we'll pierce through to the Otherworld and find bliss there, with our Creator, Matar, and never have to return to the hardships of this life again. But to grow that high and to go that deep, we must pass many tests. We must weather many storms,

91

many droughts. We must endure all those things that would nibble us down and blight us and see us crushed underfoot. Such tests serve to make our roots stronger and our stalks sturdier. So yes, we need these tests. We need these tests in order to join with Matar. It's only because Matar loves us and wants us to be with him/her/it that he/she/it gives us these many tests."

I don't know where this little rhapsody of mine came from, but it sounded so good I nearly believed it myself.

Mok pursed his thick, violet lips. He was clearly displeased. What could he possibly say to such poetry?

But then, once again, Boq's innocent logic brought me down. "Yes, so in that case, Matar must be testing the powers of our Seer," he said.

"Our 'Seer'?" I said. "To whom are you referring?"

"You see the things we can not see. That's your job. So therefore, you're our Seer. Yes."

"Oh," I said. "Thank you."

"Yes, so now Matar's testing your power," Boq said cheerfully. "And until you develop more power—more 'influence', if you will—the antelope won't return."

"Yeah, that's the problem," Mok chimed in.

The rest of the tribe stroked their chins and nodded their heads.

My stomach twitched.

"So you'd better start developing your power and quick," Mok said. "We've need the antelope back now."

Despite my wonderful speech, I'd ended up where I'd begun. Except that now I had a title and my position was even more precarious.

Damn that innocent logic.

At this point, the days became excruciatingly tedious. I could do nothing but wait and hope the antelope would return.

To make matters worse, every evening at the campfire circle, the tribe would quiz me about Matar.

Night after night, I had to handle the same damn questions. At first, the tribes-kin accepted Matar as given; they didn't need details. Boq, however, had to struggle to get his logical mind around this new business. And his questions perked the others' curiosity.

So, once again, my creative resources were taken to the limit.

First of all, Boq wanted to know what Matar looked like.

I thought it best not to say that our Creator was a hideous, pus-spewing stump. So I told him, "Matar uses many guises. Matar can look like anything and everything—a cloud, a mountain, a star, an elephant. That's because he/she/it is everything rolled up into one. Yet, when all is said and done, Matar looks like nothing at all."

"Nothing at all?" Boq asked. "That doesn't make sense."

The others grumbled in agreement.

"Sure it does, because if you saw him/her/it as he/she/it really is, the spectacle would explode you. Matar is just too much for us to take in, my friends. So don't try, don't bother—please."

Boq scratched his chin. "Well, can you at least tell us how big our Creator is?"

"Wider than the heavens, deeper than the earth. That's how big Matar is. Matar has to be that big because, like I said, Matar contains everything."

Boq scratched his chin. "So, if Matar created all things, who or what created Matar?"

"It's like this...Matar just is. Matar will always be and Matar has always been. And you can't create something that's always been."

"Huh? I still don't understand. That doesn't make sense."

"It sure doesn't," Ert whined.

The others grumbled in agreement.

"I keep telling you: Matar is not meant to be understood. So don't waste your time trying, my friends; just praise and worship our Creator and ask him/her/it for his/her/its blessing."

At this juncture, I would try, if at all possible, to change the subject.

These questions about Matar always drained my sap.

Chapter 6 : The People of Roq

Then late one morning, I awoke from a solid sleep to note a change in the air. A low murmuring came to me from far across the plain. I crept to the edge of our campsite and surveyed the horizon. Way in the distance, I spied a line of beads wobbling through the savanna heat waves. As these wobbly beads drew closer, they began to sprout legs—a disconnected centipede was marching toward our camp. Soon, Mok joined me on my left and Boq came up on my right. We three took shallow breaths and held our muscles tense. My stomach twitched. The centipede was now a group of nearly seventy men, women, and children.

By this time, all the tribespeople had gathered behind us. Kids peeked around adult legs like cats crouching in the weeds.

We'd never encountered another tribe before.

They came at us in a ragged single-file line. They walked like people who'd walked forever, like people who no longer counted distance or time. They walked like people who never stopped nor thought of stopping.

But they had to stop. We were right in their path.

Some kind of creature meandered in front of them. I'd seen goats once before, when our hunting party had wandered far into the hills. But these animals looked a bit different; they were bedraggled and scrawny; downright downtrodden—nothing like the noble beasts we'd found in the mountains.

Their owners didn't appear much better. Dry mud matted the hair on the animal hides they wore. The hollows of their eyes had a dark cast and the whites of their eyes were red. A tight latticework of wrinkles cut their leathery skin. Hard, spindly arms; legs like bulbous tree roots. Their feet were absurdly wide—the toes looked inflated.

But then, when I examined my own tribes-kin, I realized we didn't look much better; we just had a little more meat on our bones, that's all.

"What a pathetic lot," Lut said.

"They hardly seem human," Mok said.

"The savanna heat must've dried up their spirits," Aruk said.

This haggard band pulled up short about a stone's throw from us. They stared at us; we stared at them. The goats butted their owners' shinbones and chawed tufts of grass.

I nodded to Mok, then to Boq. We three men then walked as one towards the newcomers.

We halted midway between the two tribes. We waited.

The visitors then produced their three delegates: a stooped-back old man with a bluish-white cast to one eye; a broad-shouldered young blade who wore a blank expression; and a middle-aged woman with a big pot belly.

This trio walked as one. They stopped within five paces of us.

The woman rubbed her toothless gums together and stroked the hairs that clung to her chin. The young blade held a spear at the vertical.

We eyed them; they eyed us. No one dared show the least hint of emotion. No one dared to even blink. The moments crept by.

Finally, I lost patience and broke the silence. "Hi, I'm Amar," I said. "And this here is Mok, and this here is Boq."

That these people understood my words clearly indicated a connection between us. But the two tribes chose to ignore the obvious—at this meeting, and at all those that followed.

"We are the People of Roq," the woman said. "We are called the People of Roq because Roq is our god. The one we worship."

"So what is a god?" asked Boq.

"A being that exists outside time; a being that can never be destroyed."

"Well in that case, we are the People of Matar," I said. "Because Matar is our god. The one we worship."

"Never heard of her," the old woman said. "Anyway, my name is Urm, the young warrior there is Urk, and the old guy's known as Mer—he's our Seer."

"Yes, well Amar is our Seer," Boq said.

I could see that Mer was a Seer—the way he squinted and peered at me, he seemed to be trying to see into me. I felt at a disadvantage—that old buzzard looked tough; he could've built up some real power over the seasons. Though Urm was sociable, she too had an abrasive edge. As for Urk, he appeared downright deadly.

"You must have traveled quite a ways," I said. "What brings you people here?"

"Time and distance," Urm said. She spat, then rubbed the spit into the dust with her big toe. "You see, all we do is travel. That's all I've ever done and all my ancestors ever did, beginning before anyone can ever remember. You see, long, long ago, our tribe came into being in the Land of Roq. But then one day we left the Land of Roq to wander the earth. And thus we have roamed the world ever since. But someday we will return to the Land of Roq. And then we can finally stop our wandering and be at peace and have all that we ever want or need. In the Land of Roq, milk and honey will pour from the sky. In the Land of Roq, we will find the righteous life we so rightly deserve."

"Did you train those creatures to follow you around like that?" Boq asked.

"Actually, it's we who follow them," Urm said. "They have a great appetite and eat from dawn 'til dusk. And when they've shorn all the grass from one place, we must move on to the next. But when we reach the Land of Roq, our moon will be full and our life will be filled with excess upon excess."

Though we Matarians didn't feel comfortable with the People of Roq around, our innate sense of etiquette demanded that we show hospitality. So we suggested that they rest for that day at our campfire. For their part, the Roqians really wanted to travel on, but accepted our invitation out of politeness.

We stoked the fire and the People of Roq carved up a goat to celebrate the occasion. The goat meat, though somewhat stringy, had a fine flavor.

For the remainder of that day, the tribes commingled about the campfire. At first, the two groups of children stared at each other with a certain timid distrust. Then, in just a twinkling, they were rolling together in the dirt and holding spitting contests.

We adults took a subtler approach and divided up into small sets for genteel conversation. Mostly, we compared and contrasted our different lifestyles. Though no one said as much, we Matarians found the lifestyle of our visitors to be fascinating, but peculiar and inferior to our own way of life. Suffice it to say, the Roqians held the opposite opinion.

Yes, the two tribes chirped together like happy birds. But behind all our cheerful talk lay a sense of unease and wariness. My stomach wouldn't stop twitching.

And Mer wouldn't stop eyeing me. At first, he kept his distance, but then ever so slowly, he circled in, closing the net. I maintained a bead on him while I conversed with a lovely Roqian woman. Within moments of our meeting, her invigorating presence had taken me captive—in mind, body, and heart. How can I describe her? I can't. She had a tiny bony frame, dark bulging eyes, and lips with the texture of caterpillar hide. From her measured tones, I could tell she was strong-willed, yet dutiful. From her firm, light fingers, I could see she was shrewd, yet tender; passionate, yet restrained. Her name was Rewan. In odd hours alone, I still speak that name, for it fills me with a sense of warmth and wistfulness.

If only that damn Seer would have left us alone! But he hovered like a vulture.

Finally, emboldened by my new passion for Rewan, I looked him straight in his one good eye and said, "Yes Mer, can I help you with something?"

He just stood there, staring at me, nodding his head and stroking his chin. "So you're the Seer for this tribe?" he said.

"Yes, that's what I am," I said. "I handle the dreaming around here and I lead the antelope dance. On occasion, I take trips to the Otherworld and bring back information for my people. Anything else you want to know?"

I could feel the admiration pouring from Rewan's liquid brown eyes.

But that old billy goat Mer just kept on stroking his chin. "So you ever walk on fire?" he asked me.

"Now why would I want to do a thing like that?" My stomach twitched.

"Well, I walk on fire all the time," he boasted. "It helps me See."

I checked his feet. They were charred black to the ankle.

"Well, I don't need fire to help me See," I said.

Sensing confrontation, people lifted their heads and perked up their ears.

"You aren't afraid to walk on fire, are you?" Mer's voice crackled in my ear.

"I have confronted Matar—creator of us all—on more than one occasion. So a little fire walk doesn't scare me."

Perhaps if Rewan hadn't roused my emotions, I could've responded to Mer's challenge with a cooler head. As it was, the old Seer had trapped me with ease.

"Rewan," he said, "fix me a fire—I think I'll go for a stroll on the embers tonight."

My love interest—who, unfortunately, was also Mer's assistant—scurried off to do her master's bidding.

Then before I could escape, Mer settled down beside me. He now turned his gaze to the stars above and began to tell of his adventures in the Otherworld. But his Otherworld was a much different place than the one that I had visited. In succulent detail, the old Seer described a paradise. He told of all the glorious feasts he'd enjoyed there, of all the nectar he'd imbibed, and of savory sights, such as flowers so bright they burn your eye. Dwarf creatures populated his Otherworld; they bowed to him and waited upon his every whim.

I tried to appear calm and follow along, but from the corner of my eye, I could see Rewan's fire eating higher and higher into the sky. The bonfire rose until it licked the moon. At that point, Rewan beat the conflagration into submission, then spread the embers out with loving care, creating a narrow path twenty paces in length. The black chunks glowed red within.

When his assistant had finished grooming this bed, Mer stood up, stretched his arms overhead, yawned, then cracked his knuckles. He worked a crick from his neck and then took several deep breaths.

"I just love the feel of red-hot coals under my feet," he said to me.

The old codger hopped over to the smoldering plank and examined it for a moment. "It doesn't look quite hot enough," he said to Rewan.

"I think it is," she said. "Test it."

To my surprise, Mer reached down and picked up a coal with his bare hand. He bounced this dumpling on his palm, then blew on it. The ember burned a deeper red. Mer waited several moments more, then tossed the coal back down.

"I guess it'll have to do," he sighed.

Mer cracked his knuckles one last irritating time. Then, with no further ado, he sauntered down the fiery path, holding his chin aloft. Not once did that serene glaze leave his eyes. When he'd reached the end of the bed, he simply turned on his heel and walked back to the beginning. Then he hopped off the embers and spread his arms wide to my amazed tribes-kin. Oh, what a self-satisfied smile he did wear! Such arrogance!

Of course, in the very next moment, everyone turned their eyes to me. I knew full well what they expected. In fact, I almost believed that I could do the deed. Mer had done it. He was a Seer; I was Seer. True, he had more experience than me, but perhaps we shared the same magic. Whatever the case, I couldn't let that braggart beat me.

So I got to my feet and rolled my shoulders some to loosen up. I started to crack my knuckles, but thought better of it.

Then, holding my chin aloft and my spine stiff, I stepped up to the bed of fire. The waves of heat nearly bowled me over. It was suffocating. My legs began to shake and I had to widen my stance, lest my knees knock. A general nausea bled through my body. Only by exerting the greatest force of will did I manage to remain standing.

Though I'd never before petitioned Matar on my own behalf, I now asked for his/her/its aid without restraint. "Help me, Matar, oh great Creator, please help me," I said in my mind. "Come on—I'm doing this for your honor and glory. You have competition now, you know. If I fail, the tribe might go over to Roq. Then where would you be?"

I could feel the impatience of the tribespeople. I knew I couldn't wait any longer.

So I smoothed my hair back, took a deep breath, praised Matar three more times...then—jumped on the coals, both feet forward.

I immediately discovered that Mer and I did not share the same magic. A rush of fire shot up my legs, exploded my vertebrae, then took hold of my brain and tore that tender tissue in half. The embers had my feet in a firm grip. I pulled and yanked and managed to get one foot free, then the other. Then I began pumping my legs wildly, lest the coals grab my feet again. A ragged, spiraling blaze raged within me. My head roared with the flame. Wisps of flesh flew away like ash. I could see only red. The damn fire bed had no end.

Finally, I gave up and hurled myself forward in a great flying leap.

Ah, the sensation of release! I soared high; I soared above it all. Fire dripped from my body like honey. A beautiful coolness rushed over me.

But my relief was brief, my relief was false: a moment later, without warning, a fiery burst exploded my core. This pain superseded all previous pain; this pain seared every last particle of thought and feeling from my mind and my body.

My awareness blew away in a puff of black breath.

Chapter 7 : Nadla

I came back to myself slowly. My whole body hummed. Warm mist pressed against my face. All I could see was a blurred mix of green. The air felt heavy and wet inside my lungs.

Gradually, the shades of green gained sharper outline. Trees drooped over me, dangling loops of vine. All around me, foliage sprayed out in great verdant splashes. I lay in pillows of spongy moss on the banks of a blue pool. I was embedded in a lush jungle, a garden stuffed with every conceivable form of flora.

The surface of the pool was a round, opaque plane. I propped my back against a firm tree trunk and dipped my toes into the cool blue water.

"I don't know where I am," I said, "but my feet aren't burned, so I'm not complaining."

Though I knew that I should investigate my surroundings, I just couldn't seem to motivate myself. I had no hunger and felt relatively content. My mind had lost its edge. I lacked clarity. Any thought that gathered in my head soon faded. My feeble attempts to cogitate actually amused me; I felt pleased by my own laxity. "You're living in pleasure for once," I told myself. "Why ruin it?"

So I just lay back and let the chittering of monkeys and the long, loping calls of birds perforate my ears...

...until...until...I noticed a stirring on the still water. Three ripples spread out from the center to span the breath of the pool. A bubble wiggled on the surface, then burst. A jumble of stringy black weed appeared from deep in the blue depths.

This weed soon revealed itself to be a swirling mass of black hair, hair that danced softly around a perfect oval face. This woman rose straight from the deep like the substance of dream—slowly, slowly, then suddenly all in place. She stood on the surface of the water in the center of the pool—a flawless statue. Her beauty was a cool beauty. I marveled at that cloud-white skin. Unlike the women of my tribe, she had hardly a hair on her body.

The sighing undulations of her hips graced into long, intelligent legs. Water prisms shone amid the dark tendrils of her bush. Those firm, resolute breasts had nipples so taut they could poke your eyes out.

Thin, blue lips came together in a flat line. Eyes that were both blue and gray stared at me without a hint of emotion.

An easy breeze lifted me up. Mesmerized, if not catatonic, I held my arms out to this exquisite vessel. But she just stood there, stock still. Drained of all free will, I took one blind step toward her—and plunged right into the water. I was so far gone, I couldn't even think to swim.

I surrendered to the cool water; I just let myself sink softly down and down through darker and darker shades of blue.

I had nearly touched bottom when I felt two hands press against my chest and propel me gently upward. My body rose toward the surface with the unhurried movements of a sea tortoise. My consciousness dispersed like bubbles of air.

When I awoke, I again found myself lying on the bank in the spongy moss. But now the blue-lipped woman sat beside me. She looked at me as one might look at a dead fish. But I didn't care—I already loved her. For some sick, silly reason, I saw in her my plenitude, the answer to my passion.

But when I tried to tell her of my dizzy, wastrel emotions, she put two fingers to my lips. I kissed those fingers and tasted a hard electric iciness. It tasted divine. My mind traveled into ecstasy; my thoughts broke apart again and went in five different directions.

She slid her body down next to mine. Her pale white skin had the smooth elasticity of catfish hide.

She started kissing my neck. I struggled for breath. She eased herself on top of me. Without warning, my attentive stick was plunged into the coil of her womb.

Let me just say that her cold exterior was contrasted by a fine interior blaze. In an instant, my stick became something more than its usual self—something golden, something complete.

We began to fluctuate, but slowly, slowly. She craned her head back and looked at me through the droplets on her eyelashes. Her breath poured over my face in cool waves. A misty veil formed between us. My invigorated member knew security and warmth only dreamt of before. I wanted to live in this moment forever and held myself there, sweetly tightly suspended. But then without warning—and much too abruptly—my ice floes began to explode.

For several goofy moments, my arms and legs flopped about and my eyes popped from their sockets.

But I eased down quickly; I smoothed out; I went into a winter's cave behind my eyelids.

Sea-borne vibrations echoed through frosty night fog.

Some time later, I awoke again in the spongy moss with my feet hanging off the bank. A warm apathy pervaded my body. Water sluiced through my toes.

The blue-lipped woman had waded knee-deep into the pool. I tried to speak, but my breath was silence— her undulating spine held me transfixed. As the water rose to her hips, she turned and looked back at me with those blue-gray eyes. I had to summon all my will just to whisper: "Don't go."

"No, I am not going," she said. Her cool voice had the layered tones of purling water.

"Who are you? What is your name?" I forced these words out like a man choking.

"My name is not important. My name is Nadla."

"Then Nadla, please stay." I tried forcing myself up off the ground.

"No, do not follow me," Nadla said. "Wait there. I will return. Do not move from where you are. That's all I ask of you."

With a great, sloppy sigh, I surrendered to inertia; I sank back into the moss. Nadla slowly descended. As her black hair drifted down through the blue depths and then disappeared, I receded into a stupor that knew no want.

I don't know how much time passed before Nadla returned—I was too far gone to count time. But eventually, she rose once more from the pool's secret depths. Just as before, we slid together like two parts of the same whole. Once again, I dipped into the molten flow beneath her glacier. Once again, I relinquished myself to the act, exalting in its hewings, hiccups, and dripples. Once again, the love force made a fool of me. I had a mind only for its pleasure.

After culmination, I was nothing more than a happy puddle.

To my regret, Nadla did not linger, but waded back out into the water. Once again, the movement of her spine described a finer reality. When the water had reached her hips, she turned and fixed those blue-gray eyes on me and said, "Wait there. Do not move. Do not follow me. I will return. Eventually." Her words washed upon my ears like breaking waves.

"Do not move?" I echoed, giving forth a feeble laugh. "As if I could. Nadla, Nadla—I love you."

But she had already disappeared into the pool. The last wisps of her long black hair vanished in the blue.

There was nothing left to do then, so I leaned back and let my mind go with the breeze. My love for Nadla had me in a blind mist. I drifted down the river of time; I coasted through infinity.

To her word, Nadla did return. But afterwards, she wasted no time before again descending into the pool.

And so a pattern became established.

Nadla was a drop of water dangling from a leaf. I was the supplicant with tongue extended, waiting for that drop to fall, then waiting for the next drop, then waiting for the next. Desire satiated is not the end of desire. I always wanted more.

The intervals between her visits were fog. But despite my stupor, boredom eventually came to call. I found myself scanning the treetops, searching out those howling monkeys and those rainbow birds. This dark, luxurious world began to entice me with its mystery. Finally, I rose to my feet, parted the tall fronds, and dove into the jungle.

I would explore.

For—how long?—I dog-paddled through a soft sea of green foliage. Leaves caressed my legs and arms. Mist hissed against my face. In the near distance, the trees formed a shadow wall permeated only by blue haze.

The extravagance of this garden overwhelmed me. I could feel the plants breathing.

But then a horrid thought crashed my dreaming: what if Nadla returned to find me missing? She might abandon me forever. I had forgotten her warning: 'Do not move from where you are.' How could I've been so careless?

I had to get back and soon was not soon enough.

I began fighting my way through the foliage, searching for a glimmer of the blue pool through the trees. I couldn't have gone that far. Where was my bank with the spongy moss?

This frantic effort quickly fatigued me. I had no sense of direction. The jungle had swallowed me whole. The leaves pulled on my skin like leeches; branches whopped me about. My legs started to wobble—the earth was tugging me toward its bosom. Still, I kept pushing myself, pushing myself—desperate and crazed.

But finally, the weight of my fear overwhelmed me. I dipped into a swoon and crumpled to the ground.

Yet I refused to give up. I got to my hands and knees and began to crawl. I could feel my eyes pulsating. As I continued to lose strength, I had to lie down flat and slither along on my belly.

Then finally, I caught a glimpse of blue water through the foliage. When I reached the pool, I collapsed completely and buried my face in the spongy moss.

I just lay there, wallowing in the fear that Nadla would never return.

But she did return—eventually—and once again we went through our dance. However, when she first looked at me, I thought I saw the shadow of a smile pass along those thin, blue lips.

"What was that? What was that?" I asked myself. "Is she mocking me? Is she sneering? Is she laughing at me behind the veil of her face?"

"How dare you spout such blasphemy!" I answered myself. For I did not wish to look beyond the veil. No, I just wanted to bathe myself in Nadla's deep fire again and again and again.

This time, immediately after my eruption, Nadla waded into the pool without one word nor a glance back at me. As the tendrils of her black hair filtered down through the blue, I could not help but worry.

"She must know about my forest foray," I told myself. "This silence is her way of chastising me. Well, I won't take anymore chances. I won't move from my place on the bank ever again."

So I just lolled about on the spongy moss while awaiting Nadla's return.

"Why do I have to go poking about anyway?" I asked myself. "I have no growls in my stomach; no thirst in my throat—Nadla satisfies my only need. Why can't I just be content? Relax, Amar, relax. Relax and wait for Nadla."

I lowered my feet into the pool. The cool liquid felt so lovely sluicing through my toes that way. Finally, I just had to get up on my knees, dip my hands into that silky water, and drape it all over my face. That's when I happened to glimpse a silvery fish near the surface. I reached for it without thinking. But this abrupt movement made me lose my balance; I plunged headfirst into the pool.

The cold water shocked me. I started thrashing about, but all I did was create a white chaos and push myself farther from the shore. The water kept pulling me down. I flailed like crazy just to keep my head up. My lungs and throat burned. Soon, fatigue had me in its grip; it paralyzed my limbs. Though I worried that Nadla might find me, I had to rest. I had to calm myself. I would float on my stomach until my strength returned.

I let my body go lax and as I did, I began to gaze down into the foggy blue depths. The pool was so empty—not a single living thing in sight, no silvery fish, not even a wavering water plant—nothing, nothing but milky blue liquid.

As my body stilled, my mind stilled as well. And again my curiosity took hold. Before long, I forgot my fear and began parting the water before me, searching out the deeper depths. In this way, I descended into the pool.

The water caressed my body with sweet intelligence. It seemed to flow right through my skin, stroking and soothing my entire being, dissolving all care. Strangely enough, I had no need for air.

I went down and down through deeper and deeper shades of blue until finally my feet sank into the soft bottom silt. I now stood in a blue crystalline world. I felt as dumb as a stunned calf. Plumes of muck rose about my legs.

But then something came to break the magic spell. That something was burrowing through the silt, creating a long, narrow hump in the mud. I guessed it to be some creature tunneling just beneath the surface. Whatever it was, it was headed directly at me.

So I took two steps to the right to get out of its path. However, the creature just shifted its direction to compensate. So then I went four steps to the left. But again, the thing changed direction. I tried to propel myself back up, but the silt had seized hold of my feet —I was mired in muck.

The creature then began moving this way and that, zigzagging through the mud. I yanked, pried, and pulled but my feet still wouldn't budge.

The head of the hump halted right at my toes. My heart did a hiccup. I knew I was doomed. I had gone against Nadla; I had delved into the pool. Now it was only right that I pay for my mistake.

Suddenly, the silt exploded in a roisterous cloud. A serpent had erupted from the ground. The beast stood before me: a long vertical pole; its wide mouth open right in my face—a mouth filled with rings and rings of fine, sharp teeth. A crimson mouth with thin blue lips. Thin blue lips. Who did I know with thin blue lips? Nadla! So this was her secret. Oh Nadla! Darling Nadla. My beloved Nadla. You could have told me—I would've accepted you.

Oh the shame I now felt from having disobeyed her. I knew that Nadla would devour me whole; she would swallow me down, then crunch me to a pulp with her peristalsis. But my disgrace outweighed my fear. I would accept my punishment and be humble.

I closed my eyes and spread my arms wide; I gave myself up to her. But at the same time, I began to fall backward. Only then did the silt release my feet.

It was but a heartbeat later—or so it seemed—that I awoke on the spongy moss with my back against the tree. Nadla, in her human form, wadded out into the blue pool, her undulating spine whispering a thousand secrets.

"Nadla!" I hoarsed. "Nadla, I'm sorry. Please, don't leave me. I don't care what you are. I love you—that's all that matters."

She looked over her shoulder at me, past the curtain of her wet black hair. Those blue-gray eyes radiated boredom and disgust.

"You just had to know, didn't you?" she hissed.

"It was an accident. I lost my balance and fell in. Honest."

She flicked her tongue at me, then descended into the water. Tendrils of black hair drifted down through the dense blue depths.

"Oh well," I sighed. "Oh well—life goes on." I knew that Nadla would never return. But I had no tears; I accepted my fate with grace—or perhaps it was just resignation.

The fog had suddenly cleared from my mind. Gone was the stupor that had clogged my head. I almost missed it. But in truth, I'd had enough of this place. Now I just wanted to get on back to my people.

"My time here is done," I told myself.

So I dragged my sullied carcass off the ground and began to weave a path through the forest. I knew that if I didn't hurry, if I didn't fight the gnarled and sticky foliage, if I didn't care what might become of me, then I would find my way home soon enough.

However, despite my resolution, some invisible force—some unseen thread—kept tugging at me, kept trying to pull me backward.

"No," I said. "No, I'm done here. Nadla's not coming back, so why hang around?"

A weight began to press upon my shoulders. My strength ebbed. My legs wobbled. I drooped and kept on drooping until I had melted down to the forest floor. Filled with fatigue, I curled up among the decayed leaves. Then I put both palms together and placed my hands under my head.

And with a deep sigh, I dissolved into sleep, merciful sleep.

I jerked awake. I now lay face up.

Something had pulled my legs out straight. My feet felt unusually warm. For a moment, I was blinded by the splinters of sunlight cutting down through the jungle canopy. Then I saw that Nadla, in her snake form, had slipped her wide maw over my feet and ankles and halfway up my shinbones. I tried to kick free, but her jaws weighed my legs down. Those blue-gray eyes stared at me with loathing.

"Nadla, darling, what are you doing?"

I could feel the rings of spiny teeth crawling up my legs. A torrid heat seared my flesh. Shock waves pummeled my brain. My body was now completely paralyzed.

"Nadla, dearest Nadla!" I pleaded. "What about all the good times we shared? I loved you. Remember?"

But we both knew that was a lie. I had desired her, not loved her. I had immersed myself in this desire, hoping to forget my pain. No wonder she was disgusted with me.

By now, her big maw had slid up to my neck. My body was raging hot. I took one last breath and closed my eyes.

The spiny teeth pierced my face, then sank into my brain. In one eternal moment, I traveled to the other side of agony. Nadla's body became my suffocating cocoon.

I slid down her digestive tract for a short ways, then got stuck as the walls contracted. Then nothing, nothing for several moments. I was hoping that I just might wake up. I thought to myself, "Maybe that's all. Maybe that's enough. Maybe I'm done." But then I heard a gurgling sound and before I could say "oh no", the gush of her acidic juices doused me with liquid fire. My entire being roared with the pain and I gave forth a long silent scream that still echoes through time. She stewed me through and through; I boiled ferociously.

But finally–finally–the infernal waters receded and I simmered down some; the pain reduced to a scorching throb. However, my relief was brief—then the hammering of peristalsis started. I got it from all sides at once—imagine having a body covered with bruises, then imagine each one of those bruises being beaten with a rock—imagine a pounding that refused to stop. And once you've imagined all that, just remember that what I endured was worse.

But finally—finally—the pounding did cease, and though waves of pain still pulsed through my body, the ache was much quieter now; I slowly passed into a gray world of stillness and peace. Unfortunately, this calm was but an interlude. Within a few moments, an earthquake began to shake me, it shook me to the core. But finally—finally—I experienced complete release. I dropped, I bounced, I rolled to a stop. Once again I felt the cool forest shadows flowing over me. Once again I felt the rich jungle floor beneath me.

Nadla had digested me fully. I, who had tried to consume her, had ended up being consumed by her. I was now nothing more than common excrement. But I was not yet aware of my fetid state. Yes, I was in denial.

I kept telling myself to get up and get on with it. But to my consternation, I couldn't seem to move.

Naturally, I became a little anxious. But I grew even more apprehensive when I spied the monster trundling toward me. It moved on six spindly legs—six spindly legs with pointy knees and spiked feet. Its broad, flat back was covered by a dark violet shell. Two pincher horns protruded on either side of the tube-like snout.

"Another form of Matar, no doubt," I thought to myself.

But in truth, it was our friend, the dung beetle. The thing waddled right up to me without ceremony or grace and then started poking and prodding my body with its pinchers.

"Is that you, Matar?" I tried to communicate. "I can't seem to get myself going again. Can you help me, oh great Creator? Can you help me, please?"

But the monster played dumb to my request and continued on with its callous behavior.

"That is you, isn't it, Matar? Hello? Hello? What's wrong? Why won't you speak to me?"

Ah, but the dung beetle had its own agenda. First, it butted me on one side, then it butted me on the other. Then, using its horned feet, it began to mold me. It even crawled on top of me and danced about. Then it climbed back down and pushed and jabbed some more.

Those prickly feet sure did sting. I tried striking back, but nothing happened. I seemed to be constrained within the sphere of my own being. What frustration!

"Matar, Matar!" I cried. "Why must you torture me so? What've I ever done to you? Speak to me, Matar! Speak!"

But my puling supplications had no effect on the insect. It worked as if by rote.

Now the beetle tipped me upset down. What new rude business was this? The bug kept bumping me and pushing me until I'd done a complete circle. And it didn't stop there. It continued to shove me along, wheeling me around and around, forcing me up hill and down dale. A wild vertigo swung through my body. Most intolerable! Downright despicable!

I wailed; I cursed; I pleaded. But the bug would not listen. It kicked me hither and thither with total nonchalance. I told myself that I could bear no more. But then I bore some more and some more on top of that.

Anger ate away my mind and dulled my senses. I didn't even realize when we left the cool forest behind and entered the sunny open countryside.

Then finally—finally—we rolled to a stop.

"What a relief," I said to myself. My center of gravity still reeled.

But then the bug gave one last push and sent me spinning down a dark tunnel in the earth. I knew that my doom probably waited for me at the end of this road. But I didn't care—as long as it arrived soon.

And indeed, I hadn't gone far when a large taproot caught me and held me fast with its tendrils. For a moment, I experienced a frightening sense of security.

But then those delicate strands dipped into me and worked like straws to draw the consciousness from my dead body. I felt myself bleed into the sweet, porous material of the taproot. Then I began to rise and as I rose, I sucked the earthy water from the rich root pith.

As I continued to ascend, I left this warm darkness behind and entered a tube of brilliant green. Some unnameable force was pulling me up through the plant stalk. Each branch that I passed was a black knot on the green window.

I began to accelerate. There was something within me desperate for culmination; at first, this desire was an ache, an irritation, but then it became a frenzy, an impatient storm.

The black knots flashed by me. My vision was strobed by shots of green and black.

Sensing a coming crescendo, I relinquished everything—hope, fear, anger, pain. I existed only to fulfill this dream, this horrible, wonderful dream, this thing pulling me higher and higher and faster and faster until finally—

I broke out and opened wide with a soft explosion. Five thin red tubes sprang up from my heart. Each red tube had a spongy red cap and each red cap had a frosting of bright yellow.

I was a good silly happy flower. I luxuriated in the sun's loving grace.

But my pleasure was brief. Soon, a winged creature of black and yellow stripes began caroming about me. This critter was all activity and energy —a bristly thing with a raw nasal hum. Six hairy legs dangled down from the plump body.

The tiny feet of the bumblebee danced right across my tube caps. I felt so exposed. The sharp little pricks of the feet went straight to the core of my being. Nonetheless, I remained pliant, yielding, peaceful. I gave myself up as a sacrifice. My gold dust flocked to the hairy legs like iron fillings to a magnet.

As the bee lifted away, it rubbed its antennae together, blinked its multitudinous eyes, then spoke to me in a vibrato voice.

"Amar," said the bumblebee, "when you awake you will find four pouches of seed beside you – grain seed, that is: wheat, corn, millet, and one other that I'm not quite sure about. Take this gentle grain and deliver it unto your people. Tell them that these grain seeds are to be their destiny. Just as the dung beetle planted you under the earth and you sprang to new life, just as a man plants his seed into a woman and a child births forth, so your people will plant these seeds and when the growth reaches maturity, they will reap a bountiful harvest. The seed which has grown from the seed should be crushed and ground down, mixed with water and baked on the fire. You will consume the wholesome result with praise for Matar. That will be your peoples' sustenance now."

The bee then did a quick spiral and zoomed away over the field of wild flowers.

The whole land sang with life.

I hear it now; I will hear it forever.

119

And that was the end of that Otherworld journey. Anyway, that's all I remember. When I awoke, I was back in my human form, resting in that in-between place where savanna meets jungle. A warm buzz permeated my body. For once, security felt like a birthright.

However, my normal state of consciousness soon began to leak back in. I closed my eyes and tried to hold on to that peaceful feeling, but it was too late.

So I breathed a deep sigh, then pushed myself up off the ground. Though I looked all around, I could not find the pouches of grain seed promised to me by the bee.

Finally, I gave up and walked away from the jungle toward the sun-baked plain. The yellow grass whispered against my legs.

I would walk until my feet stopped. I knew that sooner or later they would lead me to something somewhere.

I walked until day became night. Then I walked through the night until day came again. Then I walked across that day until night fell once more. Then I lay down and rested my head on a rock.

By this point, I'd nearly decided that my Otherworld life was my real life and that my so-called "normal" life—this assortment of thoughts and feelings that never seemed to add up to much—was but a dream. Nevertheless, for the time being, I was stuck with it.

But don't think that I was sulking. No, after all that I'd gone through, I was actually starting to feel my strength.

Chapter 8 : The First Fight

The next morning, I looked again, but again found no pouches of seed. Had the bee lied to me?

"Well, maybe I haven't actually woken up yet," I thought to myself.

That would explain certain inconsistencies. For one thing, the night before, I had used a sandstone rock as my pillow. Yet when I awoke at dawn, I found a clump of dirt beneath my head.

What's more, I'd fallen asleep while gazing up at an open sky. But now the dusty gourds of a baobab tree hung over me.

"You're still dreaming," I told myself.

So I closed my eyes and tried to return to sleep. But a moment later, something soft, wet, and blowing nudged the side of my neck. I sprang to my feet. A black-eyed goat stared up at me. Two others tore at the grass nearby. On the other side of the baobab tree, the lost tribe of Roq sat around a campfire, gnawing on bones and picking their teeth.

I gathered together what remained of my mind and walked over to them. One look at me and they all sat up straight.

Rewan smoothed her long hair and gave me a big toothy smile.

Mer blinked his one good eye. He stood up and began circling me slowly, vulture-style.

"What's wrong?" I asked. "You all seem so surprised to see me."

"Where'd you go when you were walking the coals?" Mer demanded.

"To the Otherworld, of course. To an enchanted forest haunted by a lovely serpent named Nadla. You know the place?"

"Well, no, not exactly," he said. "But I've been to plenty of places just as good or even better." The old man puffed out his chest.

"Oh, I don't mean to say it was good. But it sure was something."

"Well, whatever it was, you got across those coals awful quick." Mer gave a dry, dusty laugh. "No, didn't take you long at all."

"I needed to build up speed," I said, "to propel myself into the Otherworld. So anyway, where're my people?"

A long silence. The Roqians shifted their eyes away from me.

My stomach twitched. "Okay, what happened to them?"

Urk the warrior rose to his feet and stared me straight in the face. "It was their own damn fault," he said.

"Go on."

"They violated one of our most sacred laws."

"Which is?"

"They stole some of our goats."

"My people wouldn't do a thing like that."

The old woman Urm spat in my direction. "The night you left, they waited 'til we fell asleep, then slaughtered one of our goats, then roasted it on a spit and gobbled it all up. When we confronted them the next morning, Mok claimed they didn't know the goat was ours. Can you believe that? Those bastards have some gall!"

The Roqians all shook their heads.

"Well, they hadn't had meat for some time," I said. "You see, the antelope had deserted us and—"

"Then we found two others missing. Mok swore that a hyena ate them. He's got a lot nerve, that guy." Urm spat in my direction again.

"So anyway, what happened after that?"

"We fought. Your guys lost."

"You Matarians are good with the spear, yes," Urk said. "But we also have the spear, plus this little thing— which I guess your people failed to notice. Until it was too late, that is." He hefted a smooth, heavy stick from the ground. A flint wedge was tied to one end of the stick with strips of vine. "Hand axe. One whack and your brains are stew."

I swallowed deeply. My stomach twitched.

"You killed all my people?"

"No, those little birds flapped their wings and flew away."

I breathed a sigh of relief. "Well, like you said, it was their own fault."

"I'll give them credit for one thing," Mer shouted. "They sure can move their feet!"

Oh, how the Roqians rocked with laughter. They threw back their heads and slapped their knees. They laid it on thick. I managed a weak chuckle.

When everyone had finally settled down, I said, "Well, I'm sorry things turned out the way they did."

"That's okay," Urm crowed. "We enjoyed kicking their butts."

That set off another roust of laughter.

I tried to smile; it hurt my face.

"Anyway, you don't have to worry," Urk said. "We won't bash your head in. We know it's not good to mess with a powerful Seer and you must be a powerful Seer to do what you did, to disappear into the Otherworld that way. Most Seers know a few good tricks—" he cast his eyes over to Mer—"but only a few have real power."

"I wouldn't know about that," I said softly. I did not wish to humiliate Mer. Anyone who could stroll across fiery coals without getting burnt had to have something going. "So where did my people head off to anyway?"

"Wherever their feet took them," Urm said. "The battle happened more than six lunar cycles ago and we've moved many times since then. You see, once our goats chew the grass down to nubs in one place, we must travel on to the next. But when we reach the Land of Roq, the grass will grow with great benevolence and the bellies of our goats will all swell like the moon."

I was anxious to get on my way, so I took this opportunity to bid the Roqians farewell. After one last glance at Rewan, I stepped back out into the sun and continued my journey across the savanna.

Chapter 9 : A New Life

I didn't know in which direction to go. So I just went. I would trust my feet to lead me back to my people. Anyway, I'd already been gone six moon cycles, so why hurry?

At nightfall, I rested. When I awoke the next morning, I again hunted for the pouches of grain seed. But again I found nothing.

And so it went through three days of walking.

Then, on the fourth day, as the sun reached its zenith, I came upon a stream. I followed this stream and let the coolness of its shade trees wash over me. This stream eventually grew into a benevolent river. This river told me stories, stories without words. I listened to the rhythm of these stories with my feet.

Afternoon shifted into twilight; twilight shifted into night.

The river then told me that I had traveled far enough.

So I climbed the embankment and took stock of my surroundings. Moonlit trees covered the ground with dappled shadows. In a clearing amid these quiet trees, I found a circle of people sitting to their evening meal. Their campfire threw sparks into the night

I slicked my hair back, then, calm as the rising moon, I strolled over to the circle.

My tribes-kin merely nodded to me and continued on with their sober feast. I tried to catch Bruk's eye as she stoked the fire, but the old cluck ignored me.

Tonight, I could forget the various infirmities of her body. I needed her care and comfort after my long, arduous journey.

"Where the fuck you been?" Mok asked.

"The Otherworld," I told him, trying not to sound too grand. "I lived for a spell in a deep, luscious jungle there. Then a snake swallowed me whole and I was reborn as a flower."

No one seemed much impressed, so I added, "And before I left, Matar gave me another important message. Everyone hear me? Another important message. From Matar. You all listening? Okay, from now on, we are to work the soil, we are to cultivate plants. We must take the seeds of grain plants and push them down into the earth. And when the sprouts break forth, we must tend them with tenderness until they reach full growth. Then we will reap a bountiful harvest. We will take the seed which has grown from the seed then crush it, grind it, and bake it on the fire. And all the while, we will praise Matar for the gift he/she/it has bestowed upon us.

"Unfortunately, the bags of special seed promised to me have not yet arrived; however, I feel certain I will wake to find them any day now."

"Heard it already." Dith bit into a roasted gopher.

"Excuse me?"

"You told us that same crap when you came through here early spring," Dat said.

"Excuse me?"

"Yes, that's right," Boq said. "One night, you just appeared from out of the darkness with this strange blank look in your eyes. Yes. You gave us the same spiel you gave just now, then turned your palms from up to down and poured seeds onto the earth."

126

"They just poured out?" I asked.

"Yes, that's right. Four different types."

"So what'd you do with them?"

"We planted them just like you told us," Lut said.

"The women insisted," Mok said.

"So how'd they do?"

"Pretty good," Parn said.

"Stunted and dry," Mok said.

"But still, we had a harvest," Ool said.

"My sisters and I like this business of planting," Bruk said. "For that matter, most of the men like it too. Most of them." She cut her eyes over to Mok.

"Yeah, well, it's a lot of trouble," he said. "It's not just the growing of it—you've also got to grind the stuff up, bake it, store it, and so on."

"But we enjoy all that," the women chimed together.

"Besides, you men still get to hunt," added Bruk.

"But now we've got to stay in one place," said Mok. "We've been lucky in the hunt lately, but when the antelope move on, then what?"

"So what'd I do after I dropped the pouches?"

"You stepped back into the darkness," Aruk answered. "This is the first we've seen of you since then."

"No one tried looking for me?"

"We figured you'd turn up eventually," old man Purl said.

"So anyway," Mok said, "we've had our little harvest, now it's time to move on." He stuck his finger in his nose. "Forget planting those lousy seeds. Plants grow by themselves—they don't need our help. This land will hold us captive. We've got to get back to the old ways."

127

"Matar told me that the seeds were to be our destiny," I countered.

"But did he say how long this destiny was supposed to last?"

"No, I just assumed that—"

"Well then, I think it's time we get back to our real destiny. It's time we move on."

No one spoke. I had the feeling they'd heard it all before. Obviously, Mok

had lost some of his control over the group. That made me uneasy—a power struggle most likely lay ahead.

"Oh come on, what's so great about this place?" Mok barked. "Don't tell me you like this mud flat?"

After a moment of silence, Boq tilted his head, scratched his chin, and said, "Gee, I don't know. Hunting seems so erratic. The antelope come, the antelope go. Is this our fate—to continually roam the savanna in search of antelope? Yes? Well, in that case, we're no better off than the People of Roq."

At the mention of the Roqians, my tribes-kin began to grumble and hiss and their eyes grew narrow and dark.

Mok frowned at the corncob he held in his hands, then tossed it into the fire. For a long moment, he stared at Boq through the flames. Then he stood up and stalked off into the night.

I cleared my throat. "Speaking of the Roqians...I happened to run into them a few days ago. They mentioned something about a little fight you guys had."

"There was a difference of opinion," Lut said.

I could hear him grinding his teeth.

"They claimed we got the worst of it," I said.

"Well, they cheated," Mok called from the darkness.

"How's that?" I yelled back.

"By using these things." Mok leapt from the shadows, brandishing a hand axe. He whipped the weapon about, then flipped it into the air and caught it with his opposite hand, then flipped it again and caught it behind his back. What a show off.

I cleared my throat. "A difference of opinion, you say? Well, the Roqians told me you killed one of their goats."

"It was dark," Mok said. "We mistook it for an antelope."

"They're missing two others," I said.

As if on cue, an irritated bleating came from the bushes.

"They followed us." Mok shrugged. "Besides, one of them gives good milk."

I glanced around at my tribes-kin. They all cast their eyes to the ground. Unlike Mok, they at least had the good grace to show shame.

"We shouldn't take what isn't ours," I said.

"But if we take it, then it is ours," Mok said.

I opened my mouth, but then I closed my mouth. I was too tired to argue. The night had begun to weigh on me.

After throwing down a quick supper, I bid sweet dreams to everyone, then dragged myself off to the tall grass.

For my first night home, I bedded down near a sympathetic fig tree. I needed something that understood me.

I had just nestled into my dreams when Bruk poked me in the ribs. I nearly leapt from my skin. She gave a cackling laugh.

I stared at her through the dappled darkness. "What is it? What's wrong with you? You weren't very friendly during dinner tonight, you know. I mean, here I am, back from a long and arduous journey, and what kind of greeting do I get? You have no idea what I have to endure over there." My whining tone disturbed me— I sounded like her mate.

"Oh yeah? Well, you go traipsing off to the Otherworld at moment's whimsy; leaving me here all alone to diddle with myself. I'm not a young woman anymore; I don't have that many pleasuring days left. And I'd like to do a little bit more with my remaining time than just diddle with myself."

"I don't choose to take those trips—I have to take those trips. It's my job."

"Whatever. So anyway...you bring me back something nice from the Otherworld?"

"Just this." I planted a wet kiss on her tough, cracked lips.

Why, oh why did I always stand on my head just to please that old woman? Yeah, I liked her a little. And yeah, I enjoyed the security of her arms. But our union was such a stunted thing.

Bruk raked her claws through her stringy hair and said, "Well, I suppose you're forgiven."

"Gee thanks."

"But the girls and I have a little favor to ask."

A feeling of weakness passed through my body. My stomach twitched. "What is it?"

"The girls and I want to stay here. We want to live in our cozy huts and cultivate this sweet soil. We want to see the seeds burst forth in the spring. We want to see the plants unfurl their tiny leaves."

I had to admit the image had beauty. "You sure that's what you want? You might get tired of it after awhile."

"Well, if we keep moving around as we have in the past, I'll need some other form of stability."

"Meaning what exactly?" Again my stomach twitched.

"That you and I should be known as a couple. I'd like a formal ceremony. In front of the whole tribe."

"But you see...you see...you see, the thing is...the main purpose of pairing off is to produce offspring. And well, no offense, but you're way past the producing age. Matar wouldn't approve. No, Matar wouldn't like it one bit." I felt a tiny pain in my chest.

"You're embarrassed of me, is that it?"

"No, no, no, of course not," I lied. "Like I told you, it's the age difference. It goes against Matar's laws. And if I got on a bad footing with Matar, it'd hurt the whole tribe."

"Then you'll help us stay here?"

She'd trapped me. Slippery though I was, I didn't see any way out of this one.

"Well, okay, I'll help, but not because I don't want to marry you."

"Of course not."

"I just want to please Matar and preserve the tribe."

"That's the same thing we want."

"Okay then. I'll talk to Matar tonight while you're asleep and get everything all straightened out."

If Bruk was the least put off by my rejection, she hid it neatly. Yes, she had manipulated me with delicacy and skill. I would not have challenged Mok under any other circumstance.

The passage of time broadens even such limited perspective as I possess. I now see my rejection of Bruk as a big mistake. She was a wise one, though usually she kept her wisdom to herself; I guess she believed in letting things run their own course. However, she would use her wisdom to bolster anyone that she stood behind. In the days to follow, I could have used such bolstering. Perhaps with her behind me, I would have stood firm. As it was, I slipped and when I slipped, I took the whole tribe with me.

The next morning, I waited until the end of breakfast before I entered the campfire circle.

I just stood there, giving my tribes-kin a solemn, blank stare. Finally, after several tedious moments, they took notice of me.

"Matar came to me again last night," I began. "He/she/it came to me with a special message. Matar said that we—his/her/its people—have now entered a new life, the life of those who tend the soil. He/she/it told me that's just how it is and how it always must be —no "ifs", "ands", or "buts". So we have to stay here, whether we like it or not. It's all part of Matar's plan. And only Matar knows what that plan is. And only Matar needs to know. So don't ask.

"And now, my brothers and sisters, before we do anything else, let us honor this special occasion. I must perform a ritual. Okay, can everyone be quiet?"

After a moment's pause, I held my arms straight up, then lifted my chin and soaked my face in the sun's warm rays. Then abruptly, I brought my arms back down, slumped my shoulders, and hung my head. (This posture was meant to suggest a dying plant.)

I could feel my audience waiting.

Slowly, vertebrae by vertebrae, I unfurled myself.
Then I struck a stance, puffed out my chest and—just
for effect—loosed a yell that broke the air into shards. I
sang like a hawk in distress, worried for its young. And
when the last ragged notes had dwindled from my
throat, I turned to my people with a look of great
gravity. Then I began this incantation:
"Just as the Hoopoe bird calls to its mate
This land has called us here.
Across mind-numbing distances
We did wander,
Lured by a high howl
Imperceptible to our ears
But heard clearly by our hearts.
We did wander, didn't we?--
Through foul water and burnt grass.
We did wander, didn't we?--
Through hot disease and death's decay.
We did wander, didn't we?--
Through suffocating heat and bad hunting.
We did wander, didn't we?--
Through rude calamity and cruel jest.
We did wander, didn't we?--
Through blazing fire ants and whiny mosquitoes.
Yes, we did wander
With foot blisters and big bunions,
Discovering a new misery
With every step.
We did wonder, didn't we?
Drawn by the honey of a melody,
A melody sung only for us, us alone,
Yes, we did wander
Until we found its source.
And so, for better or worse

This land belongs to us
And we belong to this land.
From this time forward
This land will be known
As the Land of the People of Matar."

When I had finished my lovely prose poem, I bent to my knees and scooped up two handfuls of dirt. Then I held this dirt to the sun and let it slowly trickle down through my fingers.

I repeated this scooping gesture three more times —doing it once to the west, once to the east, and once to the southern regions behind me.

And when I was done, I looked upon my tribes-kin with a mien of great serenity and said, "Let us gather together to form the full circle. For the full circle is the circle of life. And the circle of life is the circle of Matar, for Matar is the Creator of all life.

"Okay everyone, now that we're all together, repeat after me: We, the People of Matar...bless this land with our labor, with our hope, and with our future. As the land gives to us, so we give back to the land. For we are one with the land. That is how it is and how it's meant to be, today and forever; forever and ever after.

"So now, my brothers and sisters," I continued, "go to your harvest; reap the bounty of this land. Give those pure, precious grains your love, for those grains are the life and blood of us. Always remember that. Never forget it. Never."

My tribes-kin went through the day heavy with the solemnity of this ritual. All modesty aside, I'd put on quite a performance.

Yes, the tribes-kin were with me, but I still had to worry about Mok. At night, I would find him staring at me through the campfire flames, his silvery eyes gleaming with malice. I watched my back at all times.

Often I woke from a dream of a hand axe flashing down to burst open my skull.

But though I listened and I waited, I waited in vain. What stopped Mok from coming after me? After all, I'd just destroyed his way of life. Though he and his hunters continued to go out, before long the take hardly warranted the effort. The boys of our tribe could provide more meat by pitching rocks at rabbits. Finally, Mok gave up and started staying home. Though he did train our young men in the various arts prized by the warrior, most of the time he just lay around, living off the fat of the land. He even grew a little potbelly. Whenever Aruk tried to rouse his friend to life, Mok just sloughed him off with a growl.

Nevertheless, we still treated Mok as though he was our leader. I guess that was enough to satisfy him. I suppose that's why he didn't bash in my head. Prosperity had made him complacent.

And then there was the birth of his son. Rir by name. In short time, he proved to be a copy of his father. For instance, he'd hardly learned to walk when he began corralling the other children and beating them with a stick. Then later, he harnessed some of his playmates to a sleigh made of antelope hide and forced them to haul him around through the mud flats.

Though these shenanigans spurred my indignation, to my shame, I did not say a thing. I knew that Mok enjoyed his son's sport and would not take well to any criticism.

As for Boq, after his hunting duties diminished, he became something of a philosopher and a scientist. Getting his feet mired in mud didn't suit his airy disposition, so the women gave him leave from farm labor. Henceforth, he would climb the same broad-based tree every morning and drape himself in the upper branches like some lost strand of fog. All day long, he'd stare into the sky's lofty dome, watching clouds flee to their destinies while the birds cartwheeled and shrieked. From this pinnacle, his mind spun out endless spirals of logic. Sometimes, he wouldn't even come down for dinner, but lose his thoughts in the net of stars above. The result of all this high-blown cogitating was that he looked better than he had in ages. He glowed like a rainbow—yes!—and wore a smile made of ether and innocence.

I too became somewhat lax during this period. A Seer such as myself wasn't expected to work the fields. Nor did my people allow me to knead dough into bread or shape clay pots for the kilns. I didn't have to do much more than perform the crop rituals, sanctify marriages, and administer funereal rites.

So I spent the rest of my time luxuriating in the days. I drank in sunbeams and washed my hair in the wind. I studied the fine gliding flight of the vulture and wondered at the intelligence of ants. I pondered the riddles held within the distant purple mountains. I talked to the tall grass.

What good are such pursuits? you ask. What do they add to the sum of us?—and do we need it?

Well, after some reflection, I can truly say: we need these small joys as much as we need anything else. For what good is life if one can not imbibe simple wonders on a regular basis? Our workload had nearly doubled since we'd become farmers. Somebody had to offset the imbalance. Somebody had to taste the beauty of life while others toiled. So, finding no one better suited to the task, I appointed myself.

But despite these idyllic pleasures, as one season passed into another, my thoughts again turned to the Otherworld. Though life in the Otherworld was difficult, in the Otherworld, life became more real.

But entry into that world seemed to require so much pain. I was not that bored. At least, not yet.

Fortunately, my job as Seer began to draw new duties that kept me distracted. My tribes-kin figured that someone who could talk to the seeds and coax them up out of the ground might also be able to coax the sickness out of somebody's body. So now, whenever anyone had anything—even a case of the sniffles or a mild fever—I was called upon to perform. And I always complied. To have refused would've been viewed as malicious neglect—or as cowardice.

And so, I entered the precarious profession of healing the sick. For each malady, I developed a special ritual, a unique combination of talismans, poultices, prayers, and potions. If the patient's condition worsened after my treatment, if he slipped away to the world of the dead, I would simply tell the bereaved that it was Matar's will. Since Matar was our Creator, we belonged to him/her/it. And ever so often, he/she/it grew lonesome for one of his/her/its children. And when Matar called, there was no way out—you had to go. That's what I told them.

You'd think that such a paltry excuse would've provoked extreme anger. But oddly enough, the mourners usually accepted my alibi with tears of loving gratitude.

And so, in this manner, my life traced a course through three bountiful summers and four restful winters.   Other than an irrepressible urge for the Otherworld, and the ever-present shadow of Mok, I knew no trouble.

Chapter 10 :
Visitors! Disruption! Vitality!

Then one yawning day, my somnolent life fractured. Once again, trouble appeared on the horizon. My heart leapt at the sight of those blurry forms moving through the savanna heat waves.

Visitors!

Disruption!

Vitality!

I ran back to the village and told Mok. I then rousted Boq from his tree roost, drew the women in from the fields, and pulled all the craftspeople from their trade work.

In a just twinkling, we, the People of Matar, had assembled as one body upon the plain, only a stone's throw away from our vulnerable abodes

Against a backdrop of bleached-blue sky, the blurred figures ambled along in a loose single-file line.

Though Mok placed himself at our head, I shouldered in beside him, as did Boq. The rest of the Matarian men formed a wall behind us, holding their spears low in a non-threatening manner. We didn't want to provoke anyone unless absolutely necessary. However, at the same time, we all narrowed our eyes to show that we meant business—every man, woman, and child of us.

The dust that trailed our visitors thinned out over the plain. Even from this distance, I recognized that disheveled collection of skeletons. The Roqians carried the boredom of infinite distance in their shambling gait. The vacuity in their dark eyes told of endless dismal wandering. They were as tough as life itself; as resilient as the thorn-eating camel.

I knew they weren't here by accident. The invisible thread of destiny had drawn the People of Roq back to us. We had begun something with them; the situation wanted resolution.

"You see what I see?" I whispered to Mok.

"I see, I see," he growled.

The Roqians pulled up short a hundred paces from us. When I spotted Rewan amongst them, I couldn't help but wet my lips.

The two tribes eyed each other with blank stares that failed to hide mutual distrust.

I nodded to Mok and Boq, then we three men walked as one toward the Roqians. Bruk and Ool followed right behind us. I turned and shook my head at them.

"Don't be silly," I said. "Stay with the tribe. This is our job, not yours. I mean, we have to do something around here. Go on—you heard me."

They looked at each other, then shrugged and headed back to their tribes-kin.

We met the Roqian representatives—the young warrior Urk and the old woman Urm—midway between the two tribes. Urk kept pumping his jaw muscles. His left hand was clenched in a fist. Those cold, dark eyes studied us like silent death.

Mok fixed his own deadly gaze on Urk. He kept pumping his jaw muscles. His left hand was clenched in a fist.

Urm's pot belly protruded with significant authority. She perched one hand on a voluminous hip and gave us her best dirty look. Her toothless gums worked a piece of straw.

"Where's Mer?" I asked.

"Him? We had to let him go." The words purred from Urm's lips.

"What'd you mean? Where'd he go?"

"We sent him back."

"Back where?"

"They killed him," Mok said through tight lips.

"Why'd you do a thing like that?"

"The goats weren't doing so good," Urk said. "We thought maybe it was our Seer. Maybe his goat rituals had lost their power. So we sacrificed him to Roq, hoping that the great god would accept our offering and heal our herd."

I eyed the goats as they butted against Roqian shinbones. The poor creatures had thin mangy hair and raw pink skin. Their bleary eyes leaked yellow pus. The breath hoarsed in their throats.

"I don't think the sacrifice worked," I said.

"We now believe that Mer haunts us from the other side," Urm said. "He comes at night when we're all asleep and tortures the goats for spite. The ungrateful toad."

"Ungrateful?" The word popped from my mouth.

"It's an honor to die for one's people," she answered. "Anyway, that's what Mer always told us. When the goats first took sick, he suggested that we sacrifice a couple of children—newborns would be best, he said. But we told him, 'Why use children? They aren't the ones doing the rituals. Let's go to the source.' He didn't like that idea much, but he was only one vote." The straw dipped and bobbed as Urm spoke.

"So why'd you come here?" Mok asked.

"We just happened this way," Urm said. "What about you?"

"We live here," Boq said. "It's a really neat place." His natural bonhomie nearly wrecked the mood.

"Live here?" Urk frowned. "Like on a permanent basis?"

"Yes," I said. "We farm the land here. You know—plant seeds in the ground and grow things."

"But nature plants the seeds for us. You need not plant the seeds for nature."

"Well, you guys raise goats though they run free in the mountains," Boq said.

"That's different," Urk said.

I could feel the rising apprehension of my tribes-kin. We didn't want the Roqians anywhere near our site. However, if we didn't welcome our visitors it could cause problems. In addition to that, I believed that maybe, just maybe, if the tribes got to know each other better, they might actually forget their little squabble.

Did Rewan figure into this equation at all? I have to admit, she did enter my mind. I knew it was a fool's idea, but I was still foolish enough to think that the two of us might have a future together.

"Hey, I've got an idea," I broke in. "Why don't you guys stay here for the night? Refresh yourselves in our river. Let the bounty of our fields restore your strength. Then in the morning you can leave."

"I don't know," said Urk. He kept his dull eyes fastened on Mok.

"Come on, it'd just be for one night. Let's be friends again. Mistakes were made, yes, but those mistakes are in the past," then lowering my voice, I added, "Tether your goats down river. They'll be safe there, I promise."

"Of course they'll be safe," Urm said. "Who'd want to steal those sorry-ass goats?"

Oddly enough, Urm's caustic remark seemed to seal the deal. Urk acquiesced and the two tribes came together in an uneasy peace. For the remainder of that day, we renewed acquaintance while lounging about the campfire.

And perhaps we could've put our differences behind us, perhaps from that time on we could have gotten along just fine...if only the Roqians would have stopped eyeing our strong, healthy goats, taking stock of their sleek white coats, their bright pink gums, their long full shanks. They didn't bother asking how we came by the goats; they knew that we would lie.

Each Roqian man had a hand axe hanging from a thick leather belt. Though we Matarian men had our axes tucked away inside our huts, our spears were still within reach. So while the Roqian men caressed their flint axe blades, we men of Matar stroked the shafts of our spears. Yet all the while both tribes acted oh so nonchalant, conversing about such things as the weather and the pain of arthritis.

Though I knew that the Roqians wanted their goats back, I doubted they'd be so foolish as to pick a fight. Of my own people, I was less sure. Whatever the case, I knew that tonight none of us would get much sleep—suspicion ran too deep on both sides.

While all this worry was churning through my mind, I reclined near the campfire, affecting light conversation with Urm. Actually, I wanted to talk to Rewan, but the old matriarch kept getting in the way. However, my love interest remained within range. She rested her head on her hand and poured her liquid brown eyes over me. Those eyes reflected twin moons.

I couldn't help but sputter in speech whenever my gaze touched those moon eyes. According to Urm, the poor lass hadn't been able complete her instruction with Mer before his demise. As a result, she was not yet qualified to practice the Seer's craft.

"Yes, that is true," Rewan broke in. "But Amar, perhaps you, with your great learning and courage, could bring me up to snuff. From the mountain of your wisdom, I can gain the vision needed to guide my people. How 'bout it, Amar? Can you teach me?"

Oh, how those words chimed in my ears! But now I found myself in quite a quandary. If I said 'yes'—if I agreed to take Rewan under my wing—I would anger both tribes. But on the other hand, if I said 'no', I could ruin my chances for a love match. So instead, I stumbled and stammered, then switched to a different topic.

But Rewan wouldn't let the matter rest. After a few moments, she broached the subject again. And again, I dipped my head and got all mealy-mouthed.

"Well, ah, you see, ah...I mean, it's not up to...I would have to...the thing is...what wonderful weather we've been having."

Though Urm tried to stare her down, Rewan kept on pushing. "Oh come on, Amar, say 'yes'. It'll be fun. How 'bout it, Amar? Please—I need you."

Finally, Urm let out an audible sigh, then excused herself and stalked off.

"Ah, alone at last," Rewan said. Her lips curled into a soft, milky smile. She fluttered her lids at me, then rubbed her legs together with a somnolent luxuriousness. What'd happened to that demure girl who used to heed Mer with such obedience? She had laced her innocence with smoke, that's what.

144

"It's a difficult situation," I told her.

"Difficult, but not impossible," she answered.

"I just don't know what to do."

"I can see that. I can also see that you need a strong woman beside you."

Her fingers strolled over to my hand. But I dared not touch. Finally, she lost patience and rolled her forefinger across my knuckles in a manner both seductive and soothing. What remained of my better judgment then flew to the wind. I took her tiny paw and cupped it in the pool of my palm. We did not speak; we did not need to speak. Looking into her dark moon eyes, I could see a world beyond.

In that infinite moment, I finally made my decision. But unfortunately, it was not my decision to make.

Our honey music ended as Urm again plopped down beside me. This time, Urk stood over her. His jaw muscles bulged as though he carried rocks in his cheeks. His left hand was clenched in a fist.

Rewan's tender fingers leapt from my hand.

My stomach twitched.

"Urk and I just had an idea," Urm cooed.

My mistrustful mind raised its hackles.

"Yeah? What's that?"

"We thought maybe you could travel to the Otherworld and find our old Seer for us."

"To what good purpose?"

"To help us make amends with him. Then he'd stop haunting our goats and they would have a chance to heal. I think you owe us that much, don't you?"

"Well, ah, you see, ah—" the words choked in my throat—"entering the Otherworld...it's not that easy, you know."

"Yes, that may be true," she rejoined. "But it should be no problem for a great Seer such as yourself. Rewan'd be glad to prepare the embers. It wouldn't take her that long. We'd be most appreciative."

"Do it," barked Urk.

Just thinking of the fire walk made my feet tingle. "But you see, the dead don't like to be disturbed," I countered. "It might make Mer even madder."

"Well, if my people find out that you refused—" Urm glanced at the silhouettes lounging around the fire —"it might make them even madder. Girl, get the embers ready."

Rewan stood up and dusted off her knees.

Did Urm really believe that I could appease their Seer on the other side? No, she just wanted me out of the picture. A union between Rewan and I would threaten the "purity" of both tribes. More importantly, if the two of us married, they'd have to bury the axe. And neither side was ready for that.

I was in a tight spot. But I had a plan.

"Wait!" I held up my hand. Rewan stopped in her tracks.

"You will not walk the fire plank?" Urk asked in a dark voice.

"No. There are better ways of entering the Otherworld—particularly when visiting the dead." I leapt to my feet and clapped my hands overhead. "People!" I yelled. "People. Listen up. Everyone. I've decided to journey to the Otherworld. The purpose of this trip is to aid our good friends here, the Roqians. I must talk with their old Seer on the other side and try to get him to stop haunting their goats. But before I leave, let me just say one thing: the two tribes must not break the peace while I'm away."

"Why's that?" Mok shouted.

"Any disturbance would throw off the energy surrounding this event. It's what's known as 'bad influence'. I could have trouble while navigating the Otherworld."

I looked to Mok, then to Urk, hoping to receive some guarantee from them. But both men wore blank stares; their eyes were focused inward on their own hatred. I decided not to press the issue.

"Anyway before I go, I must do a ritual to help protect me on my journey. And Rewan here will assist." In my anxious state, I actually had the audacity to take her by the hand. "Will you all please join me down by the riverside."

Everyone likes a show. The two tribes trailed after Rewan and me as we walked to the river.

I stopped near the bank. Soft coils of black water slid along, rippling the moon. Though I knew the river would be gripping cold, I preferred it to the fire pit.

I took a small gopher-skin pouch, puffed it full of air, then held it between forefinger and thumb. I then instructed Rewan to pluck a reed from along the riverbank. The murmuring crowd hushed as I raised my arm.

"This reed represents the body of man," I said. "Rooted in the ground, but rising toward the sky; breaching the waters of life while anchored firmly in the earth. Rewan, hand me the reed."

I tied the puffed-up pouch to the reed, then stuck the reed into the soft loam along shoreline. "This pouch represents the heart of man; the air within the pouch represents his spirit. When we die, the spirit leaves the heart, just as the air would leave this pouch if you were to step on it.

"Whilst I am away on my journey, you must speak to the reed and say good things to it and place bread and goat's milk before it. In this way, I will gain encouragement and have nourishment while in the Otherworld."

I bowed to the reed, then turned to the two tribes and bowed to them. Not knowing what else to do, they bowed back at me.

"Because the Otherworld is a dark world, one may enter it through the dark world of this river. But I caution you—do not try to follow me; entering the Otherworld is tricky business and the result of failure is death."

Maintaining a dignified carriage, I then marched down the slope of the bank to the river's edge. I stood there a moment, trying to prepare myself for the shock of the frigid night water. Finally, I forced myself to put one foot in. Though the sudden chill shook me, I gritted my teeth and managed to hold onto my solemn expression.

Then, fighting against all reasonable impulse, I walked into the river. The freezing waters crept up my legs, then fingered my genitals, then swelled around my chest, then bracketed my neck. Gripped by the cold, my heart nearly stopped.

Nevertheless, I took one last gulp of air, then dunked my head all the way under.

My plan was simple: to swim down river beneath the cover of this dark water. When I knew myself to be a good distance from our village, I would then crawl back up the bank and slink off into the night with the stealth of a raccoon. Then come morning, while everyone was gathered at the communal campfire, I'd pop out of the bushes as though I'd just exited the Otherworld.

I would then tell the Roqians that I'd spoken with their old Seer and apologized for their lapse of judgment. I'd say that Mer would lift his curse on the condition that they travel far, far away from here and avoid Matarians from this day forth. Mer would also ask that Rewan remain behind so that I might instruct her in the ways of the Seer. She could return to her tribe only after she'd learned the craft properly. But that might take awhile, a good long while.

That's what I'd tell them.

I dove straight down, trying my best not to disturb the river's surface. It had to look as if I'd just disappeared, as if I had descended into another realm.

But the cold current slammed me hard. I fought against a dizzy swoon. Already my lungs burned. A knife point jabbed the middle of my forehead. I couldn't even see my hands in the black water.

However, I pushed all pain aside and kept on forcing my way down through the depths.

Then somewhere along the line, I began to notice specks of light—drops of bright red and blue which blew past me and popped in my ears. These tiny explosions tickled me. I went giddy and nearly started laughing.

But at the same time, I could feel spear tips twisting in my lungs. The tips drove deeper with each kick of my legs, with each thrust of my arms.

Now the drops of light began to bloom. Their pink and green petals smoothed over my skin like sweet oil. Their profound harmony allowed me to forget the spear tips.

The river current had soothing hands, hands that guided me, drawing my spirit down. I knew that I should fight against the current. I needed to level this dive out so that I could move farther down river. But a sense of inner calmness overrode all my objections; I continued my descent.

"I'm surely going to my death," I told myself. "I am surely going to die."

But at the moment, I just didn't care.

My mind blew apart like a dandelion ball.

The seeds of my mind rode away with the current.

Chapter 11 :
Good Woman of the Flower

I awoke beneath a small tree on a grassy hill. The sun was a distant yellow dot in a sky of deep blue. A gentle hum permeated my head. This was a quiet world, a world soft and cool. The long, luminous grass swayed as if underwater.

I could have lulled here forever.

But then my eye caught sight of a big flower bud dangling over my head. This bud hung down from a vine, a thick meaty vine that had coiled up the tree trunk and snaked through the branches.

A moment later—as if on cue—the heavy bud began to shake and groan. The outer covering then peeled back with a crackling sound and a luscious cluster of white petals burgeoned forth.

A flower had burst from its cocoon, revealing itself to me in all its glory. From the heart of this fleshy, white flower, a pistil extended down. A single drop of honey clung to its tip. Within this trembling drop, I could see a rainbow prism wiggling.

Then suddenly, a beam of light refracted through the honey drop and blinded me for several anxious moments. But when my vision returned, I found a most splendid sight: an illumined being of great beauty now floated above me.

Her form was but a wispy thing. Her dainty feet swayed with the breeze; her soft golden hair drifted in lush tangles. A gold gossamer gown—as delicate as spider silk—hovered about her body. Her face was milky perfection.

I found a melancholy loveliness in her eyes. Those blue-white orbs looked down upon me as though from a great height; they pitied me. I hankered to make up the distance between us.

So I rose to my knees. I lifted my hand to touch her hand. But poof!—in an instant she was gone. The flower petals quickly folded back into their leafy cocoon.

"Wait! Wait!" I cried. "Flower woman—Woman of the Flower—come back!"

I reached for the cocoon. I would strip back its layers until I found her.

But then a voice said, "You won't get me that way, so don't bother trying."

I couldn't locate the source of this voice. Those airy, mellifluous tones seemed to come from everywhere at once.

"But I must have you, Good Woman of the Flower," I said. "I must bring you back to my people. We need you; we need your beautiful light. Without you, I'm sure we're doomed."

"You will have me," the voice intoned. "But first you must return to me my silver bow and my silver arrow."

"What do you mean?" I asked. "What silver bow? What silver arrow? I've never heard of such things. What do they look like?"

"When you finally find my silver bow and my silver arrow, you'll most certainly know them."

"But how will I know them?"

"By their virtue, by their perfection, by their necessity. Without my silver bow and arrow I am incomplete and must remain locked in this shell."

"Well, okay. But how can I find them?"

"Leave now and follow the dirt path. Stay on the path. Do not falter. Do not swerve. Hear me? Do not rest until you have found the one known as Vulam. She is my sister. When you find her, tell her that she must return my silver bow and my silver arrow. You see, she took these things from me."

"And how will I recognize her?"

"Rest assured—you will know her when you see her. Now go."

"Just one more thing," I begged.

"Well, make it quick."

"I hate to ask, but I must. You aren't just another version of Matar, are you?"

"Silly human," the voice chuckled, "don't you know your own Creator?"

"No, I don't. Are you Matar?"

"I am who I am. Now go!"

With that, a great wind rose up and bristled the tree. The branches scraped together in manner both menacing and impatient.

I saw that I had no other choice but to start down the dirt path.

This trail led me over a hill to a hollow, then through this hollow and along a purling stream. The forest trees formed an archway for me. Across my shadowy pathway, the dappled light played, mixing and dissolving into a myriad of subtle, tantalizing shades.

The idea that The Good Woman of the Flower might just be another version of Matar made me sick to my stomach. I had first known him/her/it as a slimy, pus-oozing stump. So to my mind, the first Matar was still the real Matar and all other guises were only disguises.

However, this question remained: how could our great Creator ever be locked up in a shell? No, the Woman of the Flower had to be separate from Matar and that was that. She remained unsullied. My love was still pure.

And so, brimming with purpose and eager for adventure, I hurried on down the dirt path.

However, by this time, the sky had turned soot black. The sun was now nothing more than a dead gray disk.

"Oh yeah, I can see trouble coming," I told myself. "I bet it'll just get worse from here on out."

I rounded a bend and left the archway of trees behind me. In the distance, dark clouds roiled against the mountains. Erratic snakes of lightening erupted all the way down to the ground. The light across my path had fled to the shadows. Sharp rocks now ripped at the bottoms of my feet.

"This is bad," I said to myself, "but I know it'll just get worse."

And indeed, this belief was soon confirmed. Bramble bushes began to crowd both sides of the trail. Their thorny whips tore at my arms, my chest, my back. The more I struggled, the deeper they stung.

"This is horrible," I thought, "but I know it'll just get worse."

And indeed it did. In the next instant, a streak of lightening split the sky in half. Then rain spat down, lashing my back and salting my wounds. The water seeped into my flesh until I was colder than a corpse. A frozen snake encoiled my heart.

"This is worse than horrible," I said to myself. "If I take one more step, I'll surely fall to the ground, break into splinters, and blow away with the wind."

However, my love for The Good Woman of the Flower gave me the strength to carry on. For her sake and her sake alone, I leaned into the vicious wind and strove forward, gritting my teeth against the vengeance of this path.

"You endured a furious storm before and it made you a better man," I told myself. "Remember the words of The Good Woman of the Flower: do not falter, do not swerve—you must stay on the path."

Within moments of this thought, the brambles lifted away. The rain eased to a soft, comforting drizzle. The sharp rocks sank back into the soil.

As I opened my arms to the sky, the sun broke past a dark cloud. The forest trees again formed an archway for me.

"Yes, I'd endured a furious storm before," I said to myself. "But not a storm as hurtful as that storm. Surely, I've survived the worst. Things can only get better from here on out."

But I knew I was only fooling myself; I knew that I wouldn't escape so easily; I knew that much more pain and misery waited for me on up the trail.

And indeed, the sky soon darkened again. The black clouds growled as they rolled against one another.

Then around the next bend, past the archway of trees, I discovered the source of this dismal atmosphere: a glowing orange volcano cone was burping forth harsh smoke. Orange-gold lava jumped, sputtered, and plopped in the crater above. Even from this distance, I could feel the heat against my face. I winced at the smoke.

The dirt path curved along the base of this steep volcano cone. Up ahead, a pool of lava lay right in the middle of the trail as though awaiting my arrival.

"You endured fire before and it made you a better man," I told myself. "Remember the words of The Good Woman of the Flower: do not falter, do not swerve–you must stay on the path."

A luminous snake of orange lava crept from the pool toward me.

I braced myself, knowing that I had no other choice but to tread through that molten morass. So, holding the image of The Good Woman of the Flower firmly in my mind...I took a decisive step forward.

The lava snake lunged for my toe. In a split instant, orange lightning ripped up my spine and exploded my brain.

Whirling, roaring flame now engulfed me. No matter how fast I moved my legs, I couldn't move them fast enough. Fire slashed my body at all the delicate locations; it drilled a hole right through the core of my being and out the other side. I kept waiting for the pain to explode me, to blast me into nothingness. But though the pain kept climbing higher and higher, and the pressure kept building, kept building, I did not burst.

The little man inside howled all the up to the sky.

"This is surely the worst," I told myself. "It can only get better from here on out."

But the orange tunnel of fire went on and on, dashing what little hope I had left. I watched the flesh melt from my frame. My skeleton glowed red. My bones began to sag from the heat. Finally, my finger joints broke apart and my hands became unhinged.

One bone after the other fell into the golden pool—ribs, vertebrae, the pelvic butterfly. All my twigs were gone.

"So what am I now?" I asked myself. "What remains of me? I have no feet for walking, no fingers to snap, no skull to scratch, no tailbone to sit upon. Am I stationary or am I moving?"

My pain told me that I was still alive. But how long I could endure such pain? On the other hand, what other choice did I have?

"There has to be an end to it," I told myself. "There is an end to everything. Isn't there?"

Needless to say, patience was at a premium.

I now experienced myself as a pressurized speck, impacted on every side by fire.

I was ready to implode; I kept waiting and hoping, waiting for it to all be over

Then finally—finally—something of a miracle occurred; a silent miracle yet a miracle nonetheless: all thought and feeling suddenly dissolved into smoke and I flew away, soft as a feather, borne on the gentle breeze of release. I ascended with the spiraling wind; at rest, at rest for the moment at least, though not in bliss, not yet.

When I came back to myself, I was on my hands and knees in the dark path. The volcano cone now stood behind me. Its orange glow highlighted my arms and legs and feet.

A snake of lava slid down the trail toward me.

I didn't wait around, but skittered on up the trail, sheltered by the archway of trees.

Yes, I'd endured fire before, but not a fire like that fire.

"Well, I have nothing more to fear now," I told myself. "The way can only get better from here on out. It certainly can't get any worse. I'm sure to find the silver bow and arrow around the next bend."

But I knew I was only fooling myself; I knew that I wouldn't escape so easily; I knew that much more pain and misery waited for me on up the trail.

And indeed, around the next bend, past the archway of trees, a frigid wind seared my face and hung ice crystals on my eyelashes. Through the darkness, I could see another steep mountain leering up before me. This cone had a covering of thick white snow. But after the lava, that cool blanket looked downright enticing.

Nevertheless, as the frosty wind ate into my skin and howled down through the hollow of my ribcage, I grew anxious; I hurried my pace. I just wanted to get around that frozen mountain. Surely, the silver bow and arrow awaited me on the other side.

But to my dismay, I found that the path climbed straight through those snowy drifts all the way to the peak. The traces of the trail were nearly hidden beneath the heavy white cover.

"Remember the words of The Good Woman of the Flower," I told myself, "You must not falter. You must not swerve. You must not leave the path. Well, I have endured cold before—recently, in fact. And yes, that mountain may be cold, but it's nothing that I can't endure, I'm sure."

But as soon as I put one foot into the snow, an icy fire seized my leg. Blue lightening clanged all the way up my spine and stung my brain again and again.

I now began to have second thoughts, and third thoughts as well. After removing my leg from the snow drift, I stepped back and reappraised the situation.

"Yes, the Woman of the Flower is quite nice," I told myself. "And I would love to take her back to the tribe —for my own sake, as well as theirs. But at what cost? Is it really worth the pain? Perhaps it's better that I should leave the path."

Who could stop me? I looked to the left, I looked to the right. On both sides of the track, silhouetted foliage textured the night. Within those jungle shadows, frogs croaked, birds shrieked, monkeys screamed, and creeping things slithered and scraped. The leaves breathed warm air all over my face.

I then happened to spy a spiky-tailed lizard tiptoeing along a nearby branch. Its skinny tongue flicked the air.

"Who goes there?" A gravely, aerated voice came from the lizard.

"My name is Amar," I told it. "My people are the People of Matar. And who are you?"

"I am Lizard," said the lizard. "I govern this jungle. Whosoever enters must first answer to me."

"Lizard, I respect your authority. And I think I would like to enter your forest. But tell me first, what transpires there?"

"Creatures slink and slide through the night. They forage for food. They breed and raise their young. And of course, eventually, they die, as all living things must."

"Nothing else?"

"Hardly." The forked tongue flicked the air. "So do you want to join or don't you?"

What bothered me about that jungle? It looked to be far less painful than the mountain. On the other hand, it did sound rather boring. And not all that different from my regular life. But I could live with that, couldn't I? Or could I?

I did not even bother to answer the question. I knew I was only fooling myself. I knew that I had no other option.

With little regret, I turned away from jungle and back toward the icy mountain. Again, the cold wind needled my face and sang through the vicissitudes of my gut. However, this time I did not falter, I did not swerve—no, I plowed straight ahead into the snow.

The sharp, raw rime soon had me in its grip. My legs became tight blocks of ice. Each step demanded an elephantine effort. My mind groaned under the weight of this frozen night, then groaned no more—it was now locked solid. Numbness drummed through my whole body. My eyes had frosted over; I could barely see my way. Not that I gave a damn anymore. At the moment, I just wanted to drop over dead and sleep forever in warm stillness. However, my feet kept dragging me up that ice-infested mountain, kept pushing me, forcing me on, driving me, until finally— finally—I came to a complete stop.

This halting woke me from my trance. My eyes made a pathetic attempt to focus. I could see just enough to see that the mountain fell away into darkness on all four sides. I had reached the peak. The wind blew softly here, holding me in its arms, buoying my body.

I then sensed that someone or something was watching.

I looked up to find a full blue turquoise moon gazing down upon me. It seemed nearly within reach. I wanted to touch that moon, but couldn't lift my ice-bound arms.

"Go no further," I heard a voice say. It was a woman's voice with its deep sensuality. "Not one more step." But it was man's voice with its deep command.

"Are you talking to me?" I asked the blue turquoise moon.

"Who else is around? Now you just stay here with me."

"Are you the one known as Vulam?" I murmured through frost-bitten lips.

"Not a chance."

"Then I must be moving on."

"No, you stay here with me. If you stay here with me, I will make you ruler of all that you see."

"Forget it," I said.

"No, listen—this is your destiny. Heed it. Fulfill it. Obey me."

But I'd gone too far to falter or swerve. I would not be intimidated; I would not leave the path.

So I wasted no more time, but began slowly weaving my way down the mountain's backside.

"Hold on, hold on there!" the moon shouted. "Stop, I say, stop right there! I'm warning you—you'd better come back. Come back, or you'll be sorry. I'm telling you—you'll be...sssaaaaaaaaaaaaaar-rrreeeeeeeeeeee!"

As if in league with the moon, the wind now tore at me with renewed vigor. My senses began to shut down once again. Once again, I buckled down into my shell and burrowed my way through the cold.

My body and mind did not return to life until I'd stepped off the mountain and back down on level ground. Then the ice around me and within me began to break and gradually I regained my usual feeling self.

I felt like cursing a blue streak at that rimy peak. But I just didn't have words enough. So I turned away and continued on down the path under the archway of trees.

Yes, I'd endured cold before, but no cold like that cold.

"Surely, I am free now," I told myself. "Surely, I have gone through the worst of the worst. The silver bow and arrow should be right around the corner."

The night air was spiced with the fresh scent of spring. My whole world was in nocturnal bloom. I felt ready to accept my ultimate destiny.

And so, as fate would have it, just around the next bend, past the archway of trees, I spied another mountain. And oh, what a mountain it was: the trees on those steep slopes glowed with a cool golden fire. But no—on closer examination, I saw that the fire was just an illusion. There were no trees there. That golden glow came from the plated scales of a huge serpent. The beast had coiled itself around the mountain several times, forming a spiral that went all the way up from the base to the peak. Its angular head rested on a flat rock at the very top. The eyes were shut tight.

Yes, I had endured a serpent before, but not a serpent like this serpent. However, my last encounter with a snake had led to a great glorious rebirth. "So why be afraid?" I asked myself. "Why not embrace the opportunity?"

Yet I quivered and quaked as I waited for the beast to detect my minute presence. Finally, I cleared my throat.

But still, the behemoth slumbered.

So I called to the beast: "Excuse me, coiled serpent, excuse me—are you the one known as Vulam?"

A dull yellow eye popped open. The pupil was but a thin black sliver. "Who wants to know?" The voice was dry and sooty—raspy, yes, but still womanly. Even at this distance, the breath left an odor of decay in the air. This most certainly had to be Vulam.

"I am Amar, Seer for the People of Matar." I put one foot forward and cocked my hip, affecting a heroic stance. "Your sister sent me here to retrieve the silver bow and arrow. So may I have them please?"

The monster shifted its head to get a better look at me. This movement caused a rippling effect along the length of its body. A shadow passed over the golden scales, running all the way down from the head to the tip of the tail.

I swallowed hard, but the lump was stuck.

"S-s-sister? What s-s-sister?" the serpent hissed.

"The Good Woman of the Flower."

"Don't know her."

"She is a being of supreme love and light. I have decided to bring her back to my people. They need her. But I know she won't return with me until she has the silver bow and arrow. So can you give them to me please?"

"If she's so hot, why doesn't she fetch them herself?"

"Because it's my job, not hers. Her job is to give forth healing and peace."

"Is that so?" the beast sneered. "Then what is my job, oh wise one?"

"Your job is to give me the silver bow and arrow." Hah!—I'd tricked her!

"Well then, come on up and get them."

"You have them there?"

"Yes, I do."

163

"Then where are they? I don't see anything."

"I keep them in my mouth and only show them on special occasions. But if you come on up, I'll take them out. Just follow the path."

The trail spiraled up the mountainside, running between the serpent's golden coils.

Though I didn't trust Vulam, what other choice did I have?

So I straightened my shoulders and started up the path. The lump in my throat had expanded.

"Okay, here I come. Don't you move now. Okay? Okay, Vulam?"

The gold-plated scales flexed each time Vulam took in a breath. I knew that she could squeeze me into soup with one sudden convulsion of her body. So I stepped softly.

I was about halfway to the top when Vulam drew in a deep sigh that swelled her sides until her scales pressed against my shoulders and arms. I was forced to stop for a long—very long—moment. But then she exhaled a cloud of smoke and I was released.

By the time I reached the peak, my knees had started to knock. Vulam still had not lifted her head from the slab of rock in the center of the clearing. Those hooded eyes gave me a dead stare. Black steam issued from two discreet nose holes.

I had to crunch my teeth together to keep them from chattering. I figured that Vulam would soon be processing me through her digestive organs. Though great rewards might await me on the other side, I couldn't help but cringe.

"Okay, here I am," I said. "Now can I have the silver bow and arrow?"

"On second thought, I don't think my sister needs them," the snake said. "In fact, I think she already has them."

"That's ridiculous!" I shouted. "If she already had the silver bow and arrow, why would she send me down the dirt path? I've had to travel far and endure many things—each one worse than the one before. It was rough, let me tell you, it was rough. First of all, there was this rain storm—"

"S-s-spare me!" the serpent hissed.

Sooty steam shot from the nose holes. The hot plumes condensed against my face. I wheezed and I coughed. "What've you got against your sister anyway?" I sputtered. "She is beauty defined. Born of a lovely white flower, she can turn smoke into sunlit cloud and tar into honey. Is there anyone else so pure and bright? No, I tell you, no one. All others pale beside The Good Woman of the Flower!"

"You wouldn't know her if you saw her." The grungy voice harshed in my ear.

"Oh yes, I would. I'd know that wonderful woman anywhere."

"Then take a look, smart boy." And with that, Vulam unhinged her jaw and flung her mouth open wide. "She's in here. See for yourself."

An enormous black maw now yawned before me. Rows of sharp golden teeth splintered the light.

I brushed aside the swirls of steam and squinted into the dark depths of the mouth, searching for the flower woman, ready to plunge in and rescue her if need be.

"Woman of the Flower, are you in there?" I yelled.

"She's in here...in here...just look...look," Vulam echoed back to me.

But all I could see in the darkness was a small flame so far back that it touched the uvula.

"Well, if she's in there, I sure can't find her," I shouted.

"Just hold on...hold on."

I waited a moment, then I waited a moment more. By this time, I had forgotten some of my fear. I looked down to examine a chipped fingernail. How had that happened?

Then before I knew what, the distant whisper of flame leapt forward, unfurling out to become a blazing red tongue. The tip of it bit my nose. The heat of it broasted my skin. But I did not falter, I did not swerve; no, I stood firm; I stood firm though the smoke blinded me for several anxious moments.

When all had cleared, I saw a sight that shocked me to the core. A familiar figure rode the crest of that tongue—but it was a familiar figure transformed. The delicate blonde hair had been replaced by a gaggle of gray snakes and the face was puffed up like a pale mushroom. The eyes, once loving and blue, had turned dull black. And the gold gossamer gown was now nothing more than a net of ash hanging from a heavy, bloated body.

"Good Woman of the Flower! Oh my flower woman!" I cried. "Can that be you? No, that can't be you. I know an illusion when I see one."

"Yes, dummy, it is I," she said in a raw, peppery voice. She lifted her lip to show her wolfen teeth.

But I refused to give up so easily. "That's a lie!" I shouted. "The real flower woman lives in a perfect white flower, not in a serpent's mouth. The real Woman of the Flower is all beauty and light, not

darkness and decay. The Good Woman of the Flower
—"

But I couldn't think to complete my sentence. I was distracted by the graceful instrument the ash woman now held in her hands. The long staff curved back at both ends and a string was strung from one end tip to the other. Upon that string rested the butt end of a short spear. And yes, as you may have guessed, these pieces all shone a piercing silver.

But though I admired the virtue, perfection, and necessity of that instrument, I could not ignore the fact that the spear point was aimed right at me.

"So that's the silver bow and arrow?" I asked.

"I knew you would know them when you saw them," said the Woman of the Ashes.

"Well then, hand them over. I want to return them to the real flower woman."

"But I am the real flower woman, knucklehead."

I felt hurt; I felt angry. On impulse, I leapt forward and grabbed for the bow. But my reach fell short; my hand grazed the arrow tip. My thumb throbbed as though stung by a bee.

The ash woman just shook her head of snakes at me and gave forth a cackling laugh. Then she raised the bow, drew back the bowstring, and sighted down the arrow.

The bowstring made a thrumming sound. A flash of silver slashed through the air.

I felt a sudden tightness in my chest. I looked down to find the arrow shaft protruding from the area of my left breast. I waited to feel the bite of the arrow tip. But instead, to my surprise, I began to experience a golden radiance—a gentle warmth—spreading outward from my heart. I lifted my eyes to thank the Woman of the Ashes, but in that moment, the fiery tongue recoiled, pulling her back in with it.

As she disappeared down the throat, the ash woman leaned way back and loosed another silver arrow. But this one went singing high overhead and plunked right into the center of that blue turquoise moon.

I looked down at my bloody hands, then held my hands up to the moon and said, "I'm stained yet I'm pure. I'm pure, yet stained."

"So now you know!" the moon sang out. "So now you know!" That laugh—affectionate, but in a condescending way—still sounds within me.

Chapter 12 : Welcome Home

I awoke to find myself sitting on a steep mountainside in an in-between area where the trees and moss gave way to gray rock and lichen. I checked my chest: no arrow there; no noticeable wound. It was good to be back from the Otherworld.

Cloud shadows passed over the plain below. The sun shone silver on the delicate network of streams that fed into the main river. A mountain range serrated the far horizon.

I spent a few moments gathering myself together, then began to pick my way down the mountainside, navigating around the roots and rocks. I knew that once I found the river it would lead me home. I was more than ready to rejoin my tribe; I wanted to return to my ordinary life. I wanted Bruk's tough, bony arms around me; Bruk would anchor me to mother earth.

My legs still felt a little shaky from my journey through the Otherworld. My head wobbled on its neck.

Images and feelings from the trip began to twist my mind. What did I say to the blue turquoise moon? 'I'm stained, yet pure'—what the blazes did that mean? But more importantly, how could I reconcile the two conflicting versions of the flower woman?

Perhaps Matar had tricked me. Yeah, that had to be it. Matar was a jealous god; Matar wanted to keep The Woman of the Flower for him/her/itself. So...Matar had put a false flower woman before me. Obviously, Matar and Vulam were in cahoots.

At the bottom of the mountain, I found a gurgling spring filled with watercress. Here I drank my fill and washed my head. Then I set out across the plain, following the path of a slender, snaking stream.

By now, I understood that patience is not a virtue when walking. Patience involves waiting and hope. Patience tends to chase it own tail. Showing patience when you walk means you want to hurry, but don't. That just leads to frustration and exhaustion.

So now I walked with the thought that I didn't care if I ever got anywhere.

When the earth grew dark, I found a soft round sandstone and lay my head down for the night. The next morning, as the sun bloomed on the horizon, I continued tracing the path of the stream.

This stream eventually became a slow river. In time, the river began to pick up speed, getting wild— crashing against rocks and spewing up white spray.

I felt tempted to increase my pace, but managed to contain myself.

Finally, I came to a dark-brown marshy land. I knew this land; I knew I was home. I felt glad in my heart—I knew this land would care for me the way a mother cares for her babe.

In the distance, through the shimmering heat waves, I could see a grove of trees and a field where corn plants waggled their long leaves. I knew that within that grove dwelt the People of Matar.

But I needed a few more moments alone before I returned to them. I wanted to examine my mouth and eyes and see if I had changed.

But then, as I knelt down to look at my reflection on the water, something caught my eye and I pulled up short. What was that I spied beyond the grove? What was that ugly thing? It looked like a giant block of dried dead mud. It looked like a stunted plateau.

I forgot about my reflection for the moment and, with a mixture of curiosity and caution, walked ahead to get a better look.

"Could be another form of Mater," I thought. "But I'm tired. I don't want any more trouble. Maybe I'll come back later on."

But the will of my feet was stronger than the will of my head. My feet always led me toward the unknown, toward the mystery that awakens fear.

First, I entered the dusty tree grove and found the clearing where my tribe had kept their shelters. It was empty now. All that remained of their dwellings were raw blotches on the earth. Flint pieces and pottery shards littered the ground.

"So why'd they pull up stakes?" I wondered. "What happened? Did that big block of Matar devour them all?" The thrill of danger made my blood sing.

I hurried my pace. For Matar to mess with me was one thing; for him/her/it to mess with my tribe was quite another. I would challenge the behemoth.

But when I stepped from the clearing, I suddenly found three spear points poking against my throat. Three pairs of dark eyes blazed at me; three pairs of nostrils flared with anger; three sets of teeth ground with audible fury. Though I knew these men well, they didn't seem to know me. Perhaps my mouth and eyes had changed.

"My brothers, what's wrong?" I croaked. "It's me— Amar!"

Ever so slowly, Mok, Aruk, and Lut removed their spear tips from my sensitive neck. I couldn't help but notice that each man now had a long wooden bow slung over his shoulder and a quiver of arrows strapped across his back.

"So where you been?" Mok grunted.

I massaged my throat. "Is that any kind of greeting?" I asked. "You know I've been in the Otherworld. So what's going on here anyway? What happened to the shelters? And where'd that ugly block of mud come from?"

"That," said Aruk, "happens to be our finest achievement. The best thing the tribe's ever done. It's our protection, our mother. Within those walls of mud brick we now make our life. Within those walls we are safe."

"Boq got the idea one day while watching a crawfish work," Lut said, "while watching it build up the bulwarks around its hidey hole."

The four of us began to stroll toward the unsightly structure.

"But what exactly do the mud walls protect us from?"

"Roqians," Mok hissed.

"Bad people those people," Lut said.

"So what happened this time?" I sighed.

"Roqian people have bad manners," Aruk said.

"Go on."

"When you didn't return from the Otherworld, they started making fun of that reed you stuck in the bank."

"So I told them: you mess with that reed, we mess with you," Mok said.

"No reason to get steamed about it," I said.

"But you told us to take care of the reed, remember?"

"I also told you to keep the peace."

"That's not the worst of what they did," Aruk said. "Urk untied the gopher sack from the reed and hung it under his stick like it was his seed bag."

"So what'd you do then? Start bashing in their heads?"

"Come on, we're smarter than that," Mok said. "We told them some of their goats'd gotten loose. So they all took off running and when they came back, we ambushed them."

"You killed them all?"

"Nah," he sighed. "Those suspicious bastards had a spy on the lookout. He ruined our surprise."

Mok then described the ensuing battle in glorious detail—how the tribesmen had fought in hand-to-hand combat beneath the big eye of a full moon.

"So who won?" I flipped a pebble with my toe.

"We did, I guess," Aruk grunted. "Anyway, they ran off."

"But not before they stole one of our goats," Lut said.

"Those low down, dirty thieves," Mok said.

"So have they been back since then?"

"Yep." Mok jabbed the air with his spear. "But they took one look at our walls and high-tailed it out of here."

"Well, that's one positive, I suppose."

"But they'll be back." Mok jabbed the air with his spear. "I know they will."

My stomach twitched.

We had reached the walls. A gate made of rough-hewn logs swung open to admit us. I followed Mok into the dusty courtyard and surveyed the new city. My people now resided in adobe cubicles packed side by side down narrow lanes. These boxes were stacked two and three high. Wooden ladders led to the upper floors. Each abode had one small window and a doorway covered with an animal hide.

Our mud-brick city may have lacked beauty; nevertheless, it had a certain bold naked charm.

Unfortunately, the walls of the place seemed to hold the heat. It felt hot enough to cook flesh. The ambience was one of glare and stagnation. Though I tried waving them off, a swarm of flies kept buzzing about my head.

"So what happens when it rains?" I asked.

"What'd you mean?" said Mok.

"Does the mud brick melt or what?"

"Well yeah, a little. But nothing we can't patch."

Children clustered around my legs and pounded their tiny fists into my kneecaps. Old woman Ool spat from an upper window.

Boq bounded forth to greet me. A wholesome smile split his face.

"So how do you like our new home, my brother?" He grabbed me at the elbows and pinched.

"It seems kind of big. For the number of people we have anyway."

"Yes, but our numbers keep growing."

"Well then, I guess it's okay."

"I don't think you like it. Yes?"

"No, no, I'm just a little discombobulated from my Otherworld journey, that's all. I had quite a time over there, let me tell you. So anyway, how long have I been gone?"

"For two full cycles of the seasons. Yes."

I nearly dropped. "Two full cycles!" My head spun. "It hardly seemed a day."

"Here, I think you need to relax," Boq said. "Yes, let me show you to your new quarters. When we gather in the sweet calm of the evening, you can tell us all about your travels."

Boq led me through the lanes and alleys until we'd reached a back corner cubicle. We stepped into a low, dark room. The dead air felt like dry leaves in my lungs.

"We reserved this space especially for you," Boq said.

"No window?" I asked.

"We figured a Seer such as yourself wouldn't need a window."

"Oh. Okay."

Boq knelt by the empty hearth in the center of the room. I flopped myself down and spread my body out over the cool floor.

My friend traced his forefinger across the clay.

I felt that his silence held something. "So what's on your mind, my brother?" I finally asked.

Boq took a deep breath. "I've...I've been performing the rituals while you've been gone. Yes."

"That's it? That's all? That's no big deal. Someone had to do them."

My stomach twitched.

"Well, the rituals still seemed to work, though sometimes I forgot the words and had to make some up."

"That's okay; Matar doesn't mind. Just as long as you mean what you say."

"There's more."

"Go on."

"Some of the tribespeople—I won't mention any names—but certain people spoke ill of you while you were away. Yes."

"Oh? What did they say?"

"Well, for one thing, they think you spend far too much time in the Otherworld."

"I don't have any control over that. I've explained it to them before." I scratched the dry skin under my chin. "So is that all?"

"No. There's more."

Boq then told me about his sun observations. He'd discovered that the sun rose at a slightly different place on the horizon each morning. As Boq tracked its rising points, he saw that the golden orb moved back and forth across that distant edge in a predictable manner. Now he knew exactly where the sun would rise at any time of year. Where it would rise on the longest day of the year and on the shortest day. Where it would be at planting time, and at harvest time, and all times in-between.

"Based on my observations, it's now easier to plan our yearly activities," he said. "Now, we prepare for the planting ritual far in advance. And so, do a much bigger production. Something truly special. It's become a festival. Everyone gets involved. Yes, the ritual is now a joyous occasion—a sacred event for all." Boq blinked his small, childlike eyes at me.

My stomach twitched; the blood drummed at my temples. But I smoothed my voice to sound calm and reasonable. "That's wonderful, my brother. No reason to feel guilty. I thank you for all that you've done."

"But you see, here's the problem...we've kind of gotten into a groove." He dipped his head.

"No problem. The groove can remain."

176

"What I'm saying is...the people might not let you do the rituals anymore."

"Oh." I couldn't swallow past the lump in my throat.

Boq traced a circle on the floor. "Yes, they already said that I should take your place, whether you returned or not. I refused, of course. I told them that it was your job and rightfully so; that you understood these things much better than I."

"What'd they say to that?"

"They said it wasn't my decision to make. So there's nothing I can do about it. Still, I hate to see you to lose your job. Any suggestions?"

"Well, I don't know, let's see, let's see. There's got to be an answer here somewhere. Let me think, let me think...hmmm...what can we do...what can we do...hmmm...hmmm..." Though I acted quite composed, in my mind I was screaming, "What am I going to do! Without my job, what do I have left? Healing the sick? That's not enough!"

I'd never felt comfortable with my special status. Yet now, as I watched my position erode, I panicked.

Fortunately, Boq was willing to accommodate. "Hey, I've got an idea!" he shouted. "Let me do the rituals awhile longer, just until people get used to having you back. Yes. Then we can start switching off. Then eventually, you can take over completely— things'll be just like the way they used to be. Yes!"

"You enjoy doing the rituals, don't you?"

"Well, yeah, it's kind of fun." He peeked at me through his eyebrows. "I just don't want you to think that I tried to steal your job. I mean after all, you created the rituals—at least, the first ones. Yes, I've added some, but mine aren't divinely inspired the way yours are. I mean, I'm not a true Seer like you are. Yes. You have contact with Matar; I don't. But even so, my rituals don't seem to have any ill effects and the people say they like them just as much."

"Oh, stop your worrying," I laughed. "If you're happy and the tribe's happy, then I'm happy." These words nearly choked me. "I mean, what am I to expect, being gone so long? It's not like you stole my woman, right?"

Again Boq dipped his head. He traced another circle on the floor. My stomach twitched.

After a long pause, I asked him, "So how's your wife these days?"

"Oroo died last winter when her gums and teeth all turned black."

"I'm sorry to hear that."

"Yes, it was difficult for me at first. I don't know what I would've done without Bruk. Yes, but listen, Amar, I didn't go to her. It was she who came to me. I thought it impolite to refuse. And I was so lonely. Yes, Bruk and I are married now. She assures me it's all for the best."

How many times had I bemoaned my match with that desiccated, lizard-skinned old woman? Yet now my face burned red. The room tilted as I went off-balance.

"Everything okay, Amar?"

"Sure, fine, why?"

"I know about you and Bruk."

"Oh. So she told you?"

"Actually, everyone knew about you and her."

Wonderful! My humiliation would now be a public event. This upstart had not only taken my job, but nabbed my woman to boot.

"Amar?"

"What's that?"

"You seem awfully quiet."

"Oh. Excuse me. I was just thinking of all the enchanting women that I met over there in the Otherworld. Yeah, there sure were some beauties. Mention that to Bruk, will you?"

"Why?"

"She always likes hearing about my Otherworld adventures."

"Oh, okay. For a moment there, I thought maybe you were trying to make her jealous. She told me that you'd understand about us. She told me that you never really loved her. Actually, I find that kind of hard to believe. Did you love her, Amar? Yes? Did you?"

"Well, I...I..."

Fortunately, Mok picked this moment to show up at my doorway. For once, I was glad to see him.

"Brother Mok!" I yelled. "Welcome! Welcome! Come right in."

"You two're talking," he said. "I'll stop by later."

"No no. Get on in here and sit down. Tell me how you've been."

"Fair, I suppose." Mok swung the bow off his shoulder and knelt down on one knee by the hearth.

"So you never told me where you got that fine-looking bow," I said.

"This thing?" Mok thrummed the bowstring.

"You should know," Boq told me.

"Oh?"

"Yes," he said. "Some of the warriors were out on patrol one day when you suddenly appeared before them. Let me see—that would be about four moon cycles ago. Yes."

"Go on."

"In one hand, you carried a finely-carved wooden staff, which you called a bow. In the other hand, you held a fistful of small spears, which you called arrows. Yes. You said these gifts came from Matar. Then you dropped them to the ground. Yes. But you disappeared without telling us what they were for."

"Yeah, but I figured out soon enough," Mok said.

"It still hurts when I sit down," Boq said.

"So you don't remember coming to us?" Mok asked me.

"I just forgot, that's all," I told him. "So much has happened lately."

Mok fitted an arrow to the bowstring, then pulled it back. The arrow shaft made a dry, scraping sound against the wooden bow. Then Mok relaxed the bowstring. Again the arrow shaft scraped the bow.

I was picking up a strange vibe here. From what I could tell, Mok and Boq were on nearly equal footing now. Yes, Mok still had more status, but Boq wasn't that far behind. I realized that my twin had allowed this shift to occur. He didn't mind sharing power with Boq; he could manipulate Boq.

"So anyway, what'd you do over there in the Otherworld?" Mok asked me. "Must've been having a good time, you stayed away so long." Again, the arrow shaft scraped the bow.

"I'll share my story tonight at the communal fire," I told him. "I'm just too tired right now."

"Yeah, well I need to relax too," Mok said. "I need some entertainment. Defending this city, it's a tough job. So come on, what happened over there?" He reclined on one elbow and lay the bow across his legs.

"Well, it's a lot to tell," I said.

"Then get on with it."

"I really don't feel like talking right now."

"Tell him about all the beautiful women," Boq said.

Stone that Boq! No way would Mok let me off the hook now.

So, I gave up arguing, took a deep breath and began my tale.

"Yeah, well, yes, I did meet up with some real beauties over there. But one in particular outshone all the others. She was the bright sun; the rest were but stars. How can I possibly describe her fine glory? I am not adequate to the task, and yet I must try, for your sake as well as mine."

What a joy it was, telling my brothers of the wonder of the Woman of the Flower! I caressed her with my words. But of course, such sissy talk made Mok impatient; I had to cut it short.

"And so, vowing to return the silver bow and arrow to her, I set off down the shining path," I told them, "carried forth by the wings upon my feet and the gallantry within my heart."

"Without any weapons?" Mok interrupted. "That hag didn't give you anything to defend yourself with?"

"I told her that I only needed my strength and my cunning. Nevertheless, I accepted the spear that she offered me—a spear of luminous gold."

"That's it? Just a spear?"

"And for good measure, she threw in a matching gold knife."

"Okay, I guess that'll do. So you kill anybody?"

"My path was fraught with danger. Time and time again, my fortitude was pushed to its limits."

"Like how?"

"First there were these rocks. The trail had some really sharp rocks in it. They sure did hurt my feet. And on top of that, some brambles stung my skin."

"A warrior expects such things, endures such things, and never complains of such things." Mok spat on the floor.

"Well yes, of course. But just to test my mettle, I pressed my feet down onto the razor points of those rocks. And then I cursed the brambles until they whipped my back to the bone."

"So?"

"So then came the cold, cold rain. Unbearably cold —freezing cold."

"So?"

"So then lightening burst the trees asunder on either side of me."

"So?"

"So then out of the roiling black clouds came the face of a giant—scowling and growling, he was. He shook his terrible fist at me, yes he did, then he threatened me with his jagged white lightening bolt. But I did not flinch, I did not falter. No. I aimed my spear with calmness and precision. That golden rod shot from my hand in a sure, straight line and popped the giant's left eye, leaving only bloody tatters. Then, with a sharp snap of the wrist, I flipped my golden knife through the air. Before the giant could even blink, the blade had punctured his other eye—yes, that eyeball collapsed with a woeful sigh.

"He dropped his lightening bolt then and covered his empty sockets in shame. By the time his bolt hit the ground, it was nothing more than a dainty spark.

"So that was the end of that. Once again, I skipped down the trail, eager to meet my destiny."

I knew I was enjoying these lies a little too much. But I had just lost my job as well as my woman; my wounded feelings urged me to inflate.

"So then what happened?" Mok grunted.

"So then a volcano erupted from the ground and rained vicious fire down upon me. But I did not flinch, I did not falter. No, I bulled right through that inferno. My flesh and my bones all melted; I became less than a speck. But I kept on forging ahead and when I'd finally reached the end, I found myself whole once again. Somehow I'd survived intact."

"That's it? That's all?" Mok asked. "You ran through a fire?"

"Actually, there was more to it than that. Truth is, a blazing army of fire creatures then leapt from the volcano. They came at me with flaming red eyes, flaring red fangs, and fierce fiery claws. A mean, ugly bunch that bunch, let me tell you.

"But I stood my ground and with great patience, skill, and dexterity, I plucked them off, one by one, row upon row, with my golden spear and my golden dagger. And when my fighting deed was done, I stacked their bodies into one big pile and they burned each other up. In the end, all that remained of them was a handful of weak ash."

Yes, I'd told quite a whopper, and yes, I felt ashamed of myself. But I wasn't about to let Mok trivialize my feat of fire endurance.

"And then?" My twin affected a yawn.

"Then I continued on down the path and for awhile, everything was just fine. But then...but then..."

"But then what?"

How could I possibly convey the horrid torture of the ice mountain? I would need to elaborate.

183

"But then...but then I came upon a frozen peak guarded by a throng of ferocious ice warriors. However, I did not flinch, I did not falter. No, I furrowed my brow, narrowed my eyes, and yelled to them, 'Ice men, let me pass, or I will cut you into sleet.'

"But they just glared at me with their icy blue eyes and snarled with their icicle teeth. And oh, as their ice claws scraped through the air, how the wind did scream.

"I merely shook my head at them and continued on up the mountain. Whistling a cheery tune, I speared the ice men on my right. And humming a happy song, I slashed the ice men on my left. By the time I'd reached the lofty peak, the once-fearsome army had all melted away in tears of humility."

Mok just rolled his eyes. "I've got to be going."

"I thought you wanted to hear this?"

"I have more important things to do."

"But the best is yet to come."

"Yeah, sure."

"No, really. Come on—stay."

"Oh all right." Mok spat on the floor.

Summoning forth all my wit and narrative ability, I then told how I'd chopped through a dense jungle, defeating every danger known to man, until I arrived at a mountain that touched the sky. I told of the enormous serpent that ruled this mountain; I told of how the serpent tried to frighten me away by shooting blue-white ice from one nostril and angry red flame from the other.

Then in tones of humble solemnity, I described how I'd diced and sliced that loathsome creature into a thousand small snakes.

"And in its belly, among all the squirming maggots, what did I find but the silver bow and the silver arrow—which, of course, I then returned to The Good Woman of the Flower posthaste. And just guess what that wonderful lady said to me in that most blessed moment. She said, 'Amar, take the knowledge of this treasure back to your tribes-kin. They must have this prize for their very own. And do you know why they must have it, Amar?'

"'Because good people deserve good things?' said I.

"'That is right,' she said. 'Now sally forth.'

"Though I wanted to stay with her forever, I knew that I had to obey The Good Woman's command. But before I took my leave, I lifted the bow and fitted the arrow against the bowstring. Then I pointed the arrow toward the full blue turquoise moon."

"Turquoise?" Boq asked.

"Blue turquoise. Then I loosed the silver arrow; it soared through the night with the cry of a wounded bird; it struck deep into the center of that luscious moon. Then the wounded moon flew away and a brilliant sun burst forth in its place. Once again, the world beamed with the clarity of a bright, new day."

Having completed my tale in fine fashion, I offered my companions a wide, benevolent grin.

"That's it?" Mok yawned again and stretched his legs like a bored lion.

"Don't act so impressed," I said. "Just remember, if not for me, you wouldn't have that new play thing."

"Oh, but Amar, I am impressed," Mok said. "I'm just wondering why you don't you use a little of that warriorhood in this world once in awhile. This world, Amar. Where it matters."

"How can that knucklehead possibly be my twin?" I asked myself for the umpteenth time.

The arrow shaft scraped the bow.

To reach the communal hearth, you had to climb ladders to the second and third floors, then go up eight steps to a wide, square platform. This was the central point of our city—the apex. Here in the evenings we would sit in a circle around a log fire, keeping to the old way. Except that now our circle had three rings instead of one. The population boom was due, in part, to the Larvians. One night, Mok had spied them shifting through our farm fields, striping ears from corn stalks. Though the Larvians had fought bravely with their spears and flint knives, they were no match for Matarians with hand axes. Several of their broken skulls now decorated our walls to commemorate the great victory.

After the battle, we'd locked the Larvian survivors —mostly women and children—in a basement room until they'd simmered down some. The Larvians were basically placid folk, so friendly relations were soon established. Because they still had hair thick on their backs and walked stoop-shouldered, we considered these people to be our inferiors. For that reason, we didn't too feel threatened by them. Coming as they did from the hunting and gathering mode, the Larvians marveled at the complexity of our city society. Bins filled with surplus grain; a roof over their heads—they took to this life with relative ease. To help matters along, some of their women had already set up house with some of our men.

Only a few of the Larvian warriors had been spared. Through the skillful use of intimidation, Mok had transformed them into dedicated Matarian soldiers. Even so, they weren't allowed to breed with our women.

Since their god Larv was a close copy of Matar, the Larvians adopted our religious ideas without undue coercion. Though their own Seer had been killed in the cornfield battle, his head joined us during the group rituals.

No, the People of Larv had not yet reached our level of advancement and sophistication. However, their eyes still glistened with a pleasant simplicity that my own tribes-kin had lost some time back.

When I retold my tale at the communal fire that evening, the audience oooed and ahhhed at all the right places. They took delight in my wondrous feats. Their eyes sparkled upon me.

True, I had sullied my story with ice goons and fire monkeys. But one must get through to one's audience, right?

During this earthly life, I would bring back many more tales from the Otherworld. However, the legend of the silver bow and arrow would always be my biggest hit. Down through the generations, a chorus of voices would sing the song of my adventure quest.

I had embellished my story in an effort to inflate myself. Likewise, through the ages, it would serve to inflate untold others before they went into battle. Over the course of time, my pumped-up narrative would inspire countless acts of out and out savagery.

Taken in this light, should I have held my tongue?

Maybe so.

Would that have made any difference?

I doubt it.

After my welcome home at the communal fire that evening, I wandered back to my cubicle haunted by a sense of emptiness. It was dark and lonely inside. In the absence of any better bed, I curled up to sleep in the circular hearth.

I had just eased into slumber when I felt a knobby finger tracing its way up my thigh. Could that be Bruk? Had she come back to me? Had she regained her senses? I hadn't looked her way once during dinner. Perhaps she was lonesome for my comfort. Yes, that was possible. Possible, but not probable.

I sat up, grabbed my intruder at the elbows, and studied her face in the dim light. Shingles of hair sheltered tiny black eyes. A Larvian. Communication with these people was still a haphazard business. The two languages didn't quite mesh. But talk could wait— this woman's blunt approach had lit a torch. I just wanted to wrestle her into my arms and forget myself for a few delicious moments. And so—with her consent —that's what I did.

We enjoyed a delirious match that evening, though my fingers kept getting caught in the matted hair that covered her back.

Evarl and I never officially married. She crept to my room only after nightfall. I would wake to find her small eyes glittering at me in the darkness. I assumed that my people, in a gesture born of sympathy, had encouraged her to visit me. Still, she seemed eager enough, so I never felt as though I was imposing. Maybe I didn't love her, but I sure did like her a lot. And maybe that's enough.

Shortly after my return, the time came to perform one of our many rituals. Naturally, I felt a little awkward with the situation. What should I do? Hold Boq's staff while he intoned the incantation? No, I just couldn't lower myself that much; I felt low enough already.

Fortunately, Boq discerned my delicate emotional state and devised a remedy. While he led the congregation through their paces in the ritual room, I sat outside the door with a dull, solemn mien fixed to my face. Positioned at the portal thusly, I was supposed to represent none other than our protector—Matar him/her/itself. Though I worried that the Creator might take offense at my impersonation, the role was just too juicy. Pride won out.

Chapter 13 : City Life

And so, as one day followed the next, new wounds became old and somewhat forgotten. Once again, my life fell into a comfortable pattern. And once again, boredom set in. From my perch atop the city wall, I would gaze across the sun-baked plain to the mountain whose stream had led me home. That mountain now represented my deepest desire; that mountain represented the Otherworld—a place of magnificence and pain. Could I somehow get to that world without cooking my brain, burning my feet, or nearly drowning? There had to be another way.

"I sure wish those Otherworld journeys wouldn't take so long," I told myself. "When I finally get back, everything's changed for the worse. If I'd been around more often, I could've stopped this feud with the Roqians. I could have been the voice of reason."

Among ourselves, we Matarians were generally peaceful folk. Yet we didn't think twice about bashing in the head of a non-Matarian. We treated non-Matarian heads just like they were coconuts.

Did anyone else besides me see a problem here? I broached the subject one night at the communal fire. To my surprise, it was Boq—not Mok—who defended the tribe's position.

"Amar, we Matarians must protect our own," he said. "Yes. Because if we don't have each other, then what do we have? All we have is ourselves—that's all. Yes."

My tribes-kin murmured their assent. Oh that innocent logic! That dangerous logic!

"Well what about just trying to get along?" I asked.

"But how can we get along with those who won't get along with us?" Boq answered.

"Try reasoning with them," I said. "You're good at that."

Aruk cleared his throat. "But when we told the Roqians to stop messing with your reed, they laughed at us," he said.

"How do you reason with people like that?" Lut asked.

"Okay then, what about the Larvians? They didn't know that was our corn. Why didn't you try reasoning with them? They seem reasonable enough."

"Yeah, they became real reasonable," Mok said, "after we kicked their butts. You kick somebody's butt, it makes them reasonable enough. I say that's reason enough for war."

My tribes-kin murmured their assent.

"Well, just remember...you steal somebody's goat, you're going to have a fight on your hands. A fight you may not win."

"We happened to be hungry that night," Mok said. "Is that so unreasonable? To be hungry?" He held up his hands and shrugged. "They could've tried reasoning with us, instead of getting so bent out of shape."

My tribes-kin murmured their assent.

"Well okay then, because of our thieving ways, we now live penned up in a mud box. Day and night, we pace these walls, always on the lookout, forever fearful that someone will try to wrest this patch of land from us. You think that's a reasonable way to live? I say it's not. I say this mud city is a trap, a cage that we've built for ourselves."

"But Amar," Boq stressed, "as you yourself have so often told us, we are Matar's representatives here on this earth. So if we are destroyed, then Matar is destroyed. In this world, anyway."

"I, ah, I doubt Matar would allow that to happen."

"But if we were negligent in our defense, he might let it happen," said Dith. "

"Just to teach us a lesson," said Dat.

"That'd be just like him," Ool said.

My tribes-kin murmured their assent.

"Well, you see, it's like this," I said, "Here's how it is...it's like this..."

But before I could think of a counter argument, Mok said to me, "Wasn't Matar the one who gave us the seeds and asked us to stay here and farm this land?"

"Yeah, so?"

"Well then, if he wanted us to stay here, he must've wanted us to build a city. And why would he want us to build a city and not defend it? After all, it is named after him. After all, it is called the City of Matar. So Matar's responsible for the way we live. And obviously, he wants us to be voracious warriors. Otherwise, he wouldn't've given us this city to defend. Really, Amar, I'm surprised at you—contradicting Matar like that."

My tribes-kin murmured their assent.

Mok spat into the fire, then stood up and hefted his balls with both hands.

And that was the end of that. The blunt-headed brute had beaten me at my own game.

To bolster my position in the tribe, I now added another trick to my repertoire. Our new way of life created many complex domestic situations. Crises arose in every household. And when push came to shove, people often sought out my sage wisdom.

Before long, a routine became established: every afternoon, during the heat of the day, I would crawl into my dark cubicle, fold my legs under me, light an oil lamp, and then sit there staring straight ahead, affecting an attitude of high-minded solemnity.

Then one at a time, those in need would enter, kneel down at a respectful distance from me, and ask some question concerning their personal life.

Such as: "You think I should get my lip pierced? My parents object."

Or: "How can we stop the baby from wailing when my husband and I make love?"

Or: "I got lice from a Larvian woman. What do I tell my wife?"

These troubles may seem trivial to you; nevertheless, providing answers to such questions is a tricky business.

Much of the time, the question had this subtext:

Deep down, the supplicant knew that the answer he wished to hear was probably the wrong answer. Yet he wished to hear it anyway.

My job, as I saw it, was to give him the right answer, but in terms he could accept. At the same time, I had to make sure that he couldn't come back at me later on.

Take the aforementioned lice-infested man for example. (Discretion and a strict professional conduct code prohibit me from revealing his name. Anyway, it's nobody you know.)

"Oh, so you got lice, eh?" I said to him. "Well, here's what you do: tell your wife (in a joking manner, of course) that you must've picked up those critters from

193

some hideous Larvian gal—and be sure to use the word 'hideous.'"

"Oh Seer, no, Seer, I can't possibly say such a thing."

"You can and you will."

"But Seer, isn't there great danger in telling such a bold-face truth?"

"No, not if you follow it with a big laugh, as though you sleeping with a Larvian is the most absurd thing imaginable."

"Okay, okay, now I think I get it. Most astute Seer, I will follow your advice."

Perhaps you're thinking that the lice man should have lied. Wouldn't that have been best for both him and his wife? Well, I'll tell you why I didn't let the sleeping dog lie: I doubt that he would have learned his lesson that way. He would have kept on running around with those Larvian women. His wife would have been bitten badly before she got wise. Better to come clean at the beginning.

In short time, the lousy man reported back to me. "Dear Seer, I told my wife where I got the lice, then laughed my head off. Now she's banished me from the house. How could a brilliant Seer such as yourself be so wrong?"

But of course, I was already prepared for this turn of events. "You big fool!" I said. "Don't you see what's going on? One of your wife's girlfriends squealed on you. Even so, your wife—such a good woman—refused to believe her. That is, until you confirmed her suspicions."

"Well why didn't you warn me? You must've known. After all, you are a Seer."

"I answered the question you gave me. You never asked me if your wife's friends were spies and gossips."

"So what do I do now?"

"Now you must beg your wife's forgiveness. Get on your knees if need be. Say to her, "Honey, I'm big fat boob.""

"She'll just tell me to 'hit the bricks.'"

"In that case, set up house with the Larvian woman. Despite the lice, Larvian women have a comforting simplicity and can make good mates."

"Thank you, oh wise and wonderful Seer, thank you so very much. You penetrate to the essence of any question."

Did I enjoy this job? Not much. But my advice helped to provide comfort and kill doubt. I maintained the social order.

Yes, I was still a player.

Chapter 14 : Deception

In time, I accepted my boredom as an inescapable fact of life. Though I didn't feel satisfied with my lot, I didn't feel too horribly dissatisfied either. And as I grew more complacent, my longings for the Otherworld began to dim.

So naturally, at this point, a whirlwind came and blew my fragile world to bits.

This whirlwind found me sitting atop the city wall one evening, dangling my feet in the calm moonlight. Everyone else had gone to bed. The stacked cubicles dozed in the darkness. At the communal hearth, a few logs still winked and glowed red.

My reverie drifted to the morass of stars above. For the first time in a long time, I thought about the Otherworld and about all my hair-rising adventures there. I realized how much I still yearned for its amazements and grandeur, its beauty and its horror.

"Just how many realms does that world contain anyway?" I wondered aloud. "Perhaps the realm I experience depends upon my mode of entry. If I found a gentler mode, perhaps the Otherworld would treat me more gently. But is that what I want? To have things made easy for me? Is that what I need?"

My desire nearly overpowered me. I turned my eyes away from the stars and gazed down at the moon-frosted plain.

Suddenly, the hair on the back of my neck prickled. What was that I saw shifting through the shadows below? Were my eyes playing tricks on me or was that a bundle of reeds scuddling across the clearing? As I focused my attention, I spied another scuddling reed bundle, then another and another and another. There was a line of at least thirty bundles moving through the clearing between the forest grove and our front wall. One by one, they crept from the trees. The nearest was but a stone's throw away from me. It appeared to be bound around the middle with rope. On the other side of this bundle, I could clearly see a bent back and a set of waggling haunches.

"Just who do they expect to fool with this gambit?" I thought to myself.

I wasted no more time, but shimmied on down the ladder, then hurried through the streets until I'd reached Mok's cubicle. I found him cresting and dipping between the hairy legs of a Larvian woman. She was chewing on his ear, but to what good purpose, I wasn't sure.

At least, he'd had the decency to stick his wife and kid in the other room.

Though Mok was fully engaged in the act, his warrior instincts remained intact. I only had to tap his shoulder once. In an instant, he withdrew his stick and grabbed his spear, then leapt over his lover and started jabbing the air.

"Mok, take it easy—it's me."

"Get out of here," he hissed. "This one's mine."

"Forget about that—you've got more important business—rouse your men—we're under attack."

After I'd told him about the reed bundles, he said that I should gather all the women and children together, then take them to the basement room and batten down the hatch.

"And stay there until I tell you otherwise," he added.

"No, I'll fight alongside you atop the wall."

"But we're not fighting them from atop the wall—we're going out to them."

"What?"

"We'll pour out through the gate and hack those reeds into chaff before they know what hit them."

"Then what'd you build the damn walls for? You have the advantage, use it."

"The walls are merely for protection—for women and children and old men such as yourself."

"I'm the same age as you are. Now listen to me—"

But Mok quickly tired of words when war beckoned. On his way out the door, he slammed his forearm into my chest and knocked me across the room. My back smacked the hard clay wall and my breath went out with a little 'poofing' sound. It felt like I'd just swallowed a brick. Nevertheless, I did not wait, but pulled myself onto my feet, then stumbled from the room.

After I'd guided all the women and children to safe haven, I climbed back up the basement shaft and wove my way through the moonlit alleys until I came to the main courtyard. The Matarian warriors and their Larvian comrades had gathered together near the front gate. Some of the men strummed their bowstrings, testing for tightness. Others whipped their hand axes through the air to loosen their arms. Others whetted flint blades against their thighs.

High above me, I could hear Boq murmuring his prayers inside the ritual room, beseeching Matar, asking him/her/it to provide us with victory.

Mok put a finger to his lips to quiet the men, then placed his ear against the gate.

In the still of the moment, I considered my value to the tribe. If I died, who would take my place? Boq had never gone anywhere near the Otherworld. He'd never performed a healing ceremony, nor doled out domestic advice. If Mok had chosen to fight from atop the walls —allowing us to shoot down upon our enemy, like sensible folk—I wouldn't have hesitated. But as things stood, I felt I would best serve my people by not engaging in the hostilities.

So, while our warriors waited at the gate, I begin climbing the ladders that led to the communal platform. Though I'd be in close proximity to the ritual room and would have to listen to Boq's absurd prayers, from there I'd have a good view of the battle.

The reed bundles now stood in a bunch about two hundred paces from the gate. Though impatient, Mok wanted to survey the situation before sending his men out. So he hurried up the ladders and steps and joined me on the platform.

"I don't get it," he said. "What's their strategy? Why're they just sitting there? Why don't they try to break down the gate?"

"First of all, they'd wake us all up before they got in," I said. "And once they got in, they'd be trapped. This way they can make a swift retreat. They must be trying to draw us out. I bet you it's a trick." My stomach twitched. Somehow I knew I was right.

"Nah, they're starting to get scared," Mok said. "They're having second thoughts. I can tell."

"No, they're waiting. They're waiting for us. They want us to see them. I'm telling you—they're trying to draw us out. They don't know about our bows and arrows; they don't know we could shoot them down from atop the walls. If we wanted to, that is—if a certain pig-headed someone would just listen to me, that is."

"If they want us to see them, then why the camouflage?"

"You call that camouflage? I'm telling you, it's a trick. A ruse. My advice is: don't bite the bait. Stay inside. Shoot them down from atop the walls."

"No, it's no trick. They're trying to get up enough nerve to attack."

"I tell you, they're waiting. They're waiting for us to make a move. They're being patient—something you wouldn't know anything about."

"No, they think we're still asleep. Well, baby, they're in for a big surprise."

Mok rushed back down and collected his men at the main gate. My twin would not be denied his fight.

A mosquito hummed in my ear. I couldn't seem to wave it away.

At a signal from Mok, two men lifted the gate bolt ever so gently. An eternity passed in one breath-held moment.

Then abruptly—with a wild whoop and holler—our warriors burst out through the gate. They pulled up short and unleashed a swarm of arrows. The Roqians threw off their reed bundles and came at us fully armed. Force met force in the open field. In the whirl of the action, knives slashed the air, hand axe cracked against hand axe; spear broke against spear. The combat was hand to hand and toe to toe—a combination of craziness and dignity.

But these separate skirmishes soon deteriorated into one big swirling, shouting chaos. Within the boil of this confusion, I saw long blades flashing—our enemy had a new weapon. The Roqians did a neat pirouette with those blades, blurring the air with their sweeping strokes. Our men had to step lively to keep from having their guts sliced out. It was a dance both beautiful and horrific.

Yes, the Roqians' had artistry; however, Mok's fighting frenzy had set his men afire. And with the Larvians on our side, we had the enemy well outnumbered. We held our own and then some.

In fact, the Roqians soon began shuffling backward in the direction of the forest grove. With victory in sight, our men pressed hard against the enemy line, pumping their spears into the mass of bodies.

Finally, halfway to the trees, Urk lifted his head and dredged a cry from his throat that made the sleeping birds shudder. Such a tortured call could only mean one thing: full-blown retreat. The Roqian army took to its heels. Their dust smothered the scene.

When the air had cleared, I found our warriors standing at the edge of the forest, peering into the darkness of the trees, their shoulders rising and falling with their huffing breaths. They knew that if they entered the grove now, they'd be easy marks for an ambush. So they let matters rest for the time being and raised their fists and shouted to the moon in celebration of victory. Then they turned back to the battlefield to inspect the wounded—and to scavenge for long blades.

There were a few Roqians strewn here and there, but only one still groaned with life. To my horror, I recognized Urm's harshly-lined face. I was surprised to find a woman in their army—and shocked to find such an old one. Who were these Roqians? Did they think so little of their women? (On the other hand, maybe they thought more of them.)

Our men dragged Urm to the gate. Boq and I stood waiting as they plopped her down in the courtyard. Though I felt protective toward her, I knew that the old bat would've spat in my face given half a chance.

Blood leaked from her mouth. She squeezed her eyelids shut as she coughed. Her chest heaved with ragged breathing.

"Go on, kill me," she hissed, "you lickers of excrement."

"You hear what she called us!" Aruk shouted. His eyes boiled in his head. He raised his arm back and aimed his spear at Urm's heart.

"Stop!" Mok and I yelled in unison.

My twin narrowed his eyes at me. "I'm running the show here," he said. "So get along—spectator."

Though I kept quiet, I held my place.

Mok carried a long blade taken from a dead Roqian. It had been molded from a reddish-brown metal unlike any we'd ever seen.

He held the hilt between his forefinger and thumb, so that the blade dangled over Urm's head. The tip of it nicked her nose.

"Go ahead, kill an old woman," she said. "Show us what a brave man you are."

"No," Mok said, "I'm not letting you off so easy. I want to know how you people came by these lovely weapons."

Urm was a tough, ol' gal. I didn't think she would talk—even if Mok knocked the stuffing out of her, which I knew that he would. I couldn't just stand around and watch. I would have step in.

However, Urm surprised me. She answered Mok straight off. "It's what we call a sword," she sputtered. "They're made from bronze. We traded for them at the City of Ekruk." .

"So where do I find this City of Ekruk?" Mok asked.

"What? You never heard of it?"

"We don't get out that much," said Dith.

"Hardly ever," said Dat.

"Well, if you follow the river toward those two tall peaks in the west, after three days travel, you will come to Ekruk—a walled city much like your own, except bigger and nicer."

"Woman, you disappoint me," Mok said. "I was hoping to have pleasure of beating this information out of you."

Mok lifted the sword high overhead.

"Wait!" I shouted.

"She's a Roqian," he sneered at me.

But before he could deal the blow, the old woman convulsed with a bloody cough. A tremor shook her body. Then all grew still. The ornery cuss had just joined the Otherworld.

Angry at having been denied a kill, Mok whipped the blade down and severed the head from the neck with one stroke.

"Now why'd you do that for?" I asked him. "That wasn't necessary."

"I wanted a keepsake," he said.

Mok hoisted the bloody head up by the hair and gave it a shake. Our warriors let out another victory shout.

I sighed all the way to the bottom of my feet.

Though our men kept a vigilant watch, they waited in vain: the Roqians did not return the next day, nor the next night, nor the day nor night after that. Mok then lost what little patience he had and led a group of warriors into the forest grove. But if the Roqians still occupied those dark woods, they kept themselves well out of sight.

Mok brooded heavily at the communal fire that evening. He didn't speak once during dinner. His eyes were silvery dark.

My stomach wouldn't stop twitching.

Finally, Mok coughed a bird bone from his throat, spat into the fire, then stood up and hefted his balls with both hands. Everyone grew quiet. He then raised his bow and sent an arrow singing toward the moon. Though this dart barely cleared the wall, Mok gazed into the sky as if his arrow had made a long arcing flight.

"Matar came to me in dream during my nap this afternoon," he announced to the tribe. "Yes, he came to me. To me." Mok pounded his chest. "He said we must go to the City of Ekruk to trade for bronze swords. We must go, he said, and soon is not soon enough." Mok leveled those dark silvery eyes at all in the circle. "So tomorrow I'm taking my best men and traveling to the City of Ekruk."

"Whoa now, wait," I said. I knew Mok was lying about the dream; I figured that I could trap him in this lie, but I had to think fast. "You sure that was Matar in your dream? Maybe you made a mistake. I mean, do we really need those swords? Didn't we do okay the other night without them? I don't believe that Matar would have us go all the way to Ekruk for something we didn't really need."

"Well, you know how Matar is," Mok countered. "There's no explaining him."

The tribespeople grumbled in agreement.

"But what if the Roqians return while you're gone?" I asked. "The city would be defenseless, for all practical purposes. I'm sure Matar wouldn't want that."

"Matar knows those cowards aren't coming back," Mok said. "We've beaten them into submission."

"Yeah, just like last time," Ool sneered.

"But what if the Ekrukians don't take a shine to us?" I asked.

"Why wouldn't they?" Mok asked back.

I held my tongue on that one.

"So what could we give them for their swords?" Lut scratched his head.

"I bet I know something they could use," Mok said. He eyed the Larvians among us.

"I don't think that's such a good idea," I said underneath my breath. "For one thing, they are strong, hardworking folk. We need those people."

"It would have to be something you could carry a long distance," Boq said.

"Okay then, what about these?" Mok extended his bow for all to see. "If the Roqians don't have them yet, the Ekrukians don't have them either."

"But do we have any extras?" I asked.

"No, not really," Aruk said.

"Then you'll have to make some more before you go."

Mok hefted his balls again—always a bad sign with him. "Not enough time," he said. "We'll have to take what we've got.. We can make some more when we get back. Besides, the bow and arrow isn't much good in hand-to-hand combat. It's always in the way."

"They'd work real well from atop the wall," I said.

"You're such a sissy," Mok said.

"Well, you're a big fat liiii—" But I caught myself. I took a deep breath. "Okay, you say the city doesn't need protecting. You say you want to go off and trade for weapons. But what are those weapons for? For protection. See—the whole business just doesn't make sense. You're contradicting yourself."

The bonfire painted Mok's face orange-red. Twin flames danced in his eyes. "I'm doing what Matar told me to do and that's that!"

"Can't you at least wait a few days?"

"Matar said go now."

"But must you take all the warriors?"

"Yes, all of them—no telling who or what we might encounter out there."

The people began to murmur among themselves. I now saw the danger in our religion: anyone could claim contact with Matar. I would have to find a way to counteract such claims in the future.

My chest collapsed with a heavy sigh. "Oh, alright," I said. "It's up to you. But I still think you misunderstood Matar. You don't know him/her/it like I do."

"Matar doesn't belong to just one," Mok declared. "Matar belongs to all."

The tribespeople grumbled in agreement. What could I say?

"Should I perform a ritual before you go?" Boq asked eagerly.

"Yeah, sure, why not," Mok said. Then once again he hefted his balls with both hands and spat.

And once again, my stomach twitched.

So the next morning, Mok and his troupe left the protection of our city walls and began their trek across the sun-baked plain. His party included twenty-nine of our best warriors, twelve good Larvian men, and a few young Matarians, not yet of age, who just wanted to tag along. In addition, seven Larvian women carried food, tents, and miscellaneous items. To my regret, Evarl was among them.

The males who remained behind were mostly rickety old codgers or wet-nosed, bandy-chested boys.

After the troupe had departed, I began pacing my cubicle. The worry rat raced round my brain. The Roqians might be watching from some secret forest hideaway as our finest fighting men disappeared on the horizon. The children who scampered up and down our streets might soon lie crushed and bloodied.

I couldn't stop pacing. My cubicle just wasn't big enough, so I went out into the city. I paced through the maze of alleys, then along the parapets and then across the flat rooftops, and then up the steps to the communal hearth. I could not stop pacing.

For three full days, I paced. But despite my worrying, the Roqians did not jump out of the woods. For the moment, all seemed well. Nevertheless, my stomach wouldn't stop twitching. Something felt wrong. So I continued to pace.

In fact, I traveled over one rooftop so many times that the occupant below finally climbed up the ladder to confront me. She stood there staring at me with her hands on her hips, tapping her foot.

"What is it?" I barked. "I'm not taking you back, if that's what you want. You've humiliated me enough for one lifetime."

"Humiliate you? I never tried to humiliate you," Bruk said. "Amar, this roof happens to be my ceiling. I wanted to ask you to put your worried feet over someone else's head."

"Oh, so that's it? That's all I get? Just discard me like some empty corncob, sweep me out the door, toss me over the wall with the rest of the garbage."

"Okay buster, stop right there." She put her hand up. "I don't care what you say about me, my skin is old and thick. But I do care what you say about yourself. I look at you and I see a man deceiving himself. What you've done for the tribe is great indeed. Everyone knows that—even Mok. Especially Mok. Yet in your own mind, you're determined to shrink yourself down."

"I wouldn't say that," I said.

"I didn't discard you," Bruk continued. "Don't you understand that? I knew Boq didn't have the strength to handle your job. I saw how Mok manipulated him. I could see that Boq needed my help. You only needed me for a little physical comfort. I accepted that; still, at times, it hurt. Kvarl was a nice enough girl and I could see right away that she'd taken a shine to you. So I talked to her and suggested a visit."

"Oh," was all I could say, "oh."

"Any other questions while we're at it?"

"Yeah. Why didn't you tell me all this when I first got back?"

"I thought a Seer such as yourself would be able to see the situation for what it was. That's what I thought anyway."

"Oh." I dipped my head in embarrassment. "So the tribe actually appreciates me, huh?"

"Sometimes. But sometimes, they forget. Anyway, they believe in your power. You could've stopped this idiotic plan of Mok's if you'd really tried. Perhaps when you finally believe in your own power, you'll become an honest man. But oh, that may take awhile."

Bruk smoothed my cheek with her crusty hand. Those dim, gray eyes held so much wisdom. Somehow I knew we were saying goodbye. But I quickly brushed that feeling aside.

I took her hand and twined her hard, knotted fingers in mine. I wanted to ask her to forgive me—to forgive me for withholding my love. But since she didn't know, I decided to not to tell her. I was not yet an honest man."

"Go down to your cubicle and rest," she said. "Rest; don't worry. The future will answer your questions soon enough."

I thanked her, then kissed her once on the lips. Then I slunk back to my cubicle and curled up by the empty hearth, hoping for the peace of sleep.

But the worry rat still ran circles inside my brain. Finally, I sat back up. I knew that Boq would be in the ritual room, reciting prayers and burning incense. I knew that he'd welcome my presence. But the thought of listening to all that gobbledygook gave me the shimmies.

So I propped myself against the wall and let my fear have full reign.

But even worry gets weary. Soon, my head grew heavy and I fell into sleep.

But this sleep was not a full sleep. For some time, odd swirls and shapes traipsed across the gray space of my mind. Then ever so slowly, from this jumbled fog, a large sphere emerged. Within its glowing globe I watched a scene take form: Mok's troupe marched across the savanna plain in a single file line. Of course, my twin was in the lead. How he did strut!

Then that scene faded and another one gathered form. The troupe now waited at the gates of a large city. Mok straightened his shoulders, puffed out his chest, then called to the guard who stood at top of the wall. But to his surprise, the sentry just stuck out his tongue, then ducked behind the parapet. Once again, Mok cupped his hands to his mouth and called. This time, the guard wouldn't even show himself.

The Matarians then huddled together to discuss the situation.

This conference went on for several moments. Then suddenly Aruk lifted his head and perked his ears. He listened; he listened. He stretched his neck and squinted at the horizon. What he saw there made little sense to him at first: a dust cloud was coming towards them, advancing from the north. Then figures appeared within this roiling ball of dust—a horde of helmeted soldiers.

They ran at full speed, holding their swords aloft and gritting their teeth into the wind.

Aruk tapped his good buddy Mok on the shoulder. But Mok gave no notice; he just kept on talking to his warriors. Aruk tapped again and again, but my twin continued to ignore him. So finally, he grabbed Mok at the elbows and shook him to attention.

Mok took a long, incredulous look at the oncoming army. Then he snapped to his senses and began shouting instructions to the men. In a flash, he had them assembled into two lines facing north, more than a hundred paces from the city gates. Of course, he himself stood front and center. For their part, the Larvian women crouched in the rear, alert as rabbits, each one clutching a flint knife in her fist.

The horde was now but a stone's throw away from the Matarian army.

Our warriors raised their bows.

They loosed a swarm of arrows. A few of the enemy fell in their tracks. Again, our men drew back their bowstrings.

Though this batch of arrows brought down some more of the front line, those behind leapt over their fallen comrades without even breaking stride.

Mok looked to his left, then to his right. He still had time to flee the scene.

But in the next moment, the city gates burst open and a howling mass of Ekrukian soldiers charged forth. They immediately broke into two units with one group moving off to the left and the other moving off to the right.

Our men now found themselves nearly hemmed in. The Ekrukians had them outnumbered five to one. Though our arrows continued to storm the air, we hardly dented the horde coming from the north.

Mok hated to withdraw under any condition; however, the wide open city gates now beckoned to him; just a short distance away lay possible sanctuary—

and a bounty of pillagible goods. If he could beat the Ekrukians back to the gates, he could throw the bolt down, then take the city with little resistance.

So Mok drew in a deep breath, then lifted his head and ripped out a war cry that felled birds from the sky. Then he waved his warriors toward the city gates. The men needed no extra encouragement—they streaked the air with their retreat. What a moment Mok enjoyed then!—he bared his teeth in a savage smile; his eyes burned fiery wild; his hair flared like a lion's mane.

But those eyes lost their mad gleam as the gates began to yawn shut. Though Mok ran like a lynx, he slammed against the wooden gate just as the bolt whammed into place.

He then whirled about, quickly taking stock. The enemy now bore down on all three sides. They had him trapped.

Mok could see that death was hungry for him and to his credit, he acquiesced. Nevertheless, he wanted his last bit of fun. So he gave forth another war shout— the shriek of a wounded eagle— then he puffed out his chest, steadied his bow, and let fly with a steady stream of arrows. His bowstring blurred the air like a hummingbird wing.

But for every Ekrukian struck down by an arrow, two more stepped over him. As the enemy closed upon them, Mok and his men dropped their bows and raised their spears.

The Ekrukian force crashed into them like an ocean storm—one wave following another— creating a turbulent mix of arms, legs, spears, and swords. In the flurry of the undertow, the Larvian women crawled about, stabbing their flint knives into the enemy's legs and groins. Evarl tore a man's thigh open to bone.

But though our warriors fought with ferocity and skill, the rushing tide soon overwhelmed them; they began to bend.

Mok slashed wildly with the sword; his dark eyes had gone blind.

Then suddenly, amidst all the chaos, he stopped, dead still. He raised his head; he listened—for once, he listened.

My twin had caught some far-off call—some sweet music never before known to him. A beatific smile flowered over his face. A new white glow filled his eyes. What sound, what vision, had permeated his crazy head? When I recall this last image of Mok, it gives me pause. Had I failed to see some better part of the man, some finer something within him? But then, maybe it was Mok who'd failed to see that better part—something vital and pure; unknown, untouched, until his death.

The Matarian warriors disappeared beneath the final wave. From the top of the wall, the populace cheered the carnage.

As the scene faded, I pitched forward from dizziness and smacked my forehead on the floor. I just lay there, spent. "What a sick, silly dream," I told myself. But a spike in my gut told me that the vision was true.

I forced myself onto my hands and knees, but that's as far as I got. My face burned. I swallowed to keep from spewing.

"Should I tell the others what I've seen?" I wondered. "But what if it's all wrong? Perhaps the dream is just my fear coming back at me."

That thought helped to calm me. I restrained my disruptive internal functions and climbed to my feet. Again, I paced.

Outside of the group rituals, I'd rarely, if ever, petitioned Matar. I just didn't trust him/her/it that much. On the other hand, as a rule, I didn't go around blaming him/her/it for the state of things either. "It's our own damn fault and we've got to help ourselves," is what I usually told myself.

But now, with my stomach so weak that I could barely walk and my brain beating like a heart against my temples, I fell to my knees in the dark cubicle. I covered my face with my hands and I prayed: "Matar, dear Matar, if you can hear me, please listen. Tell me, is my vision true? Have all our warriors been massacred? Is the city now defenseless? Will you protect us, Matar? Will you?"

But the only thing I heard in reply was the blood drumming in my ears. "So what do I do if the dream is true?" I continued. "How can I save my people? We may not be the best, but we're yours, Matar, we're yours. Help us, please help us." Again I paused. The blood throbbed in my ears.

Finally, I gave up, got to my feet, and walked out of that dim suffocating space. Though hard sunlight still filled the streets, I could see dark clouds massed and roiling in the distant mountains. Lightening twitched within the thunderhead. The wind carried a scent of rain.

I shuffled on down the alley, keeping my eyes low, avoiding all encounters, fearing that I might expose my secret.

"If only the rain would come and wash my mind clear," I thought to myself.

But the black clouds seemed to stagnate against the mountains.

I climbed up to the parapet and gazed across at the dense forest grove. Perhaps the Roqians still waited there. Or perhaps they'd gone far away into the hills. No matter—in time they would return. They always did. But this time they would have their way with us— if my vision told the truth.

One element of the dream just didn't make sense: why would the Ekrukians attack our men without so much as a 'how do you do'?

Perhaps the Roqians had warned them about our sheep-stealing, head-bashing ways.

But another thing bothered me: from all appearances, the Ekrukian attack had been well-planned. How could they have possibly known when our troupe would arrive?

My mind whirled with confusion, doubt, and worry.

"I must rest," I told myself.

My legs wobbled as I traced my way back to the dark cubicle. The stale air hit me like the smell of disease. Man, was I worn out. I curled up by the hearth and groped my way towards sleep.

But despite my best efforts, I only struggled on the restless edges of slumber. Bric-a-brac tumbled through the gray landscape of my mind. Then in short time, a bubble appeared amid the jumble—another luminous sphere. Within its glow, I could see the Roqian warrior Urk and a bearded fellow wearing an Ekrukian helmet. They clasped each other at the elbow. Obviously, they had just struck a pact.

Then that scene faded and another one took form: Urk knelt with his head bowed before the old matriarch

Urm. His hands covered his face. Bloody tears leaked through the cracks of his fingers.

Urm looked down upon him with dispassionate eyes. Her knotted hands caressed his hair.

Then that scene faded and another one took shape: I now saw the dense forest grove beyond our city walls.

Then suddenly, I was in the scene myself; I was there, swooping like a hawk over the forest trees, the ruffles of green flowing under me, the wind ssshing in my ears. Ah, the rush of freedom! What power in my flight!

Unfortunately, some force kept pulling me down—a force that would not be denied kept drawing me down into the dark forest. I broke through the canopy of leaves, then slammed to a halt. I now hovered above a circle of men sitting beneath a big fat oak.

I immediately recognized the haggard faces of the Roqian warriors. They were working whetstones over their sword blades. To a man, their eyes burned with the same smoldering fire. The act of waiting—the tension, the stasis—had stoked their inner flames. I knew that they waited for news from Ekruk. They waited to hear if Matar's best men had fallen. Then and only then would this small band attempt to overrun our city.

The whetstones sighed soulfully against the bronze. Urk breathed against his blade and examined the shine. If asked to pick a warrior as a leader, I would have chosen Urk over Mok. The Roqian was dull, but patient and methodical. Mok was creative, but too impulsive. Though both men were bloodthirsty to a fault, Urk could hold his passion in check, making him all the more deadly.

A water drop hit Urk on the forearm. He stopped moving his whetstone. He watched the fragments of water roll off his arm, and then gazed up through the branches at the clouds above.

In the next moment, the air exploded with a downpour. The Roqians jumped to their feet, then pressed their bodies together under the oak tree. But the rain sliced right through the canopy of leaves, dousing those men to the marrow.

Abruptly I was out of the scene. For a flash, I was ssshing over the trees. Then once again, I saw the forest grove through the soft glow of the sphere.

In the next instant, that bubble burst. My head cleared. I opened my eyes.

The air had changed. The cool fragrance of fresh rain had cut through the stagnation. I flexed my nostrils and drank in the watery scent. Bold rain drummed and rattled in the alleys and on the rooftops. Children squealed with delight.

For a few moments, I just lay back and enjoyed this release. But then I recalled the image of the Roqian warriors getting drenched beneath the big oak tree. Once again, I began to pace, trying to make sense of all that I'd seen in my half-sleep. Apparently, Urk had formed an alliance with the Ekrukian leader. Then Urm had offered herself up as a sacrifice: she would allow herself to be captured by us; she would point Mok and his men toward the City of Ekruk.

After the battle, Urk had waited in the woods and when he saw our troupe start off across the plain, he'd dispatched a messenger to warn of their arrival.

Yes, the Roqians had set us up for an ambush. They had planted the bait and we'd bitten. I had to give them credit—they knew us all too well. Yes, their plan had worked to perfection: all our warriors now lay dead; our city was defenseless.

As my worries mounted, I lost what little patience I had left. Rather than be cooped up with my thoughts, I stepped out into the pouring rain.

The hard dashes of water stung my skin. Everything was a gray blur. I sloshed through the streets. Women and children ran for cover like a scatter of mice.

Near the front gate, I climbed a ladder that led to the parapet. Rain pounded my shoulders and back. Hoping to bolster myself, I recalled the biting rain that I'd endured in the Otherworld. But that just chilled me all the more. The cold water seemed to pour right into me, roaring down through the hollow of my ribcage, saturating my gut.

I hoisted myself onto the parapet. On the plain below, the hard earth had already dissolved into a pool of mush. Hooding my eyes with my hands, I peered through the curtain of rain at the forest grove. Lightening whited the trees for an instant. I coughed water from my throat. In the next flash of lightening, I saw a group of men leave the forest and begin running toward our front gate. The rain had finally beaten the patience out of Urk.

I figured the gate was secure—it would take a massive force to crack that bolt and Urk didn't have that many warriors. However, in time, the Roqians would find a way to scale our walls. I had to mobilize what few men remained among us, pathetic though they were.

But then, as I started toward the ladder, my foot slipped and I jammed my hand down hard on the top ledge.

Something cool and thick rose over my fingers. I looked down to find my hand buried deep in mud. "Well that's odd," I thought to myself. My mind remained blank for a long empty moment. Then I recalled what Mok had said: the walls had eroded a little with each rainfall. "Nothing we couldn't patch," he'd told me. However, I knew the city had never faced a storm like this rainstorm.

The walls were melting. Quick brown rivulets cut through the mud brick. I pried my hand loose and continued moving toward the ladder. Dollops of mud rolled over the boards of the parapet. The planks wobbled beneath my feet. I tried holding onto the wall for support, but my hand kept sliding down.

A board flew up and nearly smacked me in the head. My foot skidded out from under me. I clawed at the wall, but my fingers only raked through mud. I fell free of the parapet.

I swam my arms and legs in the air, trying to right myself, but landed off balance anyway and hit the ground hard on my hip. The pain jagged up my side.

I got to my feet and tried to forge ahead but slipped again and again. Mud ran in a river around my shins. I finally managed to steady myself by placing one hand on the wall. The mud coursed down my arm and coated my chest. The rain kept coming in whips.

I had to warn my people about the Roqians. If this rain continued, the walls would erode until Urk and his men could climb over with ease. The top ledge already had big gaps. Besides that, our cubicles had softened around the edges and their roofs had started to sag.

A carpet of mud slopped down the steps that led to the communal platform. Boq's ghostly form stood in the doorway of the ritual room high above me. I waved my arms over my head, trying to get his attention. He peered into the rain, but didn't seem to see me. A moment later, he ducked back into the room. Perhaps he believed that by chanting his mumbo-jumbo he could stop this downpour. I had to save him from his madness.

I sloshed over to a ladder propped against a cubicle. But as soon as I put one foot on the bottom rung, the wooden stays of the ladder cut into the soft cubicle wall. So I took my foot off the ladder and said goodbye to Boq in my heart.

The mud river running down the alley was nearly up to my knees. A thunderbolt burst overhead. I grabbed an old woman by the shoulder as she splashed past me. Ool sprayed water from her nose and looked at me with bulging eyes.

"Tell everyone you see to gather at the back corner by my cubicle," I yelled through the rain. "These walls won't hold. And I just saw the Roqians outside the gate. Tell everyone you see—the back corner by my cubicle."

"Why there?" Ool snorted.

"It's higher ground. If the Roqians break in, we can help each other over the wall. Okay now, let's get moving!"

I left Ool behind and lunged ahead through the river of mud. I screamed through the rain at everyone I that passed, telling them all to gather at the back corner. I'd soon shouted myself hoarse. Water tickled the back of my throat. I had to drag my feet up from the dregs with each step.

I thought my flesh had grown numb until a hard sheet of rain slapped me. A thousand cold needles pierced my skin. The downpour had not slackened. Funneled through the street between the outside wall and the cubicles, the river now came up to my hips.

I lost my footing and plunged face first into the water. Before I knew what'd hit me, I'd sucked in a gulletful of mud. I dredged myself to the surface, spewing ooze from nose and mouth. The lifeless body of a child bobbed past me. By now, the outer walls had eroded to the halfway mark in places. However, I'd finally reached the street that led back to my cubicle.

All this struggle had drained the strength from my body, my mind, and my heart. With every step, I battled against the current.

"Enough, Matar, enough!" My voice came out in splinters that razored my throat, yet I continued to yell. "You're drowning your own people, Matar. Don't you see that? Oh, I get it—you're doing this on purpose. You know what you are, Matar?—you're evil, pure evil, that's what. You're evil masking itself as good, decay disguising itself as beauty. Come on—come on out and show yourself. Come on, punish my blasphemy, blast me with a thunderbolt. I dare you!"

As if to tease me, a crack of lightening broke the sky into black shards.

"Come on, Matar!" I shrieked. "You can do better than that."

I waited, but this time, the sky remained quiet.

Matar understood that the worst torture is silence.

The river had suddenly reached chest level.

Something grabbed my foot. I gave that foot a good hard yank, but whatever had me held on. I became frantic and began jerking my leg; I actually grabbed my leg with both hands and pulled.

Then my foot came free and I fell backward, down into the water. For several anxious moments, I thrashed about—the current kept pulling me under.

Finally I broke the surface and managed to suck in some air and shake my head clear. Then I regained my feet and continued fighting my way upstream.

I could now see the back corner. My cubicle and the two above it had collapsed. Only a pile of mud remained in their place. To my disappointment, I found only three old women and five children hunkering atop this mud heap. They stood in ooze up to their ankles, watching the river rise towards them. I didn't have much time.

I tried to ease myself toward the outer wall, hoping to use it for support. But the current quickened alongside the wall, cutting a deeper channel. I had to lift my chin to keep my mouth above water.

My feet suddenly slipped backward. A gush of water pushed me under and hurled me downstream. I flailed about. Again the current drew me down. I thought I was a dead man. But then something struck me in the stomach and I bounced back up; I bobbed to the surface again.

I pushed myself away from the outer wall and managed to find my feet. But even at the lowest point, the floodwaters now reached my neck. Nevertheless, I kept on working against the current. Though I'd lost some ground, I could still see the back corner. By now, the river had risen over the mud pile. The women and children stood ankle-deep in water. I had to get to them soon.

But time and time again, my feet slipped and I plunged into the river.

A surge of water toppled one of the children from the mud heap. A woman lunged for the boy, but the current carried them both away. They disappeared into the muddy river.

I now fought even harder against the flood swell. But my feet kept sliding backward and I kept tumbling down into the drink. And each time I resurfaced, I found one less person standing atop the mud heap. This flood had a fiendish jealousy. Finally, only a child remained. The water was all the way up to his chest. He held his arms over his head and swayed with the swirling current.

Not far from me, a gap in the outer wall had eroded to near water level. If I could get to that gap, I could pull myself atop the wall. Then perhaps I could shimmy along the ledge until I reached the child. That looked to be my only hope.

But the current had grown even stronger near the wall. I couldn't keep my feet under me.

So then I decided to try a different tack; my thought was this: if I positioned myself at a point slightly upriver, at a place where the ground rose to a knob, I could leap from the water and, with luck, land directly in the gap. The current might just give me the extra push that I needed. That was my plan—perhaps a foolish one, but I saw no better option. The child was Rir—Mok's boy. A belligerent bully, a slave driver to the other kids. But no matter—we could share our grief over his father's death; I could comfort him. Under my caring attention, he might transform into someone honorable and good. My own life meant nothing now unless I could save him.

I eased myself over to the strategic point upriver. When I stood on the knob, the waters only came halfway up my chest. Rir called to me, but the rain mangled his voice. I braced my body against the current and focused on the gap. I started to pray to Matar, then checked myself. I took a deep breath. Then, with a great heave-ho, I shot from the water.

To my own surprise, I landed right in the gap, on top of the ledge, hitting it splat on my stomach. Unfortunately, the impact collapsed the wall there to the water line. A torrent sprang through the break, knocking me over the bulwark and swooshing me down the other side. I kicked my legs and flapped my arms, but to little use.

This waterfall crashed into a gully at the bottom of the wall. Then the rushing flood washed me along the ditch; I was its puppet, as helpless as a twig. Yes, the river laughed at me. The surging waves doused me and lapped over me and threw me into a yowling black space. My lungs burned and strained for every last particle of air. My mind went blind with fatigue.

"Just hang in there," I told myself. "Eventually, this flood will spend its force."

But the river kept charging on and the water kept slapping me about. Finally, delirious with exhaustion and grief, I decided to stop fighting. I would give myself to death. I had failed my people. I deserved to die.

I allowed my body to relax; I stopped moving my legs and arms; I emptied all the air from my lungs. I began to sink.

"Ah well," I thought. "Ah well—so this is finally it for me."

After not too long, I seemed to settle. Unable to breathe, unable to move, I lay in my mud cocoon, feeling the bands tightening across my chest. My blood grew cold.

"After all I've done and seen, I wait for death mired in muck," I thought to myself. "Such a ludicrous way to die—it's embarrassing."

Of course, when viewed in a certain light, I had lived a rather silly life: lying through my teeth on a regular basis, busting my chops trying to please everyone, and spoiling my own plans, more often than not. When I wasn't being falsely humble, I was being foolishly pompous.

However, in my next human life, I would do everything differently; I would live as one should, I'd be a decent person. I knew I could do it; I knew I had it in me. I knew how to be honest and decent. The problem was in the execution.

I could feel my body cracking under the weight of the mud; I could feel my shell breaking. It didn't really hurt all that much. Just few sharp pangs.

Yes, for some reason, life as a human was just too confusing. And if I did come back as an antelope, I doubted my life would be that much different. To begin with, they lived in groups; that would lead to trouble, most certainly. If I could pick for myself, I would choose to live life as a plant or a mollusk or any other being that truly understood its purpose.

I could feel my spirit exiting the body shell as a nebulous blue gas. I could feel myself rising as this ether eased its way up through the mud, traveling from air pocket to air pocket, aching toward daylight— hungry for sunshine like a seed struggling to burst from the soil.

Then, after a long, tight squeeze, my blue gas consciousness finally broke the surface. I hovered above the quiet earth. The cool air was a thousand tickles. I could feel my substance guiding itself, gathering itself: all the particles pulling together...assembling...forming the shape—becoming.

Chapter 15 : The Invitation

When I was all together again and my vision returned, I found myself standing on a dry riverbed in my usual human body. A tiny fault ran through the riverbed, zigzagging between my feet.

The full moon had reached its zenith. This bright white moon covered a good quarter of the sky's dark dome. I had enough light to leave a shadow.

"I guess this must be death," I said to myself. "I wonder what happens now?"

As if to answer me, the fault between my feet groaned and cracked open a little more. I stepped aside as a luminous blue gas eased from this suture.

"Another spirit," I said to myself. "Perhaps my companion. That would be nice. I could use the company."

As the blue gas oozed out, it roiled and whorled and slowly thickened into dense cloud. Then this cloud began to swirl, gradually building momentum, throwing off fluffy whips of blue fog while making a low moan. I waited with a child's anticipation; I waited for something wonderful to emerge.

But when all had cleared—when the cloud had completely dispersed—what I found before me was a short, tight tornado. It was about my same height, so I didn't feel too intimidated, though I didn't feel too comfortable either.

I thought this funnel might cease its spinning to reveal a Matar within—a miniature version of Matar the pustulous stump. I actually looked forward to such an eye-to-eye confrontation. I had some choice words ready for my creator.

But the wind funnel just kept on whirling, kept on ripping and roaring—scraping the air with its gray and black streaks and strokes. Its hot dry breath peppered my face.

"That you, Matar?" I asked the cyclone. "You hiding in there? Show yourself, or at least, speak to me. No, on the other hand, don't speak. Don't say a thing. Because I have plenty to say to you—"

As I spoke these words, the wind funnel began creeping across the dry riverbed, easing its way toward me. This slow, deliberate movement made it seem all the more ominous. That funnel had teeth—its burrs abraded the air with a metallic shriek. Those streaks and strokes were like a shifting stack of spinning blades, each one eager to snatch off a finger if I so much as touched its blurred edge.

Though I didn't wish to show fear, I had to get out of the way.

So, ever so slowly, I slid my right foot back and then my left foot back.

Suddenly, the funnel lunged at me. I leapt away, but kept stumbling until I finally tripped and landed on my tail. With no time left for dignity, I scuttled away like a nervous sideways crab.

But the funnel did not hurry after me. No, it just slid along, taking its time, as if to say, "Why rush? I can have you whenever I wish." It was playing with me, torturing me for a bit of fun. It would let me spend all my energy, then come in for the kill.

Searching for some means of escape, I surveyed the terrain that stretched past the banks of the riverbed.

The dark land was empty, open desert all the way to the horizon.

"I should at least try to make a run for it," I told myself. "I should at least try."

But I didn't. I knew it wouldn't work. I knew that the funnel was just waiting for me to make such a move.

So what other options did I have? If I stood my ground, those burred teeth would grind right through me.

"But why not let them?" I asked myself. "Get this business over with and done. Accept the inevitable and go on. After all, this is the Otherworld—I will surely find something wonderful waiting for me beyond those teeth.

"Okay, Matar, here I am," I said. "Take me. Do with me what you will. I relinquish myself to you. Hope you're satisfied."

Usually, in such frightful situations, my feet would show courage while my head would know fear. However this time, much to my shame, my feet took a different tack—my feet kept dragging my exhausted body backwards, kept trying to save what little man of me remained. The answer was obvious: I couldn't get out of it so easily. I had to put up something of a fight.

"Matar, I swear, you'd better destroy me now, because if I ever have half a chance, I'll get you—I will. I'll deliver the world from your misery, from your curse. Don't doubt me. Don't laugh. I have both rage enough and resolution enough, so heed my warning."

This was silly talk from a man humiliated and confused. Nevertheless, it seemed to work magic. As soon as I'd finished my little speech, I noticed a tightness—a heaviness—coming from my right arm. Looking down, I found that my hand was clasped around the hilt of a golden sword. Streaks of light sang along the edges of the long blade.

I knew enough to know that such a gift must be used in a decisive manner.

A distance of seven paces now separated me from my foe.

I raised the sword to my chest. Fastening both hands tightly to the hilt, I pointed the blade at my adversary. I did not delude myself; I knew the fight would not be easy. But come what may, I would not allow the sword to be stripped from me.

The cyclone continued its drudging approach. I positioned my feet; I braced my legs, bending the knees slightly so as to absorb any impact. I would let the tornado come to me—I wouldn't move a muscle.

However, the moment the funnel brushed the sword tip, the centrifugal force flung the blade sideways and me with it. I flew off my feet. The weight of the blade yanked my arms out straight. I landed hard on my stomach. Yet I kept my grip on the hilt.

My shoulder now burned with these hot stinging jabs—like a hornet had burrowed into the socket. Nevertheless, I was not discouraged. On the contrary— I felt energized.

As the cyclone raved toward me, I climbed to my knees, then went into a crouch, holding the lance at the level of my solar plexus. I felt like a warrior—for the first time, truly a warrior.

"I have gone way beyond the limits of my puny body," I said aloud. "It is a triumph of the spirit. I have mastered myself and having mastered myself, I can master anything—including you, Matar."

This time I pulled the blade way back, paused for a beat, then slashed upward at a sharp angle. Guided by the force of my will, the sword passed directly into the center of the cyclone. And the cyclone spat it right back out. As the lance continued its ascent, I found myself airborne once again.

When my back slammed the ground, the impact knocked the wind from me as well as what remained of my reasoning faculties. I was dumb as a stunned calf. I didn't have a thought in my whole body.

So I just lay there, if not at peace, then at least, at rest.

But I had just kicked the beehive.

The tornado now stopped its creeping around and began bouncing here and there, moving quickly, abruptly, to the right, to the left, forward, then back, then forward again—a predator delighting in the kill.

Lacking the willpower to regain my feet, I tried rolling away; I held my body stiff and straight and rolled and rolled and rolled. But instead of taking me away from danger, this motion merely brought me in a circle. I ended up where I'd begun. Stupid, yes, but I had no time left for self-criticism. The funnel now hovered right behind my head, drilling my ears with its high-pitched hum.

Yes, the cyclone was watching me, watching and waiting, waiting for my next move—then it would nail me, I knew it would. Why didn't the funnel just finish me off? It wanted to torture me for a few moments more, that's why. But such arrogance, as we all know, only serves to defeat the perpetrator.

I would take one more stab at it.

My hands still gripped the hilt. The blade lay across my chest; the tip of it touched my nose. I now realized that I'd used this weapon incorrectly. The trick, I believed, was to strike the tornado with a straight forward blow. Thrust to the heart of the cyclone; pierce through to its core. No more mousing around. The hit would be quick, sudden, final.

I lay there, quiet as ice. I dared not show my hand. By focusing mind, body, and spirit, I had achieved the state of grace which is the calmness of the setting sun.

Abruptly, I brought my arms up and back, driving the blade over my head, cutting through to the cyclone's dark pith.

The sword held fast. It was as if another set of hands inside the funnel had grabbed hold of the lance.

Not to be outdone, I kept a firm grip on my end. And so, as the cyclone continued to turn, I turned with it. I did three full rotations before I finally gave up and let go of the hilt.

I scooted across the ground on my rump until I could break my momentum by digging in my heels. Then I flipped over onto my hands and knees and there I froze–but not in the stance of fierce wildcat; no, it was more like the pose of a common scrubber woman.

The golden sword was still planted in the funnel, spinning as it spun; the hilt showing one moment; the tip showing the next.

At this juncture, I finally realized the obvious: sword blades mean nothing to a tornado. Throw what you will into a wind funnel: it will either toss the thing back out or suck the thing up into itself. Even if this funnel was a sentient creature, it was still a tornado and would behave as such.

Yes, I was becoming quite wise as I crouched there in my scrubber woman pose, watching the cyclone bounce this way and that: it would leap forward, then hop back, coming close enough to tousle my hair, yet never harming a hair on my head.

About this time, another stroke of wisdom struck my mind. It was the type of insight that comes when all efforts to reason your way out have failed.

The thought was thus: Was the tornado really taunting me, threatening me? Or was it actually issuing an invitation? Had I misconstrued its intentions from the start?

"No, that can't be right," I told myself. "You're just fooling yourself again with your fanciful imagination."

"Perhaps, perhaps. But on the other hand, maybe I've just been fooling myself with my own fear. I guess I'll never know until I take a chance. What's there to lose anyway?—after all, this is the Otherworld."

The moment I made this decision, the cyclone allowed the sword to slide all the way down through its body until the metal clattered to the ground. The funnel then moved away from the blade and just stood there, hanging, waiting, its streaks and strokes now blurred to a soft gray fuzz. Its hum no longer drilled my ears; now it made a sweet sound—the delicate high note of an innocent child.

As the moments crept by, the funnel began to heighten and widen. But to my new frame of mind, this increase was not meant to intimidate; the tornado merely wished to make room for me.

"In time, an invitation becomes a challenge," I thought as I got to my feet. "I have nothing to risk but the pain. And pain is but a momentary thing. I'm going in there."

I shifted woozily on my legs. But not from abuse was I drunk; no, I was high from a happy, mad decision. "I may be a crazed man," I said aloud, "but here goes I."

Flinging my arms out wide to show my good intentions—to show that I was embracing, not attacking—I ran full speed towards the tornado. I was all the way open. You could have sliced right through me without producing a wound—that's how open I was.

And so, with one flying, joyful leap, I plunged into the heart of the cyclone, right into the center of that slashing, grinding maelstrom.

Had the cyclone just suckered me in? No, my instincts were on target. It was not defeat that awaited me, but freedom, powerful freedom.

I was not torn, nor devoured—I didn't even scrape my knee. After fleeting through a rough, frenetic barrier, I was lifted, bumpered by a genial wind. The fluffy puffs of air hoisted my body easily, peacefully up —a mother buoying her tender babe. In this manner, I bounced to the top of the tornado, my stomach weak and all hollow.

As I rested on the current of air pouring up from its core, the funnel continued to grow, continued to climb toward the heavens. On my back and with my hands grasping towards the sky, I whirled around and around —giddy, pleasantly dizzy, wanting only to embrace all.

And as I spun, the moon above me also spun; that soft white glow, it spun with me, it spun in the sky's black ocean.

And as this moon spun, it began to spiral outward, began to unfurl—spreading five gentle, flowing, curving arms out through the night sea: a swirling starfish expanding. As the moon continued to unfurl, these arms grew longer and longer, reaching out through the night, and as the arms grew longer, the circle of the moon grew smaller and smaller until it finally disappeared altogether. And so, as the arms of the moon spread out across the sky, bleeding into one another, the black night—having nowhere else to go—gathered itself into the center.

As a result, what was once a circle of moon was now a circle of night. And what was once a sky of black was now a sky of white—an ocean of white with an island of night in its center.

I continued to spin and as I spun, I watched, enchanted, as the sky kept playing out this transformation. Now it was the circle of night spiraling outward, unfurling itself, becoming a twirling octopus, its gentle, flowing curving arms sweeping out through a soft white ocean. And as the arms grew longer and longer, the circle of the night grew smaller and smaller until finally, it disappeared altogether. And so, as the black arms spread out across the sky, bleeding into one another, the white moon—having nowhere else to go—again gathered itself into the center.

So what was once a circle of black once more became a circle of white. And what was once a sky of white once more became a sky of black.

Most impressive to my child's mind. Downright delightful.

And so it went—as the moon continued to contract and expand, the night continued to expand and contract, each one spiraling into and out of the other again and again and again, each one flowing into and out of the other again and again and again.

"Matar?" I whispered. "Matar."

Chapter 16 :
A Return to the Simple Life

I woke from this vision lying in the loving branches of a pine tree on a sweet mountainside. I knew this mountain already—I'd awoken here after my last Otherworld journey.

I decided to wait before climbing down. Though I didn't remember what, I sensed that something bad had happened prior to my journey. I was in no hurry to return.

So instead I began to reflect on this last Otherworld trip. As with my previous visits, this adventure seemed both profound and silly. Taken in that light, were these experiences so different, in essence, from my regular life?

Though strange sensations still hummed through my body, I knew that once I got down from this tree, I would return to being no more than I usually was— which was never quite enough.

So I just hung there in the tree. For a time, I examined the delicate fleece on the wings of a moth. Then I yawned and nearly fell off the branch. Prisms dangled in pine needle raindrops. The ground steamed with fresh rain. On the plain below, the streams had swelled over their banks and now fed swift brown torrents into the main river.

The sight of all that muddy water brought my memory back. We had lost our city. If any of my tribes-kin had survived the flood, the Roqian warriors had probably tortured and killed them by now. I was most likely the last remaining Matarian. I waited for this thought to sink in. But oddly enough, I seemed to have no strong feelings. However, I was beginning to get a little dizzy.

"Probably just the height," I thought to myself.

I decided to shimmy on down the tree before I fell.

The moment my feet touched the ground, the magnitude of the situation finally hit me. I had lost my tribe. Despite all the internal strife, the tribe had always been my home. Whenever I had emerged from the Otherworld, shambled and uncertain, I had always found security with my tribes-family. With them, the world became real again. Not hyper-real like the Otherworld, but ordinary, day-to-day, tedious-moment-to-tedious-moment real—which was exactly what I needed. True, there had been many times when I'd felt alone amongst my tribes-kin. But now, without them, I felt completely desolate.

Perhaps I could find another clan to take me in. But how could they ever know me? They would not be the ones who had witnessed my squalling birth, or laughed at my childhood growing pains, or guided me through my fumbling entrance into adulthood. Would this new tribe tease me, torment me, argue with me? No, they'd treat me with discretion and reserve. I didn't have the stomach for such fine treatment.

Though I grieved for my people, for their horrific experience of death, I grieved my own loss more than anything else. My people had gone on to another life, whereas I was still stuck in this sorry-ass world.

Sunk in self-pity, I sat down on the ground, covered my face with my hands, and wept.

"I have been lost before," I told myself, "but now, I am lost forever."

For the next few days, I wandered along the mountain slope, going no higher, going no lower. I barely had enough spark to walk. I felt almost ready to die—almost, but not quite.

And so I continued to walk.

In the evenings, I'd watch the red sun slide into the earth. Then I would lay back and gaze at the stars trembling in the black chill of night.

"Without a life to return to, I have no life at all," I told myself. "I guess I'll just keep drifting through this nether void until I become less than nothing."

Yes, I was being overly dramatic, and more than a little pouty. But there I was.

Then late one afternoon, as I meandered through the cool shadows, I saw a sight that stopped me dead still.

About two hundred paces below me, a cliff rock jutted out from the mountainside. Atop this cliff was a circle of flat stones. At first, I believed that some sculptor had set carved figures upon those stones— that's how lifeless these gray people appeared. The animal hides that they wore were stiff and heavy with gray mud. Only the shifting of their slumped shoulders proved that they still had breath. I thought they might be a more primitive tribe, similar to the Larvians.

Hoping for a better look, I dipped into a crouch and crept down the mountainside.

After a few steps, my foot cracked a twig. The sound exploded the silence. Yet nobody in the group stirred to life. I waited. Finally, one of the men leaned way back to bathe his face in the sun's dying rays. It was a haggard mask that he wore, with deep, soot-filled wrinkles: a picture of exhaustion and misery.

"Maybe I should just pass on," I thought.

Then a quiet shock ran through my body. I now recognized that shattered human. It was Aruk.

Aruk had always been our most solid warrior. Whereas Mok reeked of malice and suspicion, Aruk was robust and rather innocent for such an aggressive person. He never found fault in any of his tribes-kin.

But now I saw his strong spirit dead.

I began to identify others in the group.

There sat Ool with her pouched eyes and blubbery puddle of hips.

And on the next rock: old man Purl. He had black gums and a poor disposition, but was a wizard at the pottery wheel.

Then there was Lamarl, an adolescent boy with a concave chest and dark rings under his eyes.

And Mumurl, a girl adolescent with a petulant lower lip.

And an old woman known as Parn. She had long ago lost all of her teeth but two, so her frame was rather thin. She was the one who'd shown us how to weave reeds into baskets (though sometimes the bottoms cracked).

There was only one Larvian in the group—she would be the last of a fine tribe. This woman had pendulous breasts, bulky hips, and a cast over one eye. Sorry, but I can't now recall her name.

Despite their shabby appearance, I was glad to find my tribes-kin alive. But the one that I was happiest to see was a small boy with snail-colored skin and a bloated belly—a pathetic figure shivering on a rock. Rir had sunk his claws deep into life and had refused to let go out of pure spite. Perhaps I could bend the power within him toward good.

This hope rekindled my heart. I now advanced with soft steps toward a reunion most delicate. My people looked so lifeless, so dispirited. They might well feel ashamed of their ragged selves.

I stopped within fifty paces of the cliff rock and cleared my throat, then cleared my throat again. When that didn't work, I rolled a stone down the mountain slope.

Finally, Ool looked up with her pouched eyes and said, "Oh, it's you."

Aruk glanced in my direction. "You look like shit," he said.

Just out of curiosity, I gave myself the once-over. My skin had the pale shades and blue tones of a dead man. My rickety legs bowed inward. The hide that I wore was little more than a network of tattered scraps. My hair was all matted together with dry mud.

Well, so much for appearances.

"Are we all that's left?" I asked.

"Yes," Ool said. "The rest lie buried beneath the mud."

"Or else their bones now decorate the walls of Ekruk," Aruk said.

"So what happened to you?" Purl asked me.

"I nearly suffocated under a river of mud. I only managed to escape by slipping over to the Otherworld."

"So why didn't you save the others?" Aruk asked. "You could've taken them with you."

"It doesn't quite work that way."

"Yeah, sure."

"Really—there was nothing I could do."

"Some good you are," Lamarl said.

"Next time you go slinking off to the Otherworld, you'd better damn well take me along," Mumurl said. "I want out of this dump."

I could see that tragedy had transformed these two youths into churlish, impudent punks.

"You might not like the Otherworld so much once you got there," I said to Mumurl.

"Oh yeah?" she sneered. "Well, I don't think there's any such thing as the Otherworld. I think you're just making it all up."

"Murmurl, I know you've suffered greatly," I said, "but that still doesn't give you the right to—"

"Let the girl have her say," Aruk snapped. "We're tired of listening to you and your stupid stories about the Otherworld."

I restrained myself from using strong language. Perhaps Aruk believed that, having assumed Mok's position as tribal leader, he had to assume the surly disposition as well.

"So how'd you all manage to escape?" I asked.

"Through bad luck," Ool said. "The front wall collapsed and when the wash of mud finally spent its force, it spilled a mess of bodies out on the plain. The few who were still breathing didn't have time to bury those who weren't—the Roqians had already invaded the mud rubble of our city. We had to hightail it to the mountain."

"You haven't been back since then?"

"We don't dare come near the place. The bastards of Roq have set up camp."

"But it's ruined," I said.

"The crazy sons of bitches seem to like it there," Ool said. "But they're not the only weird birds in this world.

Let me tell you about Bruk. She didn't even try to save herself. I ran to her room when the walls started to melt. Her roof was leaking like mad. Yet there she sat with a smile on her face. 'Get out of this box, you old fool,' I told her. 'Your ceiling's about to cave.' But she just looked at me with those gray eyes of hers and said, 'I'm done here.' 'What'd you mean by that?' I asked her. 'Whatever I came here to do, I've done it,' she answered, 'And if not, it'll just have to wait.' Then she took both my hands in hers and kissed the back of each one and bid me farewell. I realized then that my dear friend had gone loopy on me. Must've been that softheaded Seer she used to bed in the tall grass. He twisted her mind all up." Ool stared at me dead on.

I decided to hold my tongue. Time would mend where words would fail.

Aruk now gave an account of the Ekrukian battle. In somber tones, he told of our valiant stand, how our brave band had fought off wave after wave of little helmeted men. Then with his eyes all dark and hollow, he described Mok's grand farewell—how my twin had whirled about, whipping his sword through the air and stabbing blindly with his spear. Coated with blood from head to foot, Mok had exalted in the glory of heroic defeat.

"Then all of a sudden, he stood stone still," Aruk said. "His face got all serene; his eyes had this strange glow like he was listening to something faraway and sweet. He dropped his weapons then and lifted his arms to the sky and stared straight into the sun's merciless glare.

"Of course, some yellow-belly punk had to take advantage of the situation. No respect for greatness.

The severed head landed right at my feet. The eyes still had that silvery gleam."

By destiny's design that lopped-off head had saved Aruk's life. Overcome with sorrow, he had dropped to his knees and clutched Mok's head to his breast.

"And so right about that time something blunt and heavy cracked the back of my skull," Aruk continued. "The dull vibrations rang through my brain, then all went black and I went splat!—face first—down into the mud, out cold. But the bodies kept falling; they covered me up, they hid me from view. When I finally awoke, I was snuggled beneath a blanket of corpses. It was nearly nightfall. Fortunately, the Ekrukians had not yet begun to rob my fallen comrades of their weapons and their heads. They were too busy celebrating. So I was able to worm myself free and sneak off across the plain, undetected. Each step was a drumbeat inside my head —I hear the dim echoes even now, though it's been nearly a moon cycle since then.

"When I finally came upon our city I found nothing but a mud ruin. For awhile, I kept myself hidden away in the forest grove and watched as the Roqians dug through the debris. I realized then why the Ekrukians had attacked us. They'd made a deal with the bastards of Roq. The bastards of Roq had set us up."

I decided not to mention my visions. That would only complicate matters. And raise unnecessary questions.

"Anyway, I got tired real soon of that sickly sight and headed for the mountains."

"And here you found your tribes-kin," I put in. "Destiny has pulled the strings and brought us all back together again. That's because the ties that bind us are richer than blood. For blood is but a physical bond.

And the bond that ties us together is a spiritual one. Am I right or am I right?"

"Save it," Ool said.

"Save it for someone who gives a damn," Lamarl said.

"If you can find anyone," Mumurl said.

"Save it for when you're dead," Rir said. The boy then stood up, hefted his balls with both hands and spat from the corner of his mouth. He had grown up quickly

"Okay, okay, I get the idea," I said. "Look, the last few days have been tough on all of us. It takes time to heal. Let's just be thankful for what we've got."

"Oh yes, let us be thankful," old man Purl said.

"Thank you, Purl," I said.

"Yeah," he continued, "let's all be thankful for lice and wet rot and cold nights and bad food and sick, swollen bellies."

The others immediately affirmed this list and added to it. I decided not to press the issue. At least this complaining seemed to perk them up, if only for a short while.

In the days that followed, though my tribes-kin remained mired in deep depression, my own spirits seemed to lift. Perhaps I was only trying to counterbalance their foul disposition. Or perhaps I saw gain where they saw loss. For one thing, we were no longer stuck behind the walls of that mud city. And gone were the days of back-breaking farm labor. We were free once again. So many times I'd longed for a return to the simple life. Though the price had been painful, I'd gotten my wish.

And so, under these reduced circumstances, we, the People of Matar, began our new life. Aruk carved a few wooden bows and honed some sticks into arrows. Occasionally an animal would lay down its life for his hunting party. The rest of the time, we maintained ourselves on a diet of roots and grubs and tender shoots. Rains came frequently on the mountain, so we built shelters on the rock cliff using branches and twigs and leaves. As long as our progress went no further, I would feel safe.

I wish I could say that Rir responded well to the loving, caring attention I gave him. But that just wasn't the case. Though I showed him every kindness, his belligerent behavior continued unabated. He especially enjoyed sneaking up behind me and whipping my legs with a bramble stem.

I'd often remind Rir that his father and I were twins. "Great men usually come in pairs," I told my nephew. But he never quite made the connection and kept on whipping my legs with his bramble stem.

However, I never gave up on him. I believed that I could boost his self-esteem by praising his father. So one night I sat him down at the campfire and told him what a fierce, dauntless warrior Mok had been.

"Yes," I said, "your dad was a man of honor and vision."

"That's a crock if I ever heard one!" Ool crowed.

I shot her a look and shook my head, but she ignored me.

"The boy ought to know the truth," she said. "His pa was a bloodthirsty fool. Don't forget—it was his cockamamie idea got us into this mess. Matar came to him? Hah! Why didn't you challenge him?"

I looked to Aruk for support, thinking that he'd defend his beloved comrade.

But he just hung his head and stared into the flames with eyes gone dead.

After hearing Ool denounce his father that way, Rir tried whipping her legs as well. I must admit, I found this turn of events rather amusing. But unfortunately, Ool seized this opportunity to release all her pent-up anger. One good tanning from her and Rir again gave me his full attention.

At least, Rir's shenanigans helped break the dull mood of my tribes-kin, if only for a few moments here and there. How they laughed and clapped when he stung my legs with his bramble whip. Or when he pelted my buttocks with dirt clods. Or when he bounced rocks off my head.

The tribe needed something near at hand to focus their anger on, so they chose me. Anytime I tried put to a positive spin on things, someone would always say, "Oh just go to the Otherworld and leave us alone."

I broached the subject one afternoon while Ool and I were digging for grubs.

"I try to help them, I really do," I told her, "but they just curse at me. Why do they always get so bent out of shape?"

Ool stabbed the ground with her stick and levered up a chunk of black dirt. "You really don't get it, do you? We're sick of hearing you chirp, chirp, chirp all day long like a little bird. You dance among us like a sunbeam. The way you act...it's disgusting."

"I just want everyone to feel better, that's all."

"Well forget it. We're not supposed to feel good. We've just lost everything we ever gave a damn about: our city, our tribe, our way of life. We shouldn't feel better—you should feel worse."

"Well, it's not my fault we lost everything," I sniffed.

"Then quit blaming yourself."

"I'm not."

"You are too."

I plucked four fat grubs from the dirt clod. They squirmed on my palm. In the early days, I would've sucked these fellas down my gullet like they were honey. But since that time I'd lost my taste for them and I hadn't been able to find it again. I had to admit, going back to the old ways was harder than I'd expected.

"So everyone hates me, huh?" I asked Ool.

"Except for the Larvian woman. But she's catching on."

After all I'd endured in the Otherworld, I should've been able to handle such abuse. Or so you would think. But abuse in the Otherworld was one thing, while abuse in this world—especially from those that I loved—was quite another. Since my return, I'd worked hard to spark a fire in my tribes-kin. And, in a way, I had succeeded. But it was a cold flame that I had kindled and I was tired of getting burnt by it. My anger was just about ready to spew.

What a morose bunch of whiners, my people!

I needed a break.

And so, that night, as my tribes-kin slept, I crept from the campsite and started up the mountainside. I would return to my people when I'd found some answers.

But the way things looked, that might take awhile.

Chapter 17 : The Sacrifice

By the light of the moon, I hauled my weary limbs up the trail. The anger within me swelled with each step that I took. The thin air harshed in my lungs, but I refused to even stop for a breath. My heart banged against its cage. My leg muscles were in knots.

Then the sun rose and cut a hole in my scalp. By this time, I had decided that Matarians were the worst people on Matar's earth. Goat stealers, skull bashers, rapers of Larvian women. We poisoned whatever we touched. The Roqians sparkled like pure white snow next to us. Our legacy would sicken a maggot.

A rock rolled under my toes. I pitched forward and smacked the ground hard on my chest. For awhile, I just lay there, held fast by an empty rage. Finally, I managed to pull myself back up. Weak in mind, body, and heart, I sat down on a flat stone and tried to think.

At dawn, the mountain peak had appeared to be a just short, easy climb from where I stood. Yet now, at mid-day, it didn't seem much closer. Though I'd passed the tree line, the white summit still loomed high overhead. Clouds snaked around its stony gray cliffs.

On the plain below, the rivers and streams created a fine network of veins. I scanned the edge of the savanna, trying to locate the mud rumble of our city. But a reddish haze obscured the horizon.

"I've had it!" I screamed. "I have completely, totally had it. With everything. You hear me, Matar? No, no, you don't hear me. No, you do hear me—you just won't grace me with an answer. You low-down dirty good-for-nothing god, you."

The mountainside did a sudden drop just beyond the rock where I sat. One good leap would send me to a certain death.

"What if I jumped, Matar? What then? I wouldn't be your whipping boy anymore, now would I? What about that! Without me around, they'd forget you soon enough. Who knows?—the tribe might even start worshipping Larv. Imagine that, Matar—being beaten out by Larv!"

Such was my mental state that I actually got up and started flapping my arms like a bird. "Watch out, Matar! Watch out! I'm going to jump. I'm warning you —I'll do it. One small step, that's all it'd take." I glanced over my shoulder as if addressing an invisible presence. "Don't think I'll really do it, eh, Matar? Well, guess what?—here goes!"

I lurched forward, then checked myself.

"Ha ha! Fooled you! Fooled you, didn't I, Matar?"

At this point, I grew sick of my own silliness and sat down again. The anger coiled in my stomach like a cold worm. Tears of rage burned my eyes. Matar had me. There was no way out.

When the bitter tears had finally dried on my cheeks, I surrendered to fate and got back on my feet. My body swayed from the weight of my anger. How could I drain that black pool from my gut?

Running away from my tribe wasn't getting me anywhere. I had not even come close to anything resembling an answer.

"Should I keep on climbing or go back to my people?" I wondered.

I couldn't think. My thoughts broke apart as soon as I touched them.

Then, through the fog of my confusion, I caught a shifting movement in the woods below me. I sharpened my focus, but now all was still. The trees stood there like dark, silent sentinels. I waited; I listened. My stomach twitched.

"You're just seeing things," I told myself. "When the mind fails, the senses falter. I'd better get on back to my people."

And so, with no more hesitation, I began picking my way back down the mountainside.

When I'd reached the tree line, I turned around to look at the white peak one last time. "Later," I said to the peak. "Later." Then I stepped into the dark forest.

Suddenly something hard, sharp, and cool pressed against my throat. I froze. The long blade was held by a hand laced with many battle scars. Urk flexed his broad nostrils. His hate-mongering eyes glared at me as if I was the bitch of all hardship. Behind him stood seven Roqian warriors. Their bronze swords smoldered in the shadows.

I recognized most of their faces. The one with the slice through his nose was Qor. And that sapling with ears the size of hands was Carq. And who could forget Ark the Simple? I felt a strange kinship with these men. After all, they'd been there for some of the key events of my life.

In this delicate situation, I thought it best to maintain an attitude of friendliness.

"Well hello, my Roqian brothers!" I exclaimed. "What good business brings you to this mountain?"

"We're hunting Matarians," Urk said.

"Well, I'm sorry to say that you've found the last one."

"You sure about that?"

"Sure I'm sure. Between the rain storm and the Ekrukians, we didn't stand a chance."

"So how'd you escape?"

"When our city flooded, I slipped over to the Otherworld. Remember, I'm a Seer. I can do such things."

"So who told you about Ekruk?"

"Like I said—I'm a Seer. I have my ways."

"If you can see so well, why didn't you see us just now?"

"I did. I just came down here to say 'hello'."

"But we're your enemy, remember?"

"I say let bygones be bygones. After all, my people did provoke you."

"True enough."

"So let's make up."

"Okay, fine. Tell us where the rest of your tribe is and we'll reconcile."

"I told you—I'm all that's left. I've looked everywhere. Trust me."

"You're a liar."

"That's not a very nice thing to say."

"You're a liar. You're not a true Seer. Maybe you were once, but you aren't anymore. If you could truly see, you'd be terrified right now."

"Oh? How's that?" I squeaked.

"Because you'd see what we're about do to you."

A chill washed over me. Still, I remained nonchalant "Yes, I can see it. I can see it quite clearly."

Urk lifted the sword from my neck and put his hand on his hip. "Okay then, tell us what you see."

"What I see is, what I see is this...you're going to recognize that I'm a perfectly harmless fool, yes, a fool —an insignificant worm who'll spend the rest of his lonely days trudging up and down this mountainside, longing for the good times gone by."

Urk didn't seem to appreciate my lyrical dexterity. For several tedious moments, he just stared at me. In that short time, I came to despise his dull, reptilian eyes. As you'll recall, in a previous statement, I praised this man's patience and valued him as a leader over Mok. But now I realized that I preferred the imagination and wild intensity of my twin. Urk was just too boring.

The Roqian leader snapped his fingers.

Two young toughs stepped forward. At a signal from Urk, they grabbed my wrists and twisted my arms behind my back. The shocking pain sent hot streaks right to my brain. My arm bones strained against their sockets.

The punks tied my wrists so tightly that the rope choked off the blood flow. Once done, they knocked me flat on my stomach.

"Get up," Urk said.

I thought of a witty retort, but restrained myself. I already had enough trouble. My hands began to pulsate.

"The rope's a wee bit tight," I said in small voice.

"Good," Urk said. Then he gave me a shove and I started down the trail at the head of the pack. If we kept to this path, we'd surely run into my tribes-kin on the cliff rock. Then they would have one more reason to hate me. Not that they'd live that long.

As the trail zigzagged down the mountainside, the footing got a little tricky in spots. But if I hesitated the least bit, Urk would give me a swift kick to the buttocks. One such time, I lost my balance and went tumbling, catching roots and rocks in my gut. The Roqians slapped their thighs and nearly went blind with laughter. But after a few moments, Urk narrowed his eyes at them and they all shut up in an instant. Roqian warriors were only allowed so much merriment.

When we neared the area of the cliff rock, I deliberately took a fall and kept myself rolling down the mountainside until my stomach got stuck in my throat and the Roqians caught up with me. But this little gambit worked: I had detoured my captors from the home ground of my tribes-kin.

Towards the end of our descent, we paused at the edge of a precipice to take a leak. The Roqians allowed me this one luxury.

While administering to myself, I gazed down at the sudden drop just beyond my feet. I realized that one big leap might project me into the Otherworld. After all, anytime I'd come within spitting distant of death, I had gained entry. And even if I did die, I would still enter the Otherworld, just on a more permanent basis. So what was there to lose?

However, something felt wrong with this idea.

"It's the easy way out and maybe that's the problem —it's too easy," I thought.

"On the other hand, what's wrong with too easy?" I answered myself. "Why make things any harder than need be?"

I knew that the Roqians would torture me and try to force me to reveal the whereabouts of my people.

Maybe that torture would push me over to the Otherworld. But then again, maybe not. However, if they did torture me and if I held out, if I refused to tell, I could elevate my death and, in so doing, elevate my life. And at the moment, I thought that my life could use a little elevating.

That's just how low I felt: that I would choose prolonged torture over an effortless death.

On the other hand, I knew that this plan, though noble in concept, would probably prove foolish in practice.

Nonetheless, jumping from the cliff just didn't feel right.

Unable to find my answer, I once again surrendered to the dictates of my feet.

And, of course, my feet would not take the easy way out; my feet led me away from the cliff's edge.

We reached the base of the mountain by twilight and set up camp in a small grove near a stream choked with watercress. My throat burned from thirst. My face, my back, my butt, and my legs all stung with bruises.

The Roqians tied me to a tree, then roasted two hedgehogs they'd caught that day. For my dinner, they tossed a few pieces of fat at me and laughed when these greasy strips slid down my face. Then they bounced acorns off my head until they finally grew bored and went to bed.

The next morning, they retied my wrists, then Urk fitted a loop of rope around my neck and we started off across the sun-baked plain. The Roqian leader kept a tight rein on me. Whenever I appeared sluggish or faint, he would give the rope a good hard yank. For a few moments, I'd choke for air and my eyes would bulge from their sockets like two white bubbles. Nevertheless, it always got me going again.

By late afternoon, we had arrived at the City of Roq, formerly known as the City of Matar. The Roqians had quickly rebuilt the place and made it their own. The new walls were twice as high and took in twice as much area as the old ones. Each corner now had a turret where a guard kept watch over the somnolent land. A big ditch filled with dark water encircled the whole business. Construction of this massive project was aided by "acquired labor" according to Urk.

A short man with a broad chest lifted a bullhorn to his lips and announced our arrival with a long warbling blow. The gates slowly creaked open. Urk jerked my rope and I stumbled forward on bruised scorched feet. Dust had given a covering soft as moth hair to my face and my arms and legs. I jerked my head, jerked my head, trying to flip the greasy hair out of my eyes. "Stop that," Urk said.

I had to admit: those goat-herding nomads had done a darn good job of settling down. Though the layout of the City of Roq was similar to that of its predecessor, the Roqians had a sense of scale and grandeur that my people lacked. The front gates exhaled onto to a plaza where a trader with a cart haggled with a stooped old woman. From the plaza, a wide avenue lined with transplanted palms led to a tower in the center of the city. This tall tapering structure had steep stairways on all four sides. At the summit was a small platform and on the platform was a ritual house guarded by vultures carved from stone.

The city still wore a soft shade of light brown. But many buildings and walls were now made of river rock. That chiseled stone, tucked neatly into place, suggested stability—solid strength. As a Matarian, I couldn't help but feel a bit envious.

The Roqian populace crowded along the avenue as Urk and I took the long walk to the tower. They gazed at me with an aura of hushed solemnity. They knew they were looking at a dead man.

Still, all things considered, I felt pretty relaxed.

"Sure, all that torture will hurt at first," I told myself, "but then I'll be free of this mortal shackle. Maybe death won't change me; nevertheless, whatever I find after my demise has got to be better than the life I'm now living."

When we had reached the base of the tower, Rewan appeared in doorway of the ritual house high above. Bending her dark, slender arm at the elbow, she gave us the signal to ascend. Then, as Urk and I mounted the wide stairway that led to the summit, Rewan descended the steps toward us. We met her halfway up.

The two Roqians clasped each other at the elbow by way of greeting.

"I found your boyfriend," Urk said.

"He's not my boyfriend," Rewan said. "He was never my boyfriend. He's a Matarian."

"Just wanted to hear you say that. Anyway, it appears he's lost his Seer's powers."

"How so?"

"He's still here. He hasn't gone into the Otherworld."

"So...any more Matarians around?"

257

"He says no, but I know better. Don't worry—we'll find them. But he'll do for right now."

We three then climbed to the platform together. From this height, the crowd below looked like nothing more than clusters of flowers.

Urk motioned for the two young toughs to come up. Then finally, he took the rope off my neck. From the looks of things, Urk and Rewan now shared power in some sort of symbiotic arrangement. To have finagled such a deal out of Urk would've required a lot of cunning, a lot of maneuvering. Yes, Rewan was savvy one.

I knew that if I could somehow rouse her love energies again, my life might be spared. It was my only hope. But though I tried to get her attention, she ignored me completely. Those dark eyes—those deep, mysterious pools that had once lured me on a sacred night—were now nothing more than flat blanks. Gone was that fresh, buoyant energy; gone was that aura of sweet secrecy. Her spine had become rigid; her jaw had a hard set. How could I expect to penetrate that grim facade?

Well, this much was for certain: I could not win my suit while on public display. I had to catch Rewan alone. But what was the chance of that?

The two toughs arrived carrying loops of rope. Urk cut my wrists free. Then he pointed to a large concavity in the stone platform. Wooden posts were set at four points around this shallow sink. In the middle of the basin was a drain hole.

"For me?" I asked. "Really, you shouldn't have."

"On your back," Urk said.

"Okay, whatever."

258

I lay down in the sink and spread my arms and legs out wide. "Not too tight," I said, just to humor them.

The two toughs tied my wrists and ankles to the posts, then gave each line a good hard yank to snug up the knots. This one kept swinging his butt right in my face. He smelled like burnt grease.

"I must say I'm surprised," I said to Rewan.

"Surprised at what?"

"At how you guys put this place back together so fast."

"We didn't put anything back together. It's all new."

"Well, congratulations on a job well done. You guys must've worked like ants. So where'd you get the stone?"

"The cliffs by the river. Other groups helped—wandering tribes we welcomed inside. Did you say 'ants'?"

"I meant that in the most positive sense. So anyway, why'd you build on the same exact spot?"

"We believe this place to be a sacred place," Rewan answered. "We believe we have finally found the lost Land of Roq."

"What makes you think that? I mean, it's nice, but I wouldn't call it paradise."

"Well, it pretty much matches the description our Seer gave us."

"You mean the old coot you guys killed?"

"Yes, him."

"So just out of curiosity, what do you plan to do with me?"

"You are a great man." Rewan gazed toward the distant mountains.

"Thank you," I said.

"And our god Roq demands the sacrifice of great men captured in war."

"Well, I've already sacrificed a lot in my life, let me tell you." I managed a weak laugh.

"Not that type of sacrifice. Blood sacrifice."

The shadow of a cloud passed over me.

I managed to swallow. "Blood sacrifice, huh? So what exactly does that entail?"

"Tomorrow at mid-day, in a special ceremony atop this tower, Urk will rip the heart from your breast. Then he'll extract your liver using the ritual knife. Then he'll chop you into little bits and hang you out to dry. Having witnessed our sacrifice, Roq will then send down his assistants—our friends, the vultures; they will carry the flesh back up to him in their bellies. If Roq finds our offering worthy, he will then bestow many blessings upon us."

"I see. So how do you know Roq is a 'he'."

"That's what Mer always told us."

"I thought you might torture me some first."

"We'd like to," Urk groused, "but Rewan—I mean, 'Roq'—doesn't approve."

"That's right," Rewan said. "Roq doesn't like it one bit."

"So anyway, what happens tonight?"

"Tonight, nothing," Rewan said. "You must wait until tomorrow."

"I can wait, I can wait." I tried to chuckle but started to cough. "I'm awfully thirsty."

"I said nothing until tomorrow." Then she turned from me with a movement so stiff and abrupt that her skin make a scraping sound against the air.

First, the two punks descended, then Urk and Rewan followed. The co-rulers matched each other step for step down the stairway.

Had Rewan forgotten that sacred night—that sweetly secret, dark-eyed night—when our lives had touched and nearly entwined? It sure did look that way. My case, it appeared, was lost.

The wicked afternoon sun drilled a hole through each eyelid. My throat was so parched that it hurt to swallow. But at least I had no trouble holding my bladder.

Those quaint expressions of Rewan's kept circling in my head: "rip the heart from your breast...extract your liver...chop you into little bits...hang you out to dry." Getting my heart ripped out—that would have to hurt. But maybe, just maybe, I would disappear into the Otherworld the moment Urk went for my pump. I tried to take comfort in that thought; however, for some reason, the idea just didn't feel right. It wasn't going to happen that way. Somehow I knew that. No matter— when the time came, the extraction would only be a moment's pain. Then I'd be free.

Yet despite my wonderful rationalizing, I still had the undeniable desire to save this life of mine, this painful, confusing, frustrating life, this puny life, this foolish life, this seemingly worthless, worn-out life. Why, why did I want to save this life of mine?

Maybe I just didn't want to give up without a fight.

Or maybe, some part of me beyond my limited awareness was still trying to accomplish something.

I considered Rewan. Did she really believe that mutilating me would gain Roq's blessing? A cold snake

261

had encoiled her heart. Maybe Urk had gotten to her. Or maybe she had bowed to pressure from her tribe. Whatever the case, she had lied to herself. But I could not judge the woman too harshly. I knew only too well how easy it was to deceive oneself.

Night came and the moon rose over the wall. Stars began to appear one by one. Despite my worried thoughts and the physical discomfort, I now experienced an odd sense of peace.

"By this time tomorrow, my tired spirit will have busted loose from its threads," I told myself. "Maybe then I can reconnect with Ellar."

The soft moon reminded me of Ellar's luminous loving eyes. The stars confirmed a deep space within me.

Soothed by the gentle hands of the wind, my mind eroded like sand.

I slipped into a parched sleep.

Abruptly, my warm bubble broke. I stuttered awake, blinking. Something plinked the middle of my forehead. I gave my neck a turtle stretch. A water drop struck my eye.

Rewan's fragrant brown eyes gazed down upon me. White moonlight crowned her hair. She held a goatskin bag plump with water.

"I thought you said nothing 'til tomorrow," I said.

She put a finger to her lips. "Sssssh. Quiet. Sounds echo this time of night."

"My back itches," I whined.

"Shut up and open your mouth."

I spread my maw wide. Sweet water poured from the goatskin bag in a thin silver stream. A cool pool expanded my cheeks.

I swallowed and swallowed and swallowed. I could feel my stomach softly bloating. "Thank you," I gasped. "Thank you so much. But why are you taking this chance?"

"I want some answers."

"Okay, but first, one question for you."

"You want to know who runs the show around here."

"Prescient. I like that in a woman."

"No, just logical. Anyway, to answer your question...Urk is the protector. That counts for a lot. But I guide the life of the people—I stage the rituals, I do some healing tricks, I dole out domestic advice. When two parties need a dispute settled, Urk and I sit down and listen to the case together. Then we confer in private and make our decision."

"But what if the two of you disagree?"

"Then we summon the one known as The Stickmeister. This fellow carries two sticks with him at all times. A long one and a short one. The Stickmeister hides the length of both sticks, then has Urk pick one. If Urk picks the long stick, he wins; if he picks the short stick, I win."

"Very clever. We Matarians never had such a system. I guess we didn't have that many disputes."

"Among yourselves, no."

I decided to let that remark pass. "So anyway, how did you become a Seer without finishing your training?"

"After Mer died, I was lost for a time—completely lost. But when I saw how much the people needed me,

I decided to invent what I didn't already know. Somehow it all worked out."

"But why the sacrifice ritual? Don't you think that's rather crude?"

"Yes, I do. To be honest, I can't stand to watch it." She groaned and shook her head. "But the old Seer started the practice. And now the people expect it. Or rather, they demand it. In their minds, not to sacrifice is to go against Roq."

"As seer, you're supposed to guide their beliefs."

"I can't get them to disbelieve what they want so badly to believe. I've tried, I really have, I've tried."

"So you're going to let them kill me?" I asked in a small, child-like voice.

"They won't accept anything less. After all, you are a Matarian. Not a very nice bunch, your tribes-kin. No —don't try to defend them. I'll admit, my people may not be the best people. But still, we don't go out of our way to make trouble. Our travels taught us a little diplomacy."

I bit my tongue on that one. This was not the time to argue. First and foremost, I had to think about saving my hide. "Well you see, we'd never met another tribe until you guys came along. We really didn't know how to act."

"So then after you met us, did you change?"

"You see, Rewan, I wasn't around all that much. Perhaps if I had been, things would've turned out differently. But even so...I saw that last trick you guys pulled—that business with the Ekrukians. That was downright dirty."

"I tried to talk him out of it, but you know Urk. He just didn't feel safe with Matarians running around loose in the world. And when he told the Ekrukians about you guys, they were only too willing to help."

"I thought you said you had some questions for me."

"Yes, I do."

"Let me guess. You want to go to the Otherworld, but don't know how to get there."

"Prescient. I like that in a man."

"No, just logical. Any Seer worth her salt would want the Otherworld. For one thing, it gives you a certain cachet among your people. But more importantly, it builds your inner resource. Take me for example. I know I may not seem like much. And maybe I'm not. But the Otherworld has changed me, it certainly has. Before, if I'd found myself in a predicament like this, you couldn't've stop me from kicking and screaming."

"And now?"

"Tomorrow, during the ritual, you won't be able to stop me from kicking and screaming. But seriously...I know it must be hard for you: you've heard all those stories about the Otherworld and you still don't know how to get there. It just turns your patience inside out. That's because it comes from a desire born within you—that's why you can't get past it. It's part of what makes you a Seer."

"You understand me so well." Her voice had a dusky tone.

"That's because you're so often in my thoughts."

"I did try walking on fire," she said, "since it worked for you that one time."

"So what happened? Did the coals burn your feet?"

"No. But I didn't make it to the Otherworld either."

"It's not easy," I said. "Especially the first time. Especially by yourself."

"I thought you'd say that."

"Do you want to go or don't you?"

She tapped her nose. "My people would be very disappointed to find you missing."

"Explain it to them when you get back. You're their spiritual leader—you've got to make them see things your way. That's your job."

"So how long would I be gone?"

"It's hard to say. Probably long enough for your people to forget their disappointment. That's my guess."

She kept tapping her nose, tapping her nose. "Well, I don't think you can just snap your fingers and get us there."

"Oh? You're sure about that?"

"I'm talking to a man tied to a blood sink."

"Maybe I want to be here. Maybe I came here— allowed myself to be captured—so that I could lead you to the Otherworld."

"Yeah, right." Her teeth were smiling in the moonlight. It felt good to see her smile again. "So how do you plan to get us there?"

I thought for a moment while Rewan gnawed her lip. I had a tough decision to make. If she let me escape, no telling what her people might do to her. On the other hand, I really did want to help her enter the Otherworld. But, like she said, I couldn't get us there merely by wishing.

At this precarious juncture—as sometimes happens when my reasoning faculty fails me—I was stunned by a flash of intuition—a flash so bright that it blinded my common sense. It was a fool's plan, the product of a mind susceptible to illusion.   Nonetheless, in that moment, I truly believed that we could do this deed; that this death-defying act would actually succeed.

"How high are the outside walls?" I asked.

"I don't know...they're pretty high."

"If someone jumped from the top ledge into the water ditch, what do you think would happen to him?"

"The moat's not very deep and it's lined with rock. If you went in head first, you'd bust your skull open. Otherwise, you'd probably only break your legs."

"Then head first it is."

"That's how you plan to get us there?   By busting our skulls open?"

"No, we won't actually bust our heads.   We'll break through to the Otherworld before that happens."

"Isn't there some other way?"

"You must risk life and limb if you want to enter the Otherworld.   That's how it works.   That's the deal. That's the trade-off.   So come on, let's get going.   Untie my ropes."

"You serious?"

"Yes, I am.   You want to go or don't you?"

"Sure I do.   But I don't want to bash my brains in. Mer went to the Otherworld all the time.   And he didn't have to do anything drastic to get there."

"So what exactly did he do?"

"He'd just wander off by himself at night.   Then come back a couple of days later."

"I never believed his stories.   He described a world too perfect—too easy.   I don't care to visit his version of the Otherworld.   I mean, what'd be the purpose?   What would one accomplish?"

"True enough."

"Look, we don't have to jump head-first. Breaking our legs would be risk enough. But hey, if that's too much for you, then forget it."

"No, no. It's not that...It's just that...Why didn't you slip into the Otherworld when Urk first captured you? I mean, if you can—if you can go over—why don't you? Certainly, your life and limb are endangered here."

"Tomorrow when the time comes, I will most certainly disappear into the Otherworld. I assure you. But—alas!-- you won't be with me."

"It just seems like...I mean, why wait 'til the last minute?"

"I hear what you're saying, Rewan. But that's not the way it works. Look, I know what I'm doing. I've done this before, remember? You with me or not?"

"I'm with you—as long as you're sure about this."

"Untie the ropes."

"Look, if you try making a run for it, the guards'll be on your ass quicker than you can spit. As is, we might have a hard time just getting to the wall. I'm really taking a chance, you know."

"Okay, I'll be honest with you. Sure, I'd like to escape. And what would I have to lose by trying? But you see, I have other things to consider."

"Such as?"

"Well okay, let's be very honest. Some time back—but really not so long ago—I met a young woman whose eyes held the mystery of the night."

"Oh?" Rewan dipped her head.

"Yes. This woman had the wind in her hair and moved with the rhythm of water. When her skin brushed mine, I could feel the rich fire flowing through her veins."

At this point, I paused for effect.

"Well, go on, you sweet-talking man."

"Yes, this moon-eyed feline reminded me of another I'd once known. Of all the women in my tribe, this other was the only one who truly understood the map of my body—and the map of my soul. She was the pool that gave my true reflection. But such closeness can often cause friction. Our love was a fiery itch and a wild irritation. Our love was—"

"Okay, okay, enough about her."

"Sorry. What I meant to say was: no one else had ever provoked such emotion in me until I met you. But all our meetings have been so enticingly brief. I kept reaching for your hand and touching only air. But let's put regret behind us. When we return from the Otherworld, I want us to be together. I want to breathe you into me. I want us to breathe together as one. Maybe our breathing will go stale before the new moon cuts the sky. But on the other hand, maybe our breathing can bring into being a new world—a righteous world, a free world—that world which I have sometimes felt, sometimes sensed, just before waking, yet have never been able to capture for myself."

"I'm not sure what you just said, but it sure sounded pretty."

"Thank you."

"But the way I look at it, I'm giving you your freedom. Isn't that enough?"

"You have a boyfriend now?"

"No."

"Then why don't you want to be with me?"

"Where? Here? In the City of Roq? Even if my people agreed, I don't think you'd feel very comfortable."

"I wasn't thinking about here."

"Then where? With your people?"

"They're all dead—remember?" What was she trying to do?—catch me in a lie?

"Then where, where would we go?"

"To the woods. To the mountains. Someplace far, far away. Things'll be different, I promise you. We'll start a new tribe, just you and I. All our children will be Seers and all their children will be Seers and all our children's' children will be Seers. We'll all see the same way; we'll share the same reality. We'll drink from both worlds; from this one and the Other. And so our lives will fill to the brim. Our lives will brim over and wash over the earth and cleanse it and make it into something good, something whole. You know?"

Rewan tapped her nose again. "No, I don't know. I kind of like living here."

"Here? In the City of Roq?"

"I don't like the way you said that."

"No offense. But your people do seem a little taciturn."

"That's just the warriors."

"But it pervades everything you guys do around here—so stiff, so formal, so military."

"We're a proud, noble people."

"Come on, do you really like being stuck behind these walls? Life used to be so much simpler, so much easier, so much freer."

Rewan folded her arms across her chest and pointed her chin up. I could see that I was losing ground.

"Well, you can't blame a guy for dreaming," I said with a sigh. "Come on, let's go to the Otherworld. Let the future be whatever it needs to be."

270

And with that, her quick little fingers began to untie my knots.

Chapter 18 : The Leap of Faith

Somehow I knew that no one would stop us.

We stepped down the stairway, hand in hand, as if immersed in ritual. The moonlight bathed our bodies with its soft white dust. The night held its breath. We moved like shadows through the dark streets.

Near the north corner, we climbed a ladder to the wall parapet.

Yes, I actually planned to jump. Though my legs had started to shake, in my heart, I still believed. What gave me such unfounded confidence? I don't know. But in that moment, the idea seemed perfectly acceptable. Perhaps by convincing Rewan, I had also convinced myself. What was wrong with her anyway? She was usually so clear-headed.

Yes, I was leading my beloved toward a very possible death. What exactly was going through my head? Well, to be honest, not much of anything. My feet were doing the thinking for me. At least, that's my excuse. When your mind can't decide, when thought is exhausted, you either sit down for awhile or else let your feet guide you. I had no time now for sitting down, so once again I surrendered to the will of my feet. My feet moved me onward and upward.

But what, you may well ask, moved my feet? I suspect it was the same force that moved Rewan's feet. The same force that kept my mind at bay also kept her mind at bay, kept her mind from screaming out, "What am I doing! This is impossible!"

This unnamed, unknown force always carries me toward danger, toward mystery, toward all those places I would've otherwise avoided.

Some unknown something is leading me, leading me somewhere—where I don't know. And "why" I don't know either. Matar, is that you? Life is such sweet torture!

The boards of the parapet sighed beneath our feet. The guard we passed gave a whistling snore. Gnats dipped in and out of his flared nostrils.

Strangely enough, for once, my stomach wasn't twitching. For once, my stomach was at rest.

We stopped near the front gates. For a few moments, we gazed in silence over the moon-lit plain. The dark forest grove murmured its secrets to the breeze.

I could feel Rewan's breath against my cheek. "So now what?" she asked. "Think we need to do a ritual first?"

"No," I said. "It's real enough already."

The waters of the moat twisted silver and black. I could see my ghostly reflection on its surface.

"Take my hand," Rewan said.

Her thin, delicate fingers gripped my hand until my knuckles popped.

We stepped from the parapet onto the cool stone of the top ledge. I tottered for a moment, then steadied myself. I tried collecting my thoughts, but could find no thoughts worth collecting.

I felt the tremors running through Rewan's arm. She looked at me with the eyes of a child, pleading for comfort and security. Though we still believed, we couldn't help but be afraid.

"Any time I've looked death square in the snoot, I've entered the Otherworld," I told her.

"There's always a first time."

"I think we'd better just shut up and jump."

We stood there for several tense moments, looking down at the water, waiting for something to move us. My knees rattled together like coconuts.

Yet deep down, I felt a strange calmness. "Perhaps, this is the peace that precedes death," I thought to myself.

"Come on, let's go," Rewan said. "I want to be done with it."

She gave my arm a gentle tug. I took a big breath.

In the next instant, I found myself plunging down through the cool rushing night. The wind filled the hollow of my stomach. But I didn't have time to feel scared anymore. I just concentrated on keeping my legs straight while aiming my feet at the moon's watery reflection. Yet at the same time, through the roar of the moment, I had the oddest sensation. Something was missing. Something within me had been displaced—a part of myself, a part of myself that was also a separate self. This other self still stood atop the wall, looking down, watching me as I fell. This other self had form, but the form was all shadow.

However, I couldn't wonder too long at this separate self. I had other business to attend to. To my surprise, as I fell through the night, I actually seemed to slow down. Yes, and what's more, I could feel my chest expanding, I could feel a soft pressure building. My whole body swelled up like a puff ball—I felt so pleasantly empty. Then, with just a poof of air, my body burst open like a seed pod. Yes, and all the tiny bits of me flickered down toward the moat with the delicacy of dandelion seed. As I scattered over the dark water, I felt the coolness of its touch. I luxuriated in the freedom of floating surrender.

My seeds were all separate eyes and though I looked all around me with my seed-eyes, I did not find Rewan. Nor I did feel her near me. Perhaps she had dropped into a nether zone. No matter—I had my own self to navigate.

As I drifted coolly on the channel in seed form, I could see the silhouette of my other self still perched atop the wall. This shadow man felt alone without me; he was confused, he lacked identity. So finally, unable to formulate a plan, he gave in and plunged headfirst from the ledge.

But as this other self descended, the attrition of the wind wore him down—by the time he'd reached the moat, he was but a single black drop.

And this drop of him hit me dead center. The ripples jostled my eye seeds, shook the moon and the stars.

Only then did I see Rewan. As she knelt down on the bank, the moonlight defined her form in smooth undulations of light and shadow. The reflection of her face shifted on the moving black water.

Did she see me? Or did she lean forward only to examine her own reflection? No matter—as she lowered her head, the tips of her hair touched the water's surface. I could feel a magnetic force emanating from each fine strand. In those precious moments, something within me began to coalesce. All my isolated particles—all my seed eyes—came together to feed like small fish at the hair tips. I tasted those sweet threads with a hundred different tongues, each one lending its own special shading. Sensation flooded my being.

Each hair fiber—each one—now acted as a straw and each particle of me—each one—now rose from the water and traveled up the tubing of a hair fiber.

In this manner, all my particles soon reached the crown of Rewan's head and once there, fused into something finely condensed.

Rewan's crown was a crown of golden fire; it burned like scalding ice. But I didn't care—I'd gone through fire before and come out the other side and besides, I just didn't care. I was within my feelings and yet, outside my feelings as well. So I did not care what pain I felt.

By the time the golden fire had finished with me, I was nothing but happy ashes, nothing but specks of soot. Yes, and these specks began to filter down through Rewan's body, through her cool, black interior, drifting down like pearls through honey: a slow and significant movement. My specks dispersed through the space of her and as they did, I could feel the memories of her body, I could feel the memories embedded in her neck and arms and lungs and hips and pubis and legs and toes. When I joined all those memories together, they became the sensation of movement through space and time: hurried, grasping, hungry—the impatient dance of an ant. But this movement was more than just the struggle to survive; it was also the struggle to become—always stretching, always longing, always forging on; famished for the nourishment of both earth and sky. Through the struggle of her life, I knew myself once more. She mirrored and echoed all my dim and constant yearnings.

But though I was saturated with sensation, I could still follow the action of the shadow man. After striking the water as a mere drop, he had spread out; he had rippled all the way to the shore, then bounced off the bank in a series of smaller ripples. As these tiny waves came together again in the center, his form was recreated; he again became a full-size shadow man.

He then climbed onto the bank in search of me, his good friend and companion. I could sense him groping his way blindly, sniffing the air like a mole, tasting the air like a snake— hunting me out.

Abruptly, he halted. His nose hovered over Rewan's bowed head for several tense moments. He could smell me within her.

And so, hoping to regain the whole, he placed his shadowy hands on Rewan's moon-white shoulders, then urged her gently, gently towards the earth— asking, not demanding; not dominating, but pleading. And so, her body and spirit acquiesced to his touch; in flesh and in soul, she accepted the righteousness of this act. Her body, which was her spirit, entreated him into her; her spirit, which was her body, enraptured him.

And so, the shadow man lay down. His dark form melted over her body like a molten metal flowing over the contours of a quiet stone. He melded deeply, relinquishing himself to somnolent desire. His abject body/spirit cried for sanctuary, whimpered for release —I could feel it. Rewan was an ocean; her waves had layered voices, her currents moaned; she crashed upon herself hissingly. She was movement without cessation; her force, eternally continuous. I grew so still in my desire to hear her that I became one with myself.

The world began with an argument—the argument between the earth and the sky—because that's the way of life. We begin this life whole, but then in response to this broken world, we start to break apart. Our separate parts then do what separate things do: they argue. This roiling inner conflict creates a sense of unease. But we don't see that conflict. We see the conflict of the world outside our skin. So instead of fixing the conflict within, we try to fix our broken world, in hopes of curing our unease.

But a broken person can only do so much to fix a broken world. Often, we just make a bad situation worse. And if we persist in our flailing efforts, we may eventually lose balance and hit the ground. A fortunate failure!—because then, in the stillness, we may hear our separate parts arguing. And because we really hate all the fuss, and really want to be whole again, we'll work to put those pieces back together. Putting back together is also the way of life.

But to what good purpose, all this breaking apart and putting back together? To some, it seems like a malicious design—or anyway, counterproductive. But I think differently. Yes, it takes much energy to put the pieces back together again—to bond, to heal, to mend. To create this energy requires finding the strength to create this energy. And that's where the beauty of the design reveals itself: once the parts are bonded back, the strength we've found remains with us.

As for the ultimate purpose of all this strength building...Well, I can't see, but I'm still looking. Maybe my eyes will eventually open wide enough. Until then, I'll confine myself to the obvious.

At this point, I am sorry to say, my memory of the event grows vague. All that I have left is the impression of separating, of drifting away from that place of perfect peace, and then of traveling through a dark liquid labyrinth, guided by some force other than conscious thought.

But perhaps it's not that important to remember everything. Anyway, some part of me has the memory. That'll have to suffice for now.

But why, you may well ask, did I have to leave that place of perfect peace? If the bond was so strong, how could I break it? Well, I don't think that anything was broken. That place of perfect peace remains within me. I may not know how to get there, but I know it's there. Sometimes I can almost feel it. And so I keep trying...which, after all, is the whole point. Isn't it?

Chapter 19 : I See the Future

At the end of this journey, I again awoke on the mountainside. My right hand rested on a bed of moss; my left hand lay on a round gray rock. The air had the sharp scent of resin and lichens, underscored with the subtle odor of snow. The white peak loomed directly above me. Ice crystals sparkled between my toes. Though I didn't recall the ascent, I realized that I might've finally reached the summit.

Rewan raised herself on one elbow. "Was it good for you too?" she asked.

"Yes," I rasped.

We reclined there, gazing at one another with empty sky in our eyes. What passed between us did not need speech, could not be spoken. My body hummed with the diffuse afterglow of love.

Time had no substance as we lounged there on the mountainside. One moment, the morning shadows lay long across the ground. Then in a blink, all the shadows had disappeared and the mid-day sun was beaming down upon us.

"Well," I said.

"Well, yes," Rewan said.

We stood up and shook hands. But I couldn't let go of her hand. A quiet yet potent force traveled back and forth between us.

"If my life were to end right now," I said, "it wouldn't bother me a bit."

"If we returned together, your life would end soon enough."

"That's okay. If we return together, I can save your life. Just tell them that I escaped into the Otherworld and you had to track me down."

"No, I can save my own hide. I'll go back alone; I've got to go back—I can't allow Urk to have complete control of the place. That's exactly what he wants. You understand—I've got to go back."

"I understand, but I still don't like it."

"I don't know that I like it all that much myself. But the tribes-kin need me. And someone's got to stop those sacrifice rituals. From now on, I'm putting my foot down. I must guide my people."

I released her hand. In the next moment, I noticed a shifting movement in the trees below us.

I touched Rewan on the elbow and pointed. "I think your people have found us."

"Oh no, not now, not yet. I'm still riding the love tide."

"Yeah, I know, me too. Look, you don't have to protect me. I'll die in peace."

"Maybe you'll enter the Otherworld before they can kill you."

"No, I don't think it works that way. It's one thing when your own choice. It's another thing when someone else chooses for you. I'm pretty sure that's the rule. Anyway, let's go ahead and get this business over with. And remember: don't try to protect me."

"I'm not making any promises."

"Hey, you down there!" I yelled. "Show yourselves and be proud about it. I have no patience with shirking shadows."

My one goal was to save Rewan. I wouldn't give her a chance to speak. I would tell her tribe that I'd taken her hostage during my escape.

But my heart leapt with joy when the shirking shadows stepped from the trees and I recognized my own tribes-kin. Aruk raised his bow, squinted up one eye and sighted down his arrow. His three companions —Lamarl, Purl, and the Larvian woman—lifted their bows as well.

I stepped in front of Rewan to shield her. "Don't shoot!" I cried. "It's me—Amar. I have returned from the Otherworld. Let us embrace and renew acquaintance."

"First business first," Aruk said. "For I spy a Roqian. Move aside, Amar. We'll deal with you later."

"I thought you said all your people were dead?" Rewan muttered underneath her breath.

"Ssssh, I'm trying to think," I whispered.

I had to make Aruk see reason. I could not live with Rewan's death.

But unfortunately, my mind wasn't quite ready for hard-edged reasoning; I wasn't all the way back from the Otherworld yet. My head was still half-filled with ether. "If you kill her, you must kill me as well," I yelled to Aruk.

"Why's that?" he asked through gritted teeth.

"Because we are the same."

"You mean to say you've turned Roqian?"

"No, of course not. What I meant was...we're all from the same tribe. I mean, really. Think about it. We're all just people here, right? You, me, Rewan, our tribe, her tribe, the Larvians—everybody—it makes no difference—we're all just one big tribe." When Aruk didn't respond, I added, "You understand what I'm getting at, don't you?"

"No."

Aruk was never one for philosophical thought.

"Don't trust them fancy words," old man Purl told him. "It's obvious, don't you see?—Amar's in cahoots with the Roqians."

"I knew it all along," Lamarl said. "He's one of them."

"Sure, I'm one of them," I said. "And one of you as well. Let us lay down our arms and live together in peace."

"Amar, maybe you should back off," Rewan said from the corner of her mouth. "They don't follow you at all. Don't worry about me. I don't mind dying."

"I'm going to make them understand me, whether they want to or not."

"Now I get the picture," Aruk growled. "All those times you claimed to be in the Otherworld, you were actually hanging out with the Roqians."

"You've got to be kidding," Rewan said. "My people would never have accepted Amar into the tribe."

"Shut up, you Roqian whore," Lamarl shouted. "We're talking to Amar here."

"Aaarrrjjjah," the Larvian woman spat.

"After you lost your position to Boq, you decided to destroy us," Aruk said. "You communicated with the Roqians while they were hanging out in the woods. You helped set up that ambush at the City of Ekruk. You led your own people to slaughter; yes, that's it; that's what you did."

"That's absurd. If you'll recall, I argued against Mok's trip."

"That was just a ruse," Purl said. "You gave in much too easily."

"Aaarrrjjjah," the Larvian woman spat.

"Okay, what about the stuff I brought back?" I asked. "The seeds. The bow and arrow. Where could I've gotten such things, except in the Otherworld? The Roqians had no knowledge of them."

"You withheld that stuff from them," Purl said, "because you didn't want to rouse suspicion. We're not saying you didn't go to the Otherworld. But you couldn't've spent all your time there. The rest of the time you were with the Roqians, playing house with your Roqian slut."

"Aaarrrjjjah," the Larvian woman spat.

"You're letting your imaginations get the better of you," I said. "Okay, here's what actually happened, here's how I ended up with Rewan: I was out walking around and the Roqians took me captive. They tried to make me reveal your whereabouts; they threatened to torture me; nevertheless, I refused to tell. They would've sacrificed me to Roq if Rewan—at great risk to herself—hadn't helped me escape. You should be thanking her, you really should. And by the way, she's not a slut."

"Just a moment ago, you claimed to be one of them," Aruk said. "Now you're telling us they held you prisoner?"

"You're not the liar you used to be," Purl said.

How could I argue with that?

"Aaarrrjjjah," the Larvian woman spat.

I realized then that further words were useless. My little speech about 'oneness' had confused them. Common sense could not pursue them now—they were determined to believe the worst about me.

"Well, aren't you going to kill them?" Purl asked Aruk.

Aruk lowered his bow. "No."

"Why not?" Lamarl whined.

"We'll wait. I wouldn't want the others to miss it."

So my case was not yet lost. I breathed a small sigh of relief.

I was all the way back from the Otherworld now. Damn it.

The hunters took great pleasure in binding our hands behind our backs and shoving us down the trail. By late afternoon, we had reached the foot of the mountain.

My people had abandoned their campsite on the cliff to begin work on another walled city. As soon as I'd left, they had once again pointed themselves towards progress. Just beyond the trees near the watercress stream stood a newly-constructed back wall and one full side. Several cubicles filled the corner where the two met. A large plot of soil sat freshly tilled.

"Just wait 'til we finish this baby," Aruk told me. "It'll be a beauty—nearly twice the size of the first one. We're using stone for the walls now, not mud brick. We've learned our lesson there. And get this—we're going to put the communal platform on top of a tall tower right in the center of town. Yep—right smack dab in the middle. We'll have a long stairway running all the way up it."

I thought about the stately tower in the center of the City of Roq. Coincidence, no doubt. I decided to not to mention it.

To my disappointment, none of my tribes-kin questioned the notion that I was a traitor. I started to argue my case, but quickly lost heart. Rewan had the good sense to keep quiet. She merely gave me a sad smile.

My people hammered stakes between the stones in the back wall, then strung us both up, side by side, our arms and legs spread wide, our feet well off the ground. Then they just stood there with their arms folded, shaking their heads and clicking their tongues. The ropes dug into my wrists.

Rir bounced a pebble off my forehead.

"I never would've believed it, Amar," Ool said. "Now I know why you tried to keep us down."

"I never tried to keep you down. I always tried to lift you up."

"Then why'd you want us to become hunters and gatherers again? You call that lifting us up?"

"We used to like to hunt and gather."

"You didn't want us to build another city. You didn't want us to prosper. You were afraid that we'd rise up against the People of Roq."

"Amar's innocent," Rewan finally said. "I assure you —my tribes-kin don't even like the mention of him."

"Shut up, she-beast!" Ool shouted. "We know that you lured Amar over to your side with your womanly charms, but he still has to account for his actions."

Rir bounced a pebble off my forehead.

"Okay, go on, go ahead—shoot me and be done with it," I sighed.

"No," Aruk said. "You are a Seer of some power. It wouldn't be wise to shoot you. We're just going to leave you hanging there. If Matar wants you to live, he'll save you."

"Any chance for food and water?"

"Ask Matar."

Such sarcasm. Aruk certainly had changed.

"As for the Roqian, we'll let her own god save her."

"In a demented way, that's fair," I said.

But then, to my horror, Aruk raised his bow. He aimed his arrow at a spot right between Rewan's eyes.

"Wait!" I yelled. "I thought you said—"

"If her god is truly strong, he will stay this arrow."

"Oh yeah? Well what if he strikes you down instead?"

"I've killed Roqians before and he's never struck me down. Why would he start now?"

"Because Rewan's a Seer. She has direct communication with her god, Roq."

Aruk lowered his bow and wrinkled his brow in thought. After a few moments, he gave up and lifted his bow again. "Whatever happens, happens," he proclaimed.

"Okay, but what if her god decides to crush us all?" I asked. "Roq could take a bolt of lightening and smash us to smithereens just like that."

Aruk lowered his bow again. He squinched up his eyes. Once again that slow brain of his tried to reason through the situation.

After several thoughtful moments, he again raised his bow.

"No need for worry," he announced. "Her god is not the real god. Matar will protect us. True, he has often failed us in the past. But I guess he had to test us, like you said. Anyway, I'm sure that in this case, Matar will bless the righteous action of my arrow." Aruk drew back the bowstring.

"Hold on!" I cried. "We're not done discussing yet."

"Oh yes we are." Aruk sighted down the arrow.

"No, listen to me. Everyone. I have some important news. I spoke with Matar again the other day. Right atop this mountain here. And at that time, he/she/it delivered unto me a set of laws. Laws created for his/her/its people."

"You're just making that up," Purl said. "You're scheming to save your Roqian girlfriend."

"Okay, you may have your doubts about me. But you must admit, Matar has provided for his/her/its people in the past. And how has he/she/it provided for them? Through me. And not through anyone else. So hear me out this one last time. One last time before I'm gone—before you lose your direct link to Matar. Okay everyone?"

Rir bounced a pebble off my forehead.

"Okay," Ool said. "Go on. I'm curious as to what bunk you'll try to feed us this time."

"But make it quick," Mumurl said. "I want to see this Roqian dead."

"Okay, the first law is this: one should not kill another human being."

"We're not," Parn said. "We're letting you live as long as Matar sees fit."

"This law includes humans from other tribes as well."

"That'll never work," Aruk said "What if another tribe attacks us?"

"Then you make an exception."

"Okay. Any other exceptions?"

"A few. But here's what I'm trying to say: because we've broken this law in the past, Matar made us to suffer. And if we kill Rewan now, it'll just make things worse. It'll make things worse right when things are starting to get better. Is that what you want? Is that what we need? Is it worth all that grief just to murder this poor, innocent woman?"

Aruk relaxed his bowstring and lowered the bow. "But if we didn't know about the law, why did Matar make us suffer?"

"Well, ah...um....—Matar thought you knew better without being told."

"I sure do get sick of Matar sometimes," Ool said.

"Aaarrrjjjah," the Larvian woman spat.

Rir bounced a pebble off my forehead.

Again Aruk lifted his bow. "Well, law or no law, I'm sure Matar will understand," he said. "After all, this is a Roqian. She worships Roq. Surely Matar won't mind if we kill someone who worships the wrong god. After all, her tribe has killed a lot of Matar's people. No, I don't think Matar will mind the least bit."

At that moment, I suddenly realized the limits of our religion. Fear of Matar could only restrain my people to a certain point. If they really wanted to do something, they'd do it, regardless of what Matar had said.

I looked to Rewan. I could see that she expected death. No sudden exits to the Otherworld. She knew she would die and stared at her executioner with stolid acceptance.

That brave woman stared at her executioner with stolid acceptance. But then she turned her eyes to me and her face softened. In her brown eyes, I found the purity and strength of love. She understood that this death would be just another step in her stairway.

Straining against the rope that held my wrist, I reached for her hand and she reached for mine and for a brief moment, our fingertips touched. In that moment,

I knew that her last breath would be my last breath and that gave me peace.

But as I gazed into Rewan's calm brown eyes, waiting for the gift of death to arrive, the moments passed and I began to pick up a new vibe—a shift in the energy surrounding this event.

Rewan and I were no longer the center of attention. My tribes-kin now watched the dark, silent figures standing on the piles of stone brick behind them. Clothed all in black, these specters numbered more than forty strong. They wore black hoods with tiny eye slits, black broad-sleeved tunics, and black pants woven of a coarse fabric. The tunics were embellished with two rows of small black bones down the front—a nice touch, I thought.

Each specter carried a long bronze sword and a round bronze shield. A steam of sweat rose from their uniforms under the hard afternoon sun.

My tribes-kin stood stone-quiet; they understood: this was the end.

As for myself, having just stared death square in the face, I regarded this scenario with some detachment.

"Drop your bow and release that woman!" a shrouded warrior shouted.

Aruk lowered—but did not drop—his bow and arrow.

Though muffled by the hood, the voice was easy to recognize.

"That you, Urk?" I asked.

"Yeah, why?"

"Just checking, that's all."

My people actually seemed to relax now. They were used to the Roqians.

In fact, Mumurl put a hand on her hip and, in her whiny adolescent voice, said, "Why don't you freaks show your faces? You ashamed of your ugly mugs or what?"

"The People of Roq are a proud people!" Urk growled. He whipped off his hood and threw it slap to the ground. His jaw muscles bulged with tension.

"On second thought," Mumurl said, "you can cover it back up."

Urk grabbed the girl by the ear and jerked her down to her knees.

"Yeeeeeoooow!" she screamed. "You're hurting me!"

Urk grinned, then gave the ear another hard twist.

"Urk, release her," Rewan shouted.

Urk looked at Rewan, then at the girl, then back at Rewan. "Why?" he asked in a petulant voice.

"Because we have a peace treaty with these people."

"Oh, is that so? Then why'd they string you up?"

"It's part of a ritual. A reenactment."

"Reenactment of what?"

"The death of spring."

"Well, it looks like the real thing to me."

But Urk let go of the ear. He kicked Mumurl to the ground.

"Yeah, that's right," Aruk said, "we made a treaty." Though he was a warrior through and through, Aruk knew when to back down.

"No, Rewan, there is no treaty," Urk said. "You can't run off with an enemy prisoner, fraternize with his tribe, participate in their rituals, and then, when I catch you, tell me we've just made a treaty with the lousy bastards. That's not how it works, babe."

"Okay look, I took a trip to the Otherworld. That's right. I finally made it. I forced Amar to take me there. And guess what?—while in that world, I met none other than the maestro himself, the one and only—our god, Roq. And Roq commanded me to make a treaty with these people. So I did. End of story."

"Roq or no Roq, you've got to check with me first."

"Well, blazes!" I yelled. "You people've done spoiled the ritual with all your blabbering. We were trying to create a certain ambience, you know? And now you've gone and ruined it. Here Aruk, cut us down. We'll have to do the ritual later."

Urk eyed Rewan. "I'm telling you, you can't make a treaty unless I agree."

"I can too."

"Can not."

"Can too."

"Can not."

"Can too!"

"Can not!"

"Can too."

"Can not, can not, can not!"

"Okay, I tell you what," Rewan sighed. "When we get back to the city, we'll settle this by picking sticks."

"No, we'll do it now," Urk said, then he turned and shouted, "Where's the Stickmeister? Bring me the Stickmeister!"

A short, round-shouldered figure hopped down from a mound of stone brick. Urk pulled the man's hood off. Underneath was a pudgy head with a cut across one eyebrow.

"The sticks!" Urk said. "Bring forth the sticks."

The pudgy-headed man undid the flap of his satchel and extracted two smooth white sticks of unequal length. Then he turned his back to us and began shuffling the sticks from one hand to the other.

"So why'd you bring the Stickmeister with you?" Rewan asked Urk. "You're not supposed to keep him with you. He's supposed to remain neutral."

"Sometimes I get stuck trying to make a decision. Not too often, but it happens. Anyway, you weren't around and I didn't know if you were coming back, so stop your barking."

"I just hope you're not marking the sticks. You'd better not be marking the sticks."

"I don't get it," Aruk said.

"If he picks the short stick, we have a treaty," Rewan told him. "If not, well, I'm sorry."

The Stickmeister now rotated back around, holding his fists together at chest level. The end of one stick stuck out from each fist. His tunic's broad sleeves hid the opposite ends.

Urk flipped his lower lip with his finger while trying to decide which stick to pick. His mind shifted this way and that, searching for intuition. The life of my tribe hung in the balance.

Urk believed that he would not be at peace until he'd wiped the earth clean of Matarians. But I knew that our extinction would not cure his disease—he'd just find something else to fear.

In reality, he should have been worrying about his buddies, the Ekrukians. Sooner or later, his tribe and that tribe would squabble, relations would break down, and then there'd be war. When that happened, the Roqians would do well to form alliances with other tribes. Our position at the base of the mountain would prove valuable to any ally. With our aid, the Roqians could control the mountain pass and cut off a crucial supply route from their enemy.

On the other hand, despite our lowly state, perhaps the Roqians had good reason to be concerned about us. We would soon have a new walled city and surplus grain in our storage bins. The able-bodied among us would mate with feverish fury so as to build up our numbers. Those numbers would be increased by the nomads— often war victims on the lam—who would arrive at our gates, bedraggled and begging for sanctuary. We'd accept these folk into the fold, not so much out of kindness, but because we needed the extra bodies for farm labor, for breeding purposes, and for our defense.

In short time, our new city would become a prime destination for those using the mountain pass. And so we would prosper—providing food, water, and lodging for traveler and domestic beast alike.

Eventually, Aruk would hand the reins over to Rir. In both word and deed, he would be his father's son— and then some. His greedy fire would demand feeding. Our affluence would not satiate his hunger; my influence would do nothing to curb his gluttonous desires. His greedy fire would demand blood and gold. Burning with stories of his father's defeat and brimming with aggression, Rir would take his warriors on a rampage across the plains, ripping through anyone and anything that got in his way. He would smash, claw, and slash until he'd subdued the entire valley. Then he'd sweep over the mountains to ravage the lands beyond. And when he reached the sea, he'd have his men build boats. They'd wreck havoc up and down the coast until their decks overflowed with plunder.

By the time our empire reached its zenith, everyone in the known world would hate our guts.

And so, united by their animosity, our enemies would storm our gates as one force to crush our city. Only a few Matarians would escape this carnage.

Once again, we would have to endure decay and starvation. The cornucopia we'd enjoyed would again be replaced by lice, wet rot, cold nights, bad food, and sick, swollen bellies.

However, these hardships would only serve to make us meaner and tougher.

It would only be a matter of time before we charged down off the mountain to recapture the city and reclaim our former glory.

Once again, we would reap a blessing of abundance. Once again, we would smite, skewer, and bludgeon until we'd subdued the entire valley and the lands beyond.

And so, in this manner, the tides of prosperity would surge and recede across the generations of Matarians. Look once and see us in command of the world. Look twice and see us hunkering in crevices like rats. We'd flourish, then decline; flourish, then decline —on and on and on through time: a redundancy with no end in sight. Our history would be a tale of turbulent monotony.

Could anything be done, in the here and now, to break this pattern before it built momentum? Could I bring something back from the Otherworld that would help make things right? Based on past experience, that prospect seemed doubtful. Though I'd found peace in the Otherworld, I'd not been able to transfer that peace to my people.

Each generation would have its Mok or its Rir. War is a hard habit to break. It only takes one Rir to destroy a generation.

The situation, as I saw it, was hopeless.

The Stickmeister still held his sticks out. Urk continued to thrum his lower lip while waiting for intuition.

Finally, he gave up and tapped the Stickmeister's left fist. The Stickmeister opened his hand to reveal the short stick. A collective sigh issued from my tribes-kin. We had a treaty—at least for the time being. We would not be killed. Not today anyway.

"Okay, now get us down from here," Rewan said.

To his credit, Urk accepted the loss. He snapped his fingers. Two henchmen stepped up and sliced the ropes that held Rewan's ankles and wrists.

"Cut me down too while you're at it," I told them.

The henchmen hesitated. They looked to Urk; Urk looked to Aruk. Aruk hung his head and gave a dispirited shrug.

The henchmen whacked my ropes and I crumpled to the ground, sore in every limb and emotionally vanquished.

Urk and Aruk now stood toe to toe. Though their faces were blank masks, in their eyes you could see the glint of mistrust.

"And so we have joined together in a truce," Urk growled.

"Treaty," prompted Rewan.

"Treaty," repeated Urk.

"And so we have joined together in a treaty," said Aruk. "May this union be joyful and not weigh heavy upon our minds and our hearts." He spat from the corner of his mouth.

Urk ground his teeth so hard you could hear them squeak.

"Shake hands," Rewan prodded.

Urk hesitated, then extended his hand. Aruk looked at the hand for a moment, then finally met it with his own.

They held this grip until their arms shook and the veins bulged out on their necks. Nevertheless, they managed to keep the pain hidden behind their blank masks.

"Come on, you two, that's enough," Rewan finally said.

Both men couldn't help but look a little relieved as they broke the handshake.

Urk then gave a sign and all the Roqians got into formation.

We watched as they began to file out across the plain. Rewan just stood there, staring at me, tears brimming in her moon-dark eyes. She waited for the end of the line, then with a last wave goodbye, she turned from me and stepped out onto the savanna.

I knew I'd probably never see her again—unless, of course, we met in the Otherworld.

After the Roqians had all left, the vacuum of silence was enough to make your ears pop. Aruk studied the ground and shifted his weight from one foot to the other. Rir started to toss a pebble at me, but Ool stayed his hand.

"Still think I'm a traitor?" I muttered underneath my breath.

"No," Aruk said. "I'm sorry. That wasn't right of me. I guess we've just gotten a little paranoid with all that's happened."

The day's excitement had stirred up our appetites. So we all sat down on the piles of stone brick and had a supper of dried venison strips. No one could think of a thing to say. My stomach wouldn't stop twitching.

At the conclusion of this sober meal, Aruk slapped his thighs and said, "We still have some daylight left. Let's get back to work on the walls."

I stood up and hefted a brick. Aruk touched my arm. "That's okay Amar. Why don't you just relax. You've had a rough day of it. Here, take my cubicle, use my mat, get yourself some rest. There'll be plenty left to do tomorrow. Besides, you're the Seer. You needn't do this sort of thing. Save your energy for your Seeing duties."

"I don't mind doing some good hard labor. You need all the help you can get." I'd tried not to sound sarcastic with this last remark—and failed.

"Tomorrow, my brother, tomorrow."

"Well, perhaps you're right. Tomorrow then."

Aruk gave me a gap-toothed grin and nodded his head. For a moment there, his eyes shone with that innocence of old—but only for a moment.

"Actually, I think I'll take a little walk in the woods," I said. "Just a short walk. I need to stretch my legs a bit."

"Yes, of course, Amar. We understand. You Seers need your walks and your ruminations. The mind expands in solitude."

I could feel my tribes-kin watching me as I left the grounds of our new city and entered the mountain forest. I knew what they were thinking. They were thinking they'd seen the last of me.

I knew they might be right.

Once I'd stepped into the woods, the tension fell from my body and I could breathe again. But the feeling that remained wasn't exactly what you'd call "peace". After all, my tribes-family had wanted to kill me. Sure, we'd smoothed things over, but how long would that last? What if our new crops failed? What if our new walls collapsed? What would happen when the peace treaty fell apart? In my role as religious leader, I could be blamed for anything and everything. The Roqians had sacrificed their Seer after a run of bad luck and, in due time, had prospered. My tribe might well seek the same results.

On the other hand, I was, after all, getting to be a rickety old man. I had no desire to cling to this life. I wasn't afraid of death. If my tribe didn't kill me, something else would. So why worry?

But did my people really need me anymore? This construction project had them breathing light again. They'd finally stopped wallowing in the ashes of defeat. I now saw my mistake: we couldn't go back to the old ways; it was too late.

But if I left, who'd perform the rituals? I had slowly come to realize their true importance. Through these small dramas, we enacted what we felt at a deeper level; we gave recognition to truths only dimly sensed before.

On the other hand, I'd recently witnessed the future of my tribe and seen only violent repetition. I wanted no part of that legacy.

I decided to keep on walking. Too many grand and rapturous and terrible things had passed in such a short period of time. If I returned now, the humdrum would quickly ensnare me.

Perhaps I would walk until I became one with the trees, until I melded with the earth, until I resided at the core of our world. Yes, that's what I'd do—I'd walk until I had assumed the solid consciousness of a rock. That would be my new life. True, every day of my rock life would be the same, but so what?—I'd be at one with the world.

My mind continued to spiral out these dizzy designs as I trod through the snow toward the summit. I was deep into the night. The darkness was a violet glow near the snow's white surface. My feet had numbed. I no longer felt the stinging cold, nor the bite of the sharp flint rock beneath the drift. Wisps of purple cloud swirled all around me; they climbed up my trunk like vine tentacles.

I had finally reached the peak. But though I stood at the very apex of our world, all I could see were whorls of freezing purple mist—purple above me, below me, all about me.

So what do you do once you've made the summit? Where do you go? My feet had brought me to this point, so now I let them bring me back down. I could do nothing but obey my feet.

I would return to my people whether I wanted to or not. Could I change our fate? That was too much to hope for. On the other hand, with the right kind of effort, maybe, just maybe, I could bend the river of our history ever so slightly. From that slight shift, in time, big things might come. I had to at least give it a try. I had to.

I awoke the next morning near the new City of Matar construction site. Four full pouches lay on the ground beside me.

I sat up and looked all about. The silhouette of a small figure blended into the trees. The boy Emo, walking a crooked step, had slipped through a crease and back into the Otherworld.

I stood up to follow.

###

sky rope poetry:
>http://skyrope.wordpress.com

to hear those poems read aloud:
>https://soundcloud.com/mythsteps

searching for the new mythology:
>http://mythsteps.wordpress.com

dream steps bloneironic:
>http://dreamsteps.wordpress.com

find "Michael R. Patton poetry"on YouTube

for discussions, dissensions & praises:
>livingbell@yahoo.com

ready to stop a cannonball
with his bare hand